W9-AMU-538

ENTER A WORLD

where cartoon characters ('toons) live side by side with humans and speak in word-filled balloons.

MEET

Roger Rabbit, fuzzy, up-and-coming comic-strip star . . .

The DeGreasy Brothers, sleazy owners of a cartoon syndicate, who have Roger by the ears . . .

Jessica Rabbit, Roger's sexy,, humanoid-'toon ex-wife, former star of 'toon porn . . .

Doctor Beaver, 'toon psychiatrist, featured in VD pamphlets . . .

Sid Sleaze, slimy, porno-comic-strip producer
. . . and a wacky crew of humans, 'toons, and humanoid-'toons . . .

JOIN

Eddie Valiant, L.A.'s toughest, third-rate gumshoe, as he tries to solve the murders of Rocco DeGreasy *and* Roger Rabbit in this wildly original and hilariously spellbinding new mystery . . .

WHO CENSORED ROGER RABBIT?

You'll never read the funny papers in the same way again!

"ZANY!!"

Boston Herald American

WHO CENSORED
ROGER RABBIT?

GARY WOLF

BALLANTINE BOOKS • NEW YORK

Copyright © 1981 by Gary K. Wolf

All rights reserved under International and Pan-American Copyright Conventions. Published in the United States by Ballantine Books, a division of Random House, Inc., New York, and simultaneously in Canada by Random House of Canada Limited, Toronto.

Library of Congress Catalog Card Number: 81-8861

ISBN 0-345-30325-3

This edition published by arrangement with St. Martin's Press

Manufactured in the United States of America

First Ballantine Books Edition: November 1982
Third Printing: July 1988

To Bugs, Donald, Minnie,
and the rest of the gang at the
B Street Smoke Shop

1

I found the bungalow and rang the bell.

My client answered the door.

He was almost my height, close to six feet, but only if you counted his eighteen-inch ears. He wore only a baggy pair of shorts, held up by brightly colored suspenders. His shoulders stooped so badly, he had to secure his suspender tops in place with crossed pieces of cellophane tape. For eyes, he had twin black dots, floating in the center of two oblong white saucers. His white stomach, nose, toes, and palms on a light brown body made him resemble someone who had just walked face first into a freshly painted wall.

"I'm Eddie Valiant, private eye. You the one who called?"

"Yes, I am," he said, extending a fuzzy white paw. "I'm Roger Rabbit." His words came out encased in a balloon that floated over his head.

The rabbit ushered me into his living room. The angular furniture reminded me of the upward-reaching spires in caves. That, combined with an extremely low ceiling and stale air, gave the room the closed-in nature of an underground burrow. Perfect interior design for a rabbit.

The bunny opened a liquor cabinet and brought out an earthenware jug emblazoned with three X's. "Drink?" he asked.

Since 'toons could not legally buy human-manufactured liquor, most drank the moonshine produced by their country cousins in Dogpatch and Hootin' Holler. Potent stuff. Few humans could handle it.

Although no stranger to strong drink, I knew my limitations well enough to pass.

"Mind if I do?" the rabbit asked.

"Fine with me," I said.

The rabbit cradled the jug in his elbow and guzzled down a healthy swig. Almost instantly, twin puffs of smoke shot out of his ears, drifted lazily upward, and bounced gently against the ceiling.

Quite nonchalantly, the rabbit pulled a large butterfly net out from behind the sofa, snared the bobbling whiffets, and shook them free through an open window. They joined forces, floated merrily skyward, and expanded into a soft, billowy cloud.

"Cumulonimbus," the rabbit remarked, as he watched the evidence of his indulgence drift away.

The rabbit closed the window and drew the drapes to protect his frail parchment skin from the drying effects of the early morning sun. He hippity-hopped across the room to his desk, returned, and handed me a check. "A retainer. I hope it's large enough."

It certainly was! At my regular rates, the check would buy my services for nearly a week.

"Maybe I'd better outline my problem," said the rabbit. "I know all the cash in the world wouldn't persuade a private eye to take on an unjust cause."

I nodded. If the rabbit only knew. I had undertaken numerous unjust causes in the course of my career, and for a lot less than all the cash in the world. A lot less.

The rabbit picked a walnut-inlaid cigar box off a mushroom-shaped coffee table. "Carrot?" he asked.

I looked inside. Sure enough, carrots, carefully selected for uniformity of color, size, and shape, and alternated big end to little end so that the maximum number of them could be squeezed inside. Each bore a narrow, gold and red paper band proclaiming it a product of mid-state

Illinois, generally acknowledged as the world's finest source of the orange nibblers.

I declined.

The rabbit selected a chunky specimen for himself and gnawed at it noisily, freckling his chin with tiny orange chips that flaked off in the gap between his front incisors. "About a year ago, the DeGreasy brothers, the cartoon syndicate, told me that if I signed with them they would give me my own strip." He laid his half-eaten carrot on an end table beside a display of framed and autographed photos, some human, some 'toon. They included Snoopy, Joe Namath, Beetle Bailey, John F. Kennedy, and, in a group shot, Dick Tracy, Secret Agent X-9, and J. Edgar Hoover. "Instead they made me a second banana to a dopey, obese, thumb-sucking sniveler named Baby Herman."

"So find yourself another syndicate."

"I can't." The rabbit's face collapsed. "My contract binds me to the DeGreasys for another twenty years. When I asked them to release me so I could look for work elsewhere, they refused."

"They give you any reason?"

"None. Being somewhat an amateur private eye myself, I did some legwork." He displayed a hind limb that would have looked exceptionally good dangling from the end of a keychain. "I nosed around the industry and uncovered a rumor that someone wants to buy out my contract and give me a starring role, but the DeGreasys refuse to sell. I want you to find out what's going on. If the DeGreasys won't star me, why won't they deal me away?"

Sounded horribly boring, but one more look at his check convinced me to at least go through the motions. I hauled out my notebook and pen.

Normally I would have asked some questions about his background and personal life but, since I only intended to give this case a lick and a promise anyway, why bother? I asked for the DeGreasys' address, and he rattled it off.

"I'll stay in touch," I promised on my way out.

"See you in the funny papers," joked the rabbit.

I didn't smile.

2

I stopped off at a newsstand and bought a candy bar for
lunch and a paper to read while I ate it, making sure to
get a receipt for my expense report. I turned to the comic
section and found the Baby Herman strip.

The rabbit appeared in one panel out of the four, barely
visible behind the smoke and flame of an exploding cigar
given him by Baby Herman.

I folded the paper shut. Hardly an earthshaking caper,
this one. A fast buck and not much more. But what did I
expect? Hobnobbing with a rabbit only gets you to Wonderland in fairy tales.

I met the DeGreasy Brothers, Rocco and Dominick, in
their offices high atop one of L.A.'s most prestigious sky-
scrapers.

The two were human, although almost comical in their
marked resemblance to one another. Their ridged fore-
heads formed a wobble of demarcation between bowl-
shaped haircuts and frizzy eyebrows. Their noses would
have looked perfect behind a chrome horn bolted to the
handlebars of a bicycle. Smudgy moustaches curtained
their circular porthole mouths. Their biceps looked to be
barely half the size of their forearms. And they had feet
large enough to cut fifteen seconds off any duck's time in
the hundred-meter freestyle.

4

Had the DeGreasy boys been discovered frozen beneath some Arctic tundra, a good case would probably have been made for their being the long-sought missing link between humans and 'toons.

But, as funny as they looked, when I checked them out, they had come up professional and efficient, the most astute guys in the comic-strip business. I gave my card to Rocco, the eldest, who passed it across his handsome antique desk to his brother Dominick.

Not wanting to spend a minute longer than necessary on this case, I came straight to the point. I told them Roger Rabbit had hired me to find out why they refused to honor their contractual obligation to star him in a strip of his own.

Rocco chuckled, then scowled, the way a father might when he sees his youngster do something irritating but cute. "Let me explain our position with regard to Roger Rabbit," he said, without the slightest trace of rancor. His precise manner of speech and his six-bit vocabulary gave me quite a surprise. From his looks, I expected Goofy, but got Owen Cantrell, Wall Street lawyer, instead. "My brother Dominick and I signed Roger specifically because we felt he would play well as a foil for Baby Herman. We never made any mention of a solo strip then or since."

Rocco leaned toward me, displaying in the process an impressive array of his stars' merchandising tie-ins—a Superman tie bar, Bullwinkle Moose cufflinks, and a Mickey Mouse wristwatch. "Roger frequently concocts absurd stories such as this one. We tolerate his delusions because of his great popularity with his audience. Roger makes a perfect fall guy, and his fans love him for it. However, he does not have the charisma to carry a strip of his own. We never even considered giving him one. Right, Dominick?"

Dominick's head bounced up and down with the vigor of a spring-necked plastic dog.

Rocco got up, opened a file drawer, and pulled out a sheaf of papers, which he handed to me. "Roger's contract. Read it through. You'll find no mention of a solo strip. And it stipulates a very generous salary, I might add." He closed the drawer and returned to his chair. "We have treated Roger fairly and ethically. He has no reason whatsoever to complain."

I flipped through the contract. It seemed to be in order. "What about the rumor going around that somebody wants to buy out Roger's contract and make him a star?"

Rocco and Dominick exchanged quizzical glances and shrugged more or less in unison. "News to us," said Rocco. "If someone did approach us with an offer for Roger, if it made financial sense, and if Roger wanted to go, we would gladly sell him off. We're not ones to stand in the way of our employees' advancement, and there's certainly no shortage of rabbits to replace him."

He stood and ushered me to the door. "Mister Valiant, I suggest you consider this case closed, and next time get yourself a more mentally stable client."

Sounded reasonable to me.

3

I took a few random jogs. The trench coat, broad-brimmed hat, and large sunglasses matched me move for move.

A tail.

I picked up my pace, turned a corner, and ducked into a doorway.

Seconds later my tail came around the corner after me.

I let him get three paces past, then jumped him, grabbing his arm. I twisted it behind his back and slammed him against the nearest wall.

"Who are you, and what do you want?" I hissed, applying some persuasive pressure.

"I was only curious about how a real detective operates,"

read my tail's balloon. "I just thought I'd tag along. Kind of observe from a distance. I'm sorry if I fouled up your modus operandi."

I released my grip, and snatched away the broad-brimmed hat, exposing a set of carefully accordioned eighteen-inch ears. "Look," I told the rabbit, honing the hat against his concave chest, "when I have something worthwhile to report, I get in touch. Otherwise you stay away from me. Clear?"

The rabbit smoothed out his ears. However, the left one sprang back into a tight clump giving his head the lopsided appearance of a half-straightened paper clip. "Yes, I understand." He fiddled with his ear, fiddled with his sunglasses, fiddled with the buttons on his trench coat, until finally he ran out of externals and began to fiddle with his soul. "My entire life I've wanted to be a detective."

Sure. Him and ten million others. 'Toon mystery strips suckered them into believing that knights-errant always won. Yeah, maybe Rip Kirby bats a thousand. But I consider it great if I go one for ten. "Forget it," I said. "Besides, I'm not so sure how much longer I'm going to stay on this case." I reported my conversation with the DeGreasys, adding that they'd suggested him as poster boy for the Failing Mental Health Society.

He took it in stride. "I never said they put in writing that bit about me getting my own strip," he countered. "They made the offer verbally, and Rocco repeated it several times since."

"Anybody besides you ever hear him?"

"Sure. He said it once at a photo session in front of Baby Herman and Carol Masters, my photographer. Just ask them. They'll remember. As for my being crazy, yes, I see a psychiatrist, but so do half the 'toons in the business. That hardly qualifies me as a full-blown looney."

"I don't know," I said, figuring to cut it off here. "The whole mess sounds like a job for a lawyer."

"Please," the rabbit begged. "Stick with it. I'll double your fee."

Such persuasive words. "All right. You double my fee, and I stay on your case." I turned and walked away.

The rabbit plopped his hat into the chasm between his ears and bounded after me, hopping so fast his word balloons whipped across the top of his head, snapped loose with sharp pings at the base of his neck, and bounced off across the sidewalk. "Let me help you," he said when he caught up with me. "It would mean a great deal to me. Please."

"No way," I stated flatly. "I work alone. Always have, always will." Call me rude, but I say what I mean. If people want sympathy, let them see a priest.

At least he got the message. He did an abrupt about face and shambled away.

4

Apparently the strip business paid babies a whole lot better than it paid rabbits.

Baby Herman lived in an honest-to-God, balconied, marble-pillared, stone-lions-at-the-front-gate mansion tucked neatly away in the kind of neighborhood where middle-class rubbernecks ride bicycles on Sunday afternoons.

His place covered nearly enough land to qualify it for statehood. The house proper sat far back on the property, and a jumbo herd of bib-overalled 'toon goat gardeners puttered about the grounds, nibbling back the grass and shrubs.

The ultimate 'toon status symbol, a human servant, in this case a butler in full regalia, opened the door. He ushered me through to a den furnished in sophisticated playpen.

A Barcelona chair rested beside a rocking horse. Abstract metal sculptures straddled wobbly towers of alphabet blocks. A fine, post-impressionistic painting hung just above a wooden peg supporting a tatty security blanket, one end well chewed.

Baby Herman, two feet high, wearing only a diaper, and bald save for one dark hair sprouting from the precise center of his crown, sat in a highchair in front of the TV. A good portion of his lunch—strained peas, puréed beef, and applesauce—still clung to his chin and to the tray in front of him.

He was watching his own show, giggling happily every time one of his 'toon foils took a clout to the chops.

The butler announced me as Eddie Valiant, private investigator representing Roger Rabbit, then left me and Baby Herman alone.

I had no idea how to proceed. I didn't have much of a way with kids. They generally react to me as they would to the man who shot Bambi's mother.

On the TV screen, a tuxedoed raccoon struggled vainly to extricate himself from the inside of a trombone. Baby Herman laughed uproariously and pounded his tray with a silver spoon, splattering the front of my coat with a fine layer of goo. I steeled myself for a long, hard afternoon.

Just then the butler returned bearing a cigar box, full of robust Havanas. I helped myself. And so, to my surprise, did Baby Herman.

"Kind of young for that stuff, aren't you?" I asked.

"Hah, hah," appeared over Baby Herman's head in the lettering style found on a preschooler's handmade valentine. He lit up and exhaled a cloud that would have done credit to a locomotive. "That's rich. Just how old do you think I am?" When he turned his head so I could examine his profile, he also twisted his word balloon around one hundred and eighty degrees, thus flopping his words into mirror images of themselves.

"I never play guessing games."

"Come on. Just this once. Try."

"Sorry."

"OK, then I'll tell you anyway." Baby Herman unsnapped his tray and climbed to the floor where he stood, puffing his cigar, one chubby hand on each hip. "I'm thirty-six. Don't look it, do I?"

I admitted that he didn't.

"Most people guess me between two and four. Of course, most people don't know enough about 'toons to realize that some age and some don't."

"And you're one of the lucky ones?"

Baby Herman plopped down on his hind end and zigzagged his fingers across the rug. "Depends on your point of view. Eternal youth isn't everything it's cracked up to be. Imagine going through life eating mush, wearing diapers, and sucking on plastic doodads." He displayed the teething ring hung on a gold chain around his neck. "And women. Need I even mention women? Here I sit with a thirty-six-year-old lust, and a three-year-old dinky." He climbed aboard his rocking horse and began a bouncy journey to nowhere. "Why does the funny bunny need a detective? He decided to file for divorce? That what you do? Bust into motel rooms and shoot quickie photos of cheating wives?" An obscene musing encased in a fluffy, cherubic balloon floated above the kid's head. It bobbled around playfully awhile before impaling itself on his single wiry hair, and bursting in a shower of dust that layered his shoulders with the fine powder unknowledgeable humans mistook for dandruff. He immediately conjured up a second image even worse.

"Roger Rabbit has a wife?"

"He did until she left him." Baby Herman dismounted his rocking horse and waddled out from under his pornographic fantasy. "Jessica Rabbit." His second vision turned to sand and dirtied the carpet behind him. "Gorgeous creature. Does a lot of commercials. Wouldn't mind taking her for a hop myself."

"How long they been spilt up?"

"I guess two, maybe three, weeks."

"What caused the breakup?"

"How should I know? What do I look like, Mary Worth? I mind my business, let other people mind theirs." He crawled to the wall and pulled his blanket off its peg. He bundled it around his legs, torso, and head, enveloping himself so completely that only the end of his cigar remained uncovered. "Confidentially," he whispered from out of the snuggly depths of his blanket, "I hear she left Roger for Rocco DeGreasy."

Rocco DeGreasy and a female 'toon rabbit? Sounded ridiculous, but I'd heard of guys with stranger tastes in women. "Actually, I'm not really interested in Roger's wife. I'm investigating Roger's treatment by the DeGreasy syndicate. I understand you heard Rocco promise Roger his own strip."

The blanket bobbed up and down. "Sure. Day before yesterday at a photo session, but only because the bunny was threatening to hit him over the head with his lunch box. It was the first time they'd met since Roger's marital breakup. Roger accused Rocco of putting pressure on Jessica to leave him. Rocco denied it, and Roger went for him. Carol Masters, our photographer, jumped in between them and kept them apart. Rocco came up with that bit about giving Roger his own strip mainly to cool him off, but it didn't work. I never saw Roger so riled. He kept threatening to kill Rocco. Can you imagine that coming from a pussycat like Roger Rabbit? After Carol finally got Roger calmed down, Rocco offered to drive him home. He suggested they could sit down there and discuss their differences rationally until they had them all worked out. A fair and classy guy, that Rocco. Anybody else would have canned Roger on the spot."

"Did Roger and Rocco leave together?"

"No, Roger stormed out of the studio in a huff. Darned inconsiderate of him. We still had half a day's shooting left that we had to cancel. Threw my feeding and naptime schedule into a complete tizzy."

"So Rocco wasn't serious when he offered Roger his own strip."

"Nope. Rocco was scared, plain and simple. When

Roger threatened to kill him, I believe he meant it, and
Rocco believed it, too."

The butler entered and gave the lumpy blanket a courtly
bow. "Don't forget your two-o'clock photo session, sir."

"Right." Baby Herman unwrapped himself and stood.
"I'm doing some baby-food spots." He ground his cigar
out on the rug. "I sold eight million jars of that junk last
year. My wholesome image." He extended his pudgy arms
to Eddie. "Carry me to my limousine?"

Outside, I set him into an infant seat strapped in the
right front bucket of a white Mercedes. "Hey, detective,"
said Baby Herman as I shut the door. "I like you. You
come back sometime, and we'll have us a party. I'll supply
the funny hats, the cake, and the noisemakers. You supply
the broads. Just make sure they go for younger men."

Baby Herman waved bye-bye, and his Mercedes pulled
away.

5

I'll say one thing for the rabbit, he certainly was a per-
sistent little bugger. As soon as I got back to the city, I
spotted him again, hanging maybe half a block back,
matching me move for move. He wore a trench coat
slightly open, exposing purple lederhosen and an orange
shirt. His hat brim scaled up on both sides against fully
unfurled ears. Inconspicuous? Maybe at a clown convention. Certainly not on Sunset Boulevard at two in the
afternoon.

I debated whether or not to brace him again and give
him another ultimatum. He'd probably just ignore it the
same way he had the last. Obviously not one to give up

easily, that Roger, a trait I admired in anybody, 'toon rabbits included. What the heck, if he insisted on wasting his time hopping along in my footsteps, let him. So long as he kept his distance and didn't interfere.

I entered a big downtown office building. The rabbit ducked behind a lamp post across the street, doing his best to appear unconcerned in the presence of a small poodle sniffing at his hydrant-red sneakers. On the building's directory, I found the listing for Carol Masters, photographer.

I boarded a humans-only elevator and rode it up to Masters's floor.

I opened the door to her studio and ran smack into a pile of props big enough to challenge Sir Edmund Hillary.

Masters herself, a human, thank God, since I didn't know if I could handle another 'toon today, stood in the studio's only uncluttered space, a rectangular whitewashed area about ten feet long by five feet wide, positioning her lights and camera.

She had her lean, athletic body nicely displayed in tight jeans and a blue T-shirt sporting an autographed photo of Casper the Friendly Ghost. Baby-soft brown hair played tag with her shoulders. Her tongue underscored her concentration with a thin layer of moisture traced across her creamy red lips. For the sake of male sanity, I hoped she changed perfumes after sundown, since the one she had on could send every male within sniffing range out into the streets to bay at the moon. The lenses in her big, round glasses were the kind that reacted to skin temperature, changing color according to the wearer's mood, going from dark amber to a rosy pink. Right now they fluttered somewhere in between, not happy, not sad, just doing a good day's work. "Something I can help you with?" she said.

I laid a card on her and waited for her to read it. She held it up between us, as though comparing the written description with the real thing. Apparently I measured up to my printed notice, since she motioned for me to sit.

Rummaging through the prop pile, I hauled a chair out

from between a plastic palm tree and a bus-stop sign. I reversed and straddled it so I faced her across its back. "I represent Roger Rabbit," I told her. "I'd like to ask you a few questions concerning his relationship to the syndicate."

"Ask away." She opened a corner cupboard and, from behind half a dozen jugs of 'toonshine, produced a bottle of Burgundy, which she held up with an empty glass.

I nodded.

She splashed out a healthy slug.

I tilted it back, tossed it down in one fast swallow, and extended my empty glass for a refill. "You photograph the Baby Herman strip, right?"

Carol joined me this round, sipping her wine slowly. "I photograph Baby Herman, yes, as well as a number of other DeGreasy strips."

"And you were present a few days back when Roger went after Rocco DeGreasy with a lunch box?"

She nodded. "Roger accused Rocco of pressuring his wife to leave him. I've never seen a rabbit so angry. If I hadn't stepped between them, I think he might have done Rocco some serious harm."

"Any truth to Roger's allegation?"

She studied a hanging photo of Roger Rabbit. It bore the cutesy-pie inscription you'd expect from a professional buffoon. "A sweet bunny, that one," she said fondly. "My absolute favorite subject. No big-star hangups. Never moody or temperamental. A joy to work with. I absolutely adore him." She flicked on several spotlights to see how many dark corners she could illuminate without lengthening her own shadow. She pulled over two easy chairs, one for Dagwood, one for Blondie, and set a floor lamp between them. "I believe Jessica left Roger of her own free will without the slightest bit of coercion from anybody."

"Why do you think that?"

I had seen men break other men's fingers with less force than Carol used to snap in her wide-angle lens. "Who knows?" She squinted into her camera, but jerked her face instantly away, as though repulsed by the nastiness she saw on the other side. "A real bitch, that Jessica. You ever meet her?"

"No. Kind of hard for me to picture so much allure and such a devious nature in a female rabbit."

"Rabbit? No, don't be misled by her name. She isn't a rabbit. She's humanoid. Does mainly high-fashion, cosmetic, and car ads." She went to her file cabinet, removed a portfolio, and passed it to me. "Jessica Rabbit."

A knockout. Every line perfection. Creamy skin, a hundred and twenty pounds well distributed on a statuesque frame, stunning red hair. Easily able to pass for human. "What did someone like this ever see in a 'toon rabbit?"

Carol retrieved the photos and studied them for a moment, as though trying to decide whether to return them to her files or pepper them with voodoo pins. "Nobody knows. Before Roger, she dated humans and other humanoid 'toons exclusively. Their marriage came as a total shock to everybody who knew them." She slipped Jessica's photos back into the darkness where she seemed to feel they belonged. "For about a year it appeared to work. Jessica totally changed. She quit her carousing, quit bad-mouthing her rivals, knocked off her on-the-set temper tantrums. She even went to several of Blondie Bumstead's Tupperware parties." She made a bowl out of her hands and extended it toward the right-hand chair. Then she decreased the cup of her hands to about the size of a rancid tart. "Suddenly, almost overnight, the old Jessica came roaring back. Shrieking at her photographers. Backstabbing everybody who disagreed with her in the slightest. She and Roger broke up shortly thereafter, and she went back to living with Rocco DeGreasy."

"She went *back* to living with him? You mean she had lived with him before?"

"Sure. She left him to marry Roger. Considering that Roger had just stolen Rocco's girl, nobody in the industry could understand why, a few weeks after the marriage, the DeGreasys signed Roger to a long-term contract. Everybody figured that Jessica must have gone to them on

Roger's behalf. Rocco would have done anything, even given Jessica's new husband a contract, if he thought it would get her back." Carol picked up my card and reread the inscription, apparently concerned about my competence to practice my stated profession. "I'm surprised your client neglected to tell you any of this."

"He apparently didn't consider it relevant." I walked to the window, where I could see the rabbit still trying to protect his sneakers from the poodle in the street below. "Guess I'd better ask him why."

"Will you talk to Jessica, too?"

"Probably."

"Then let me give you some advice. Be careful. She has a nasty way of sinking hooks into photogenic men." Carol smiled, pointed her camera at me, and clicked the shutter. My luck held. The lens didn't break.

"Thanks for the warning. When I see her, I'll be sure and wear my armored undies. One last question. Have you heard the rumor that someone wants to buy out Roger's contract and give him a starring role in a strip of his own?"

"Yes, I've heard it. Rumors like that spring up with alarming regularity in this business. Most often they prove totally false. For Roger's sake, I hope this one's true, but I wouldn't bet on it."

Before I left, I got her home address and phone number, just in case I decided later to ask her a few of the more personal questions that kept jumping to mind every time I saw her move.

6

I slipped out of the building through a side door, crossed the street, and came up on the rabbit from behind.

"Surprise," I growled. I grabbed the rabbit's arm and hustled him unceremoniously down the street.

I whizzed my reluctant companion past several human-only and several 'toon-only bars before we came to a grubby hole-in-the-wall saloon, maybe twenty feet wide and thirty feet long, willing to serve both species. The bar, tended by a puffy-eared, flat-nosed human, ran the length of the right-hand wall. A bunch of derelict 'toons held down one end. A bunch of derelict humans pegged down the other. The saloon's only interior decoration consisted of several framed newspapers welcoming Lindbergh back from Paris, a subtle play on the common belief that certain humans—Babe Ruth, Mae West, the Marx Brothers, and, of course, Lindbergh—were really humanoid 'toons who had crossed the line.

I marched Roger to a booth, sat him down, and slid in beside him, trapping him against the wall.

A 'toon waitress came over. In her younger days, she probably got mistaken for Dixie Dugan. Nowadays she carried forty pounds too much flab, three pounds too much makeup, and the resemblance leaned more toward Petunia Pig. "What'll it be?"

17

"Boilermaker for me," I said, "and a 'shine for the fur ball."

She waddled to the bar to fill our order.

The rabbit wiggled himself some breathing room. "I'm sorry," he said, misinterpreting the reason for my anger. "I know you told me to keep my distance, but I couldn't resist. My entire life I've been a clown, acting out jokes for a living. Here I saw the chance to get involved in something serious for a change, and I took it." His right-hand fingers started a frisky jig on the booth top, which his left-hand fingers couldn't resist joining in. "You can't imagine how exciting it's been for me just to follow you around and watch you work. Granted, I disobeyed your order. For that I apologize. But, to be honest, I'm delighted I did. I haven't had this much fun in ages."

"I'm glad I brightened your humdrum life," I said sarcastically. "Maybe you'll do something for me in return."

The rabbit doubled up his ears so they wouldn't collide with the booth top when he nodded his head. "Name it."

"Tell me about your wife," I said with enough frost in my voice to turn the rabbit's nose blue.

"My wife?" The rabbit's word balloon miserably failed its maiden flight, collapsing half-deflated across my shoulder.

I grabbed it, squashed it into a hourglass shape, and tossed it in front of him. "Jessica Rabbit." I pointed to the mangled balloon. "Your wife. Remember her?"

"Oh, of course. Jessica!" Roger plucked the name from out of the air above him and extended it to me pillowed in the cup of his palm. "Jessica. She's my wife."

I rolled the name into a tiny ball and flicked it into orbit off the end of my thumb. "And also Rocco DeGreasy's current romantic interlude. How come you didn't tell me about her?"

The rabbit twiddled the stubby ends of his ears. "I didn't think it was important."

I tilted my head back and rolled my eyes. Melodramatic, I know, but dealing with 'toons seemed to have that effect on me. "Your wife plays patty cake with one of the guys you work for, one of the guys who you say reneged on your contract, and you don't think it's important? My friend, you got a lot to learn about what makes the world go round."

"Well, how come you didn't pry it out of me?" said the rabbit, turning untypically militant in his own defense. "I mean you've got some responsibilities in this case, too."

The waitress brought our drinks. While I fished out my wallet, she snabbed a few stray ear puffs floating across the low ceiling.

"So maybe we both made a mistake," I said, figuring there to be zip percentage in arguing with a bubble-brain like Roger. "What say we chalk it off to experience, and start over?"

"Fine with me."

"Great. Let's begin with how you and Jessica first met."

The rabbit crossed his oblong pupils as though reading the high points of his life off a crib sheet taped to the rear of his nose. "We met one day at a photo session."

"At Carol Masters's place?"

"Yes. Jessica had just finished shooting a liquor ad, and I was there to do a supporting role in a Jungle Jim strip. This was, of course, when I was still doing bit parts, before I signed with the DeGreasys. We chatted for a while. Nothing of any great import. Mainly trade gossip, who got his contract dropped, who got a new strip, who got married, who had kids, who got divorced. Normal small talk. We seemed to get along pretty well, so I asked her to dinner. I didn't really expect her to accept, not with her being a humanoid and me a barnyard. But she did. We went to this cozy Italian place and had a delightful time. We talked and laughed and played kneesies under the table. She came back to my place for a drink. I made some popcorn, lit a fire, and played her a song on my piano. Then, more as a gag than anything else, I proposed to her. Got down on bended knee, the whole works. To my great surprise, Jessica accepted. We flew to Reno and tied the knot." He commemorated the happy event by looping his ears into a bow and bugging his eyes out into two perfectly matched hearts.

"You mean Jessica married you on your first date?"

"Yes. I could hardly believe it."

Same here. "How long after your marriage before the DeGreasys gave you a contract?"

"Almost immediately."

"How did it happen?"

"One night, right after Jessica and I got married, we were sitting in our living room listening to our stereo. I told her how much I envied her. How it had always been my fondest wish to be a well-known star. The next day, out of the blue, Rocco DeGreasy called up, said he had seen me in some of my supporting roles, said he thought I had enough talent to carry my own strip, and offered me a contract."

"Did you know about Jessica's previous relationship with Rocco? That she had left him to marry you?"

The rabbit nodded slowly. "But I don't think she ever really loved him. I think he had something on her, something dreadful he used to hold her to him. A girl as wonderful as Jessica would never voluntarily stay with anyone as awful as Rocco."

"Any chance Jessica might have been influential in getting you your contract?"

"I don't know." Roger's ears turned as limp as stalks of old celery. "I always secretly suspected she probably had gone to Rocco about it, but I never asked her outright. I was afraid to. I desperately wanted to believe I had gotten it based on my own merits, not because Rocco thought it might win Jessica back. Anyway, for a while I was the happiest bunny alive. I had Jessica, and I had a contract with the biggest syndicate in the business, and I had their promise to make me a star."

So much for that part of Roger's life where everybody had sung in tune. Now for the later sessions, where the notes had turned sour, and the strolling violinist had left in disgust. "What caused your marriage to break up?"

The rabbit's ears flopped over double and wobbled side to side, like a television aerial trying unsuccessfully to align itself with a very faint signal. "It was a real mystery. We had been married about a year when, about two weeks ago, almost overnight, Jessica changed from a kind, wonderful, caring person into a shrewish, raving witch." Roger's body sagged.

"You don't have any idea what caused the change?"

"None. She refused to discuss it or even to admit that she was any different. I suggested a marriage counselor, but she said no. She moved out on me and moved back in with Rocco DeGreasy."

"You seen her since?"

"No. I've tried to talk to her a couple of times, but she avoids me. I understand she's contacted a lawyer and put a divorce in the works." His eyelids dipped to half mast in memory of his dear departed, and he saluted her with a long drink of 'shine. His ear puffs, when they appeared, came out in a curving column of spheres, resembling the smoke from an underpowered locomotive chugging up a long, impossibly difficult hill.

"OK. Now that we've covered your marital squabbles, let's do your assault on Rocco DeGreasy."

The rabbit's pupils bounced back and forth across his eyes like the electronic blips in an arcade tennis game. "I knew I should have told you about that. I knew I could never hide it from you. Not from a pro." His thought-balloon formed an image of a wooden hammer that whopped a few licks of sense into his head. "It happened the first time we met after Jessica left me. I accused Rocco of somehow blackmailing her into it. Know what he did? He laughed at me. He didn't even answer. He just laughed at me. Tell me, Mister Valiant, do you know how miserable it is to have a person laugh at you?"

It seemed an odd statement from someone whose main function in life was to make people laugh at him, but I didn't feel up to tackling the philosophic implications of it. "Look," I said, "I'm not so sure this is really my kind of job. It seems to me that maybe what you ought to do is to take this up with your 'toon union labor board. You need an arbitrator, not a private eye."

"I already threatened to do that, I did, but Rocco warned me that it might have unfortunate consequences."

"Any idea what he meant?"

"Sure. He meant his brother Dominick." Roger shuddered the way you do when an icy draft slips down the back of your neck. "I'm not a brave rabbit, Mister Valiant. I'm not about to buck Rocco and Dominick by myself. That's why I came to you."

I cradled my head in my hands. What had I ever done to deserve this? Other detectives get the Maltese Falcon. I get a paranoid rabbit. "You should have told me about your marital problems before," I said self-righteously, half-hoping I'd provoke the rabbit to fire me.

But the rabbit accepted my scolding with remarkably good grace. "Well, I would have, except you didn't ask. When we first met, you were so taciturn and in such a hurry. Who am I to second guess a private detective? I assumed a close-mouthed, speedy approach must be your style. I assumed you were a pro, and you knew what you were doing. And I guess I was right. I mean you did find out about everything anyway."

"Yeah, I sure did," I said with glum resignation.

The rabbit dropped his voice so low his word-balloon barely cleared the booth top. "Where do you go next, Mister Valiant?" The words inside the balloon flickered on and off like a decrepit neon sign. "Are you going to see Jessica?"

"Yes, I am. First thing tomorrow morning."

The rabbit bowed his head and sent up a scrolly, illuminated balloon that could have been ripped straight out of a prayer book. "Well, when you do, would you give her a message for me? Would you tell her I still love her? Tell her I miss her very much, and I'd like to give her another try. Tell her that I'm sorry for whatever it was I did to offend her, and I promise to change. I promise to do anything she wants, if only she'll take me back. Will you tell her that? Please?"

I didn't stick around much longer. It depressed me to see a grown rabbit cry.

7

*A TV-commercial director hand-signaled the ten camera-*men evenly spaced along a roped-off length of Rodeo Drive.

His production assistant, perched on a tower halfway down the street, flipped on a specially rigged wireless relay box and set a driverless, open Mercedes convertible rolling along the street at forty miles an hour.

A stubby helicopter overtook the Mercedes from behind and assumed a position just above the driver's seat.

A trim, flight-suited female, wearing a leather flying helmet and aviator goggles, with a rope coiled around her left shoulder, appeared in the helicopter's cargo door. She secured one end of the rope to a pin ring on the helicopter's interior bulkhead, threw the remainder of the rope out the door, and shinnied down it toward the moving car. She lowered herself into the front seat, took the wheel, and applied the brakes just in time to prevent the car from crashing into a stationary truck positioned cross-ways in the street ahead.

The helicopter saluted her with a side-to-side dip, and sped away.

A most impressive operation, easily the equal of any-thing I'd seen in the Marines. Almost a shame that strate-gic responsibility for conquering other nations couldn't be switched from Washington to Madison Avenue. The

United States might today be bottling Coke, packaging cornflakes, assembling Pontiacs, battling crabgrass, and eradicating underarm odor in suburban Moscow, Peking, and Hanoi.

The director, decked out in polo pants with side flaps large enough to put him into contention for head bull in a herd of elephants, conferred with a man wearing enough gold chains around his neck to shackle half the prisoners in a Southern road gang. The chain man framed the final scene between his thumbs and forefingers and gave an exaggerated nod.

"That's a keeper," yelled the director. "Let's break for breakfast while we check the rushes."

The car backed, turned, and squealed to a stop alongside the curb in front of where I stood. The girl driver pulled herself free of the cockpit and swung athletically across the door and out. She unsnapped her goggles, peeled away her helmet, and gave me my first, real-life look at Jessica Rabbit.

Her photos, as stunning as they were, hadn't begun to capture the full scope of her beauty. Curly hair the color of a lingering sunset. Porcelain skin. Incendiary gray-blue eyes. Lips the softness of pink rose petals. And a body straight out of one of the magazines adolescent boys pore over in locked bathrooms. The kind of woman usually portrayed floating down the Nile on a barge, nibbling at stuffed pheasant and peeled grapes, enticing some beguiled Roman into conquering half the civilized world on her behalf.

All of which only served to deepen the mystery. What had a woman like this ever seen in a dippy 'toon rabbit?

I approached her. "Mrs. Rabbit? My name's Eddie Valiant. I'm a private investigator. I'd like to have a word with you about your husband."

"My husband?" She inclined her head, squinted her eyes, and up-tilted the corners of her mouth into the amused yet perplexed expression of someone confronted by an especially ridiculous riddle. "I'm afraid you have the wrong person. I've never been married. I have no husband."

Surely I couldn't have made a mistake. There couldn't be two women this gorgeous. "You are Jessica Rabbit?"

"Correct."

"Then what, if I may ask, is your relationship to Roger Rabbit?"

"Who?" In the best Orphan Annie tradition, Jessica demonstrated her innocent bewilderment by revolving her eyes upward and tucking them out of sight underneath her open eyelids. "Roger Rabbit? Sorry, I never heard of him." A blatant lie, no question about it, and, as though to illustrate what happens to people who lie, her brilliant smile dribbled off her chin and fluttered to the ground like a bicuspid butterfly. I reacted the way I would have had she dropped her hankie. I reached down, scooped up her smile, and handed it back, only to find that, while I had been bent over, other assorted portions of her anatomy, including both ears and her nose, had also fallen off. I gallantly scrambled to retrieve these bits and pieces for her too, but they disintegrated before I could reach them. I stood upright just in time to witness the rest of her disappear the same way.

My hand still shaped to the bow of her smile, I circled the spot where she had stood, kicking my toe against the concrete. Not a smidgeon of her remained.

Suddenly I heard bemused, husky, feminine laughter behind me. "I take it you've never seen a doppelgänger erode before?"

I turned around and found myself facing—*Jessica Rabbit!*

Of course. What I saw wasn't really her. It was a mentally projected duplicate of her, or doppelgänger as 'toons call them. Identical to her in every regard, physically and mentally, but existing only by the energy of her mind. 'Toons can create doppelgängers more or less at will. They merely relax, channel their thoughts in that direction, and magically one of them appears. 'Toons use them as doubles in risky shots. When you see a 'toon stuffed into a trombone or run over by a steamroller or crushed by a falling safe, it's really a doppelgänger. And she was right. I never had seen one erode before.

"Isn't it kind of traumatic to see a part of you just wither away like that?"

"Not particularly. No more so than I imagine it might be for you to throw one of your fingernail clippings into a trash can. Oh, I'm sure there are primitive tribes in Africa or somewhere who treat their doppelgängers as mystic offshoots of their soul, but we modern, civilized 'toons regard our doppelgängers as animated mannequins, nothing more."

She leaned gracefully against the Mercedes's rear fender, instinctively adjusting her posture to display herself to best advantage. She needn't have bothered. A woman as beautiful as this could have stood on one leg, flapped her arms, stuck out her tongue, and still held my interest. Like most humanoid 'toons, Jessica suppressed her word-balloons and spoke vocally only, thus enhancing ever further her human image. "I heard you tell my doppel that you wanted to see me about Roger. What's his problem now?"

"What was his problem before?"

She replied quickly, as though she had been asked the same question so many times that she had committed the answer to memory. "He couldn't cope with being a celebrity. He turned moody, conceited, belligerent. So I left him."

A bit of a discrepancy there between Jessica and her husband. Had it been Jessica Rabbit or Roger who had undergone the Jekyll-to-Hyde transformation that had scuttled the marriage? By rights, I should believe my client. That was by rights. From experience, I knew that the one caught with the stolen macaroons often wound up being the same one who had hired me to stake out the cookie jar. "You might be interested to know that Roger says he want a reconciliation. He says he's willing to do whatever it takes to get you back."

She crossed one perfect arm over the other. "If that's

why he hired you, to come here and tell me that, I'm afraid he's wasted your time. I left Roger for someone else."

"I guess that translates to Rocco DeGreasy."

She dipped her chin and held it there, the way a fighter would to protect himself from an uppercut. "That's right, though I don't see where it's any concern of yours."

Good looks could distract me only so long. "Roger hired me to investigate irregularities in his contract. Rather an odd coincidence that his estranged wife would have such a close relationship with one of the people who gave it to him. You have anything to do with the DeGreasys signing Roger?"

She shook her head, pushed herself away from the car, and assumed a square stance that, even in its belligerence, gave a certain graceful beauty to her tiny clenched fists and firmly set jaw. "Absolutely not. I never understood why they did it. Roger has no talent whatsoever. I suspect Rocco thought it would please me and perhaps win me back. Or possibly Rocco feared Roger might move to another part of the country and take me with him. A contract tying Roger down might have seemed the easiest way to prevent that."

"Did the DeGreasys ever promise Roger his own strip?"

Too bad she suppressed her balloons. Her tinkling laugh could have reoutfitted a Swiss bell-ringer. "No, never. That's nothing more than a story Roger concocted. You should not take Roger too seriously. He does see a psychiatrist, you know."

"You ever hear of anyone wanting to buy out Roger's contract and give him his own strip?"

"Yes, I heard a rumor to that effect, but I can't imagine anyone wanting to star Roger in anything. Believe me, the rabbit has absolutely no talent. None."

The director interrupted us before I could follow up. "Jessica, sweetheart," the director said, "the agency man wants to shoot a slightly different angle. Could you give us another doppel?"

"Of course. Would you excuse me?" she said to me.

She stepped into a nearby dressing trailer and several minutes later emerged as twins.

"Ready to shoot," she told the director.

The two indistinguishable Jessicas climbed into the helicopter and flew off into the morning sky.

While I waited for her to return, I located the nearest pay phone and called my client, hoping to maybe clarify a few of the inconsistencies Jessica had lobbed into the ballgame.

Roger answered in a state of near panic. "My God, am I glad it's you! You have to get over here. This isn't just a matter of a broken promise anymore. It's escalated drastically."

"How so?"

Roger gulped audibly. "Somebody just tried to kill me."

8

I sat in Roger's living room doing my best to swallow a chuckle. "Somebody attacked you with what?"

"A custard cream pie," Roger repeated, nervously fidgeting with the pie tin balanced on his lap. "I was on my way home from an early photo session at Carol Masters's when somebody jumped out from behind a tree and smacked me in the face with a custard cream pie."

"It must have been a practical joke. Nobody could kill you with a pie."

"Oh, you're wrong. Indeed, they could. In the classic comic pie toss, somebody plops you in the kisser, coming straight in to get maximum splatter, and then pulls up short so as not to mash in your nose. The pie tin slithers off, and that's it. But not this fellow." Roger fanned out his fingers and scrunched them into his face to demonstrate the angle of attack. "He came in from about shoulder level so the custard blocked off my mouth and nose, then he gave it kind of a half twist so the whipped cream flew up and covered my eyes. And he didn't let go. He held that pie so tightly against my face that I couldn't breathe. I kicked him a hearty one in the shins, and I guess I connected, because he grunted, dropped his pie, and ran away."

"You get a look at him?"

"No. He had turned a corner before I got my eyes scooped off."

"Human or 'toon? Could you tell that?"

"No. I'm sorry. I checked around for witnesses but drew a blank." He held up a standard nine-inch aluminum pie tin covered with half an inch of dried custard. The custard had solidified into a perfect outline of his mouth and nose. "I did retrieve the weapon, though." He handed me the tin.

I examined it front and back. No prints evident, but it did bear the stamped-in name and address of a nearby neighborhood pie shop. I wrapped the tin as best I could into my handkerchief. "I'll check it out," I said, "even though I suspect this was most likely nothing more than a juvenile prank."

"Prank?" Angry whipcords of steam puffed out of the rabbit's nostrils and heated his nose to the color of an apple. "How can you say prank? It was those DeGreasy brothers. They tried to smother me. If we don't stop them, they'll try again. And next time they might not miss."

"Believe what you want, just be aware that in my opinion this pie guy has no connection with your other predicament, and chasing after him will most likely be a big waste of effort." Pie tin in hand, I got up and headed for the door, where I stopped, turned, and almost as an afterthought said, "By the way, I talked to your wife today."

Roger couldn't have brightened up any quicker had he

plugged his tail into an electrical outlet. "Jessica? You saw Jessica? Did you give her my message?"

"Yes."

"And what did she say?"

I hit him with it the only way I knew how—hard, fast, and straight to the chops. Leave tact to the slick talkers wearing pressed three-piece suits. If you had a terminal illness, I'd tell you point-blank not to start any all-day suckers. "She's not coming back to you. And she says the reason she's not is because it was you, not her, that changed. She said you used to be a fun guy, but that, after you got your contract, you turned into an ogre. She said she couldn't take it, so she left you."

"She said that? Jessica said that?" The tiny dots that gave color to Roger's skin coalesced into splotches so large that, given an ear bob and a transplanted tail, he could have passed for a calico cat. "Well, that's the silliest thing I ever heard. Me? An ogre?" He launched a partial balloon, but the feigned hah-hah inside fizzled out through the balloon's stem and, with a resounding *blat*, splattered across the rug.

"She also said a few other things."

"Such as?"

"I'm not so sure you want to hear them."

"I'm a big bunny. I can take it."

"Suit yourself. She said you were nuts. She also said you had no talent."

"She doesn't mean that, not any of it. Rocco is pressuring her to say those things."

"She also insisted that you made up the part about the DeGreasys promising you your own strip."

"Widdle on that Rocco DeGreasy!" Roger's word balloon had originally contained something far stronger, but, always conscious of his family-rated image, he had hastily X'd it out and replaced it with a statement less profane. "He has some evil hold over Jessica. For the year Jessica and I were together, we were as in love as two people can be. There was no faking how she felt about me. She couldn't possibly have reversed herself so quickly. Rocco forced her to leave me, and he's forcing her to say things about me that she doesn't mean. I want you to find out how he's doing it, and I want you to make him stop." Roger crossed his hands over his head but couldn't cork the flood of tear-shaped balloons blubbering out of him.

I nodded as though I really took seriously this whole monumental bit of goofiness. "Exactly what I planned to do next."

9

Carol Masters wasn't at her studio, so I tried her at home. She lived in a partially 'toon, partially human neighborhood that real estate agents called ethnically enriched, and urban renewers called blighted. Depending on which way you happened to be facing—toward the gossiping, front-stoop 'toon and human housewives or toward the babbling, back-alley 'toon and human drunks—either term could apply.

Carol's apartment occupied half a floor in what had been, in the late forties, a fashionable row house. Now it and the houses linked together on either side of it resembled a rickety roller coaster already well over its summit and plunging pell-mell on its long run downhill.

Carol's door-bell wires drooped stiffly out of their housing like twin copper fangs, so I rapped on the door. Carol answered it, dressed as she had been at her studio, and invited me in.

I took an immediate liking to her home decoration. No wall to wall furniture to trip you up every time you went to the kitchen for a late-night beer. No chintz to gather dust. A few comfortable chairs placed for easy face-to-face

conversation, some scattered end tables, and a colorful
rainbow painted across two walls, culminating on each
end in framed displays of Carol's photographs. Her record
collection filled most of a six-foot-long shelf, bluegrass to
the center with a few rock records tacking down either
end.

She told me to pour myself a drink while she finished
processing some photos in a darkroom she had rigged up
in her bedroom closet.

I checked my watch. I never drink until after six. It was
then four-fifteen. Close enough. I buried the bottom of a
glass under three fingers of bourbon, walked into the bedroom after her, and sat down on her bed.

There wasn't much to be said for this room's decor. Her
clothes, mostly sweaters, shirts, and jeans hyphenated at
irregular intervals by a few frilly party numbers, hung on
a trapeze-style bar suspended from the ceiling. She had
cameras, lenses, carrying cases, and other equipment I
couldn't identify scattered everywhere. I could smell her
photographic chemicals even through the closed closet
door.

She came out after a few minutes carrying some wet
prints. "Let me just put these in the dryer," she said. She
placed the prints into a small contraption set on top of
her dresser.

I came up behind her and looked over her shoulder at
her prints, five copies of the same Baby Herman strip.
"How come you don't do this at your studio?"

"I work when the mood strikes me," she answered.
"There's no punching a time clock when it comes to
creativity."

I didn't quite see the creativity involved in smelling up
a bedroom by running off five identical prints, but who
was I to question art? "How did you get into this business?" I asked while she finished loading the dryer.

"I started out processing film for a small comic book
publisher. He gave me a chance to shoot some complete
episodes, I liked it, was good at it, and so went upward
from there."

We went back into the living room where Carol poured herself a duplicate of my drink and sank into an easy chair that was slipcovered in a pastel print. It nearly swallowed her small body whole. "Is this visit business or pleasure?"

I passed up the other easy chair in favor of a wooden kitchen chair which, as usual, I straddled in reverse. "Let's start with business. I'm just wrapping up Roger's case. If you could clarify a few minor points, that should do it."

"However I can help."

"Give me some background on the syndicate. How long have you worked for the DeGreasys?"

"About five years."

"You like it?"

"So-so." Carol kicked off her sneakers, put her feet on the front of her chair cushion, and wrapped her arms around her knees, compressing herself into a compact bundle of prettiness—pretty feet, pretty hands, pretty chin, pretty nose, pretty hair. Anyone seeing her like this, elfin and vulnerable, might be tempted to write her off as a harmless piece of fluff, a cream puff. Until you saw her eyes. The kind of cool, luminous eyes that peek out at you through jungle shrubbery and size you up for lunch. "I could do a lot better financially and have a lot more artistic satisfaction as a freelancer, but I still have five years to go on my contract. I've offered to buy myself out, but the DeGreasys won't play. Or rather one of them won't."

"Rocco?"

"Right. He's the corporate hard-nose. He personally negotiates every contract, and he ties down every loose end. Nobody gets out of a Rocco DeGreasy contract unless he lets them out."

"And if somebody tries?"

"That's where Dominick comes in. He's the muscle man."

"Sounds like a very dynamic duo."

"They do tend to balance out each other's weaknesses."

"You ever heard of Dominick DeGreasy attacking anyone with a pie?"

She got a big yuck out of that. "A pie? Hardly. He's
more the brass knuckles type. Why do you ask?"

I snickered once or twice as I described Roger's run-in
with the pie man. I told her it sounded like a practical
joke to me, but to justify my retainer I had to at least
go through the motions. "Know of anyone who might
want to smother Roger with a pie?" I found it impossible
to ask such a question and sound serious.

Carol didn't laugh, though. She burrowed sideways into
her chair and bounced her answer off the wall. "No, no
one. Roger hasn't an enemy in the world."

I treated my next question pretty much as a joke, too.
I asked her if she had seen anyone hanging around outside
her studio this morning when Roger left, maybe someone
packing a loaded pie.

No, she told me without so much as cracking a smile,
she hadn't seen anyone. She got up, poured herself another drink, but didn't offer to do the same for me.

Better lay off, I figured. The lady obviously had no
sense of humor. "I talked to Jessica Rabbit this morning,"
I said soberly. "She gave me a slightly different version
of the story I got earlier from you."

"How so?"

"According to her, it was Roger who underwent the big
personality change that broke up their marriage. She says
he became an ogre. You see any evidence of it in your
work with him?"

She twisted the ends of her hair around her index
finger. "None. She's lying. Roger's the same sweet bunny
now as he's always been."

"She also said that Roger made up that bit about Rocco
DeGreasy promising Roger his own strip. She says the
rabbit has no talent."

Carol slammed her drink down on her coffee table. "I
don't know whether or not Rocco promised Roger his own
strip. If Roger says yes, I believe him. Roger wouldn't lie.
As for Roger's talent, the rabbit's absolutely loaded with

it. He deserves a strip of his own. I can't see why the DeGreasys don't give it to him. Rocco's a tyrant, but he does know natural ability when he sees it. Which is a lot more than I can say for Jessica. Not having any talent herself, I would guess it's probably hard for her to recognize it in others."

"Funny but you're the only one with a good word to say about the rabbit. I always wonder when I see one person bucking the crowd. In my experience, the majority's usually right."

She got out of her chair and traveled toward me in the kind of half-circle a ballistic missile takes on its way into enemy territory. She pointed at me, standing so close that, if either of us moved forward by so much as an inch, her fingers would hit my nose. "Now I understand. You're going to dump Roger, aren't you? He hired you to help him, and you're going to abandon him, instead. You're not in this for truth and justice. You're in it for the money!" She jabbed me in the chest with a fingernail sharp enough to pin me to the wall. "Well, no matter what anybody says, in my book, Roger is one fine rabbit, and he deserves a lot better than he seems to be getting from you."

I grabbed her tiny hand. "I don't think you understand, lady," although quite clearly she understood only too well. "He's my client, and I care about him, sure. But I'm beginning to suspect he's a certified nut case. He does go to a psychiatrist, you know. Instead of a detective, I think he might need a padded room ten feet square."

She pulled back her hand and held it rigid and slightly away from her, as though it had to be sterilized before she could use it again. "Of course, Roger's a touch goofy. He's a *cartoon rabbit!* What do you expect him to be, Albert Einstein?"

She yanked open her front door. I went through it sideways, to prevent her from kicking me in the pants on my way out.

In a crazy sense I had to envy that fruitcake rabbit. I sure never had a friend that devoted to me.

10

*Rocco crossed his legs so that two teeny-weeny trolls, grip-*ping opposite ends of a third troll dipped in shoe polish, could seesaw across his immense upraised oxford. When they had finished with him, the troll threesome scurried over to me, took one look at my hopelessly scarred steel-toed brogans, dismissed me as a lost cause, and went back to general cleanup.

"Let me get this straight," said Rocco, aiming his index finger at the guts of my theory. "You're actually suggesting that I or my brother Dominick attempted to assassinate Roger Rabbit yesterday with a custard cream *pie?* Is that the gist of your accusation, Mister Valiant? Do I have that one hundred percent correct?"

I had to admit it did sound a lot less likely coming from him than it had from the rabbit.

Rocco leaned back in his chair. "Look at the contents of this office, Mister Valiant. Look. The original, framed comic strips on the walls cost an average of fifty thousand dollars each. My desk. A priceless antique. These trolls. Fifty dollars a day. My suit. Six hundred dollars worth of custom-tailored linen. I have wealth, status, a successful business. Why, Mister Valiant, why on Earth would I jeopardize all that by assaulting a rabbit with a custard cream pie?"

At least I had that one covered. "Roger threatened to kill you during a fight at Carol Masters's. Maybe he scared you so badly, you decided to get him before he got you."

"Are you serious?" He poked his pork-sausage thumbs against his chest. "Me, frightened of a rabbit?"

He was right, of course, and I knew it. This whole line of questioning gave me a near-terminal case of embarrassment. The only reason I decided to have one last go at Rocco before I bailed out was so there could be no Carol Masters walking around saying I hadn't given the rabbit his money's worth. "Maybe it sounds farfetched, but so does a lot of other stuff in this case. For instance, why did you give a contract to the rabbit who stole your girl? Why did Jessica suddenly leave Roger and return to you?"

Rocco went to his bar and poured two Scotch and sodas. He collared the nearest troll, upended it, and swizzled it through both glasses. Rocco handed one of the glasses to me, wrung the troll out over the sink, and draped it across the faucet to dry. Another troll trotted up with a butterfly net ready to snare our ear puffs. Lovable rascals, trolls, but a bit short in the smarts department.

"You wonder why Jessica came back to me?" Rocco said, scooting the troll's net away with his head. "I suspect she simply grew tired of Roger's eternal lunacy. I provide her with cultured, refined companionship. You can't get that from a rabbit. As to why I gave Roger his contract, also simple. Naturally I was miffed when Jessica and Roger eloped. Who wouldn't be? But I never let my personal life interfere with business. Baby Herman needed a stooge. I pegged Roger Rabbit as the perfect choice, the eternal sidekick, a fluffy Gabby Hayes." He waved his arm in a circular gesture, which grew in circumference to encompass the office, the building, the street outside, the entire world. "Oh, I've heard the rumors. That I signed Roger only to win back Jessica." His laughter exposed two rows of teeth remarkable for their resemblance to weatherworn tombstones. "I'd like to hear anyone explain how I could expect to regain Jessica by turning her new husband into a big success."

"I don't think Roger would classify being fall guy to Baby Herman as a big success."

Rocco clicked up a notch from joviality to mild annoyance. "I've discussed that with Roger at great length. He does not have the talent to support his own strip. Period." He sat down at his priceless antique desk and fondled the lapels of his six-hundred-dollar, custom-tailored suit. "Tell you what. Even though I've gone over it with him a hundred times before, I'll be glad to meet with Roger and explain it to him yet again. Lately he refuses to come here, so I'll even spare him that. I'll go to his house. Any day he wants. Just tell him to let me know when, and I'll be there."

Rocco fluttered his fingers through a bypassing troll daydream, a wispy, multicolored affair of abstract content, the kind of trendy socialites imbed in Lucite and display on étagères. "As for the incident with the custard pie, I think we can probably categorize that as another of Roger's hallucinations."

"It was no hallucination. I saw the pie tin myself."

"Yes, I'm sure you did," said Rocco. He closed his eyes and folded his hands across his chest. Cast him in lead, stick a clock in his stomach, and he would easily have fetched six bits as a novelty buddha in any el cheapo second-hand store in town. After a few seconds he came back to life, rummaged through his desk, removed an address book, and copied out a name, which he passed across to me. "Do me this one favor. Here's a noted 'toon psychiatrist, Doctor Booker T. Beaver. You may have heard of him. The syndicate uses him for public-service comics—VD pamphlets and family-planning brochures the medical associations distribute to the free clinics. Roger goes to him. I think a few words with Doctor Beaver might put this whole pie episode into proper perspective. Do that. Talk to Doctor Beaver. And, if you still suspect me afterward of having any connection with this bizarre pie-flinging incident, I'll be more than happy to do whatever you want, even take a lie detector test, to convince you of my innocence. Is that a reasonable approach?"

It certainly was, and I figured I'd better go along with it since it was probably the only reasonable approach I was likely to encounter in this screwball case.

11

Roger's psychiatrist agreed to see me after office hours. In person he presented as imposing a demeanor as a 'toon beaver could. He moved slowly and with great precision, so that the layer of fat that plumped out his lower body gave him an air of portly dignity rather than jiggly over-indulgence. He kept his broad, flat, oblong tail tucked up and away in a special pocket sewn on the underside of his white jacket, a gimmick that made him resemble a cross between the hunchback of Notre Dame and a ping-pong paddle. His head hair, the same slightly muddy brown as a river bottom, was parted down the middle and combed to each side, hiding his stubby ears. He waxed his scraggly nose whiskers and twisted them into a handlebar so curvaceous that, in bad light, he might be mistaken for a Harley Davidson. Yellow-tinted aviator glasses camouflaged his ridiculously bulging button eyes and broke up the solid arch extending from the tip of his nose to the top of his head.

To satisfy his cravings for something to gnaw, he kept a number of mahogany wood turnings in an antique umbrella stand beside his desk. A solid silver dustpan and whisk broom took care of the wood chips.

His medical diploma, dated twenty years earlier, proclaimed him a graduate of TCU, 'Toon Christian University.

His word balloons resembled the scrawly prescription forms you take to the drugstore. "Naturally," he said, "since Roger is a patient, I can't discuss his case clinically, but if he's in trouble of some sort, and I might be able to help, I would be only too happy to oblige. So long as I compromise no professional ethics in the process, of course." He ran his nose the length of a wooden pencil, then devoured it as casually as someone eating a piece of candy. He plucked the eraser discreetly off his lips and dropped it into his wastebasket. "What seems to be the problem?" he asked with great solemnity.

That nearly put the capper on it. How could I conduct a serious interrogation of a psychiatrist who snacked on pencils? I thought about the retainer and pressed forward. "My main concern is an incident involving an attack with a custard cream pie."

When the beaver leaned back and stroked his severely receding chin, his white coat flapped open to reveal a three-piece, dark-blue pinstripe suit, expertly tailored to disguise his spreading paunch. "Ah, yes, I'm quite familiar with it," he said after a short period of contemplation.

"You are?"

"Most assuredly." Doctor Beaver rolled his front paw across a desktop dispenser containing a giant ball of extra-heavyduty dental floss, a necessity for those prone to munch on mahogany. "Let me phrase this as delicately as possible. Roger has undergone a tremendous amount of strain recently. His continued role as a subordinate to Baby Herman. His marital problems climaxed by the loss of his wife. In my opinion, Roger must be considered a very sick rabbit, fully capable of concocting the most fantastic stories to rationalize his failures in life. There exist a number of quite complex psychological theories which explain such behavior. To put it into layman's language for you, Roger has become incapable of separating reality from fantasy. One of Roger's most persistent nightmares involves an attack of some faceless aggressor wielding a pie. He's reported it to me numerous times. Although he normally specifies lemon meringue."

"But I saw the empty pie tin."

"I'm sure you did." The beaver tilted his bullet-shaped head forward on his squatty neck and tweaked a stray kink out of his moustache. "Most likely Roger either hired someone to hit him with it or did the deed himself and fabricated the attacker. He's done such things before with other of his nightmares. Acted them out, that is. At my encouragement, naturally. I consider it quite beneficial to dramatize these deep-seated terrors, to disentangle them from the subconscious, to confront them head on, to see that they're nowhere near as frightening in actuality as they are when kept locked in the mind. Roger's never acted out the pie episode before, though I've urged him to do so quite often. I have a hunch I'll hear him confess to it at his next session. It would be a major breakthrough."

I doodled a few large cuckoo birds in the margin of my notebook. The beaver's comments clinched it. Roger Rabbit was as looney as a bedbug. If my next stop turned out as I expected it to, I could legitimately consider this case closed.

First thing the next morning, I brought Roger's pie tin to the pie shop whose name was stamped on the bottom. Sure enough, the pie man remembered selling such a pie to none other than Roger Rabbit.

The pie man took fifteen cents out of the register and handed it to me. The deposit, he said, for the tin.

I gave it to him, took the money, and felt I had earned every last penny.

12

From the pie shop I went directly to Roger's place. As I walked to the front door, a gray-and-white tour bus rumbled past, the human passengers inside craning for a better look at how the other half lived. "I'm only visiting!" I nearly shouted when a few of the bus-borne sightseers snapped my photo.

I banged my fist heartily against Roger's front door. To my surprise, it swung open a few inches and then snapped shut, as though hinged by a stout rubber band. I reopened it and pushed it inward, but encountered the same elastic resistance. "Hello, Roger, you in there?" I called out through the narrow crack. I received no response. I braced my feet and pressed against the door with both hands. The door eased open enough for me to see the obstruction, a musical scale, one end sprouting forth from the inside of Roger's grand piano, the other free end looped across a hat rack beside the door. I put my shoulder to the door and shoved. The scale held for a moment and then parted, allowing me to enter. I gathered up the scale and examined it. It didn't read music very well, but then this was no Beethoven symphony, either. Rather it appeared to be a simple version of "When You Wish Upon a Star." I wrapped the scale around my arm between elbow and thumb, knotted it at the end, and hooked it across the edge of the piano bench. That way Roger could iron it flat later, snip it into eight-inch segments, and paste it into his piano book for future reference. What a considerate guy I am, even in the face of the big kiss-off. "Roger," I called out. "You here?"

Again I got no response.

I ventured further into the house, through the front hall, past the living and dining rooms. No Roger anywhere.

Then I stepped into a connecting hallway containing the stairs leading to the second floor.

There I found Roger.

The rabbit lay sprawled chest down across the stairway banister. Only the finial at the banister's end prevented his body from sliding off to the floor. Triangular flaps, the kind you get when you push a pencil through a piece of paper, ringed a gaping bullet hole in Roger's back. I laid my fingertips across the rabbit's fuzzy wrist and felt for a pulse. Nothing. I rolled back the rabbit's eyelids to expose twin black olives adrift in two oblong saucers of curdled cream.

No doubt about it. Roger had gone to bunny heaven.

I leaned against the wall and evaluated my alternatives. I could turn around, walk out, phone the cops anonymously, and never talk about 'toons, think about 'toons, or get involved with 'toons ever again. That was the logical choice.

Then there was the other alternative, the one that forced me to accept the unpleasant conclusion that I, Eddie Valiant, private eye *extraordinaire,* had made a colossal boner. If I had taken the rabbit seriously, if I hadn't been so anxious to grab his money and dump him down the toilet, Roger Rabbit might still be alive.

I had done Roger a great disservice, and Roger had died for it. Nobody, not even a dippy 'toon rabbit, deserved to pay that high a price. While I couldn't resurrect the bunny, I could at least do the honorable thing—see the case through to conclusion, find out who censored Roger Rabbit, and why.

I climbed the staircase and took a closer look at the

hole in Roger's back. It was an exit wound indicating he had been shot from the front. Most of his blood had come out through the downward facing wound in his chest. Except for an almost unnoticeable trickle, the wound in his back had hardly bled at all.

I sighted around in a half-circle to see if I could pinpoint the source of the fatal shot.

Looking through the doorway into the kitchen, I saw a smoky balloon barely visible on the floor on the near side of the stove. I went into the kitchen, stuck a pencil under the balloon, lifted it up, and sniffed it. It smelled faintly of gunpowder. I shook the folds out of it so I could read it. It contained one word. *Bang*. I stretched my hand across it to measure its size. It reached from the tip of my pinky to several inches beyond my thumb. At least a .45 caliber, possibly even bigger. I returned the balloon to the floor.

I eyeballed an imaginary line from the kitchen to the point on the staircase where Roger must have been standing when he got hit. Then I went to the wall to look for the bullet. I found it immediately, burrowed in exactly where I had calculated it should be. One large hole, companion to the big-bore balloon. Remembering previous police accusations of evidence tampering, I resisted the temptation to dig out the slug.

Instead I turned to Roger. The rabibt wore a brightly patterned green, red, and yellow lounging jacket, maroon house slippers the size of swim fins, and baggy orange pants secured to his ankles by elastic bands. Nothing unusual about any of that.

Nothing of interest in his pockets, either. About two dollars in change, a few wilted carrot stems, his housekey, and a gigantic comb.

There did appear to be something underneath him, though.

Gently, I took Roger by the shoulders and lifted him off the banister. Sure enough, hanging over either side of the railing like a sheet of congealed wax, I found a balloon containing Roger's last words. Roger must have mumbled them immediately after being shot, and then fallen across them when he died.

I lifted the U-shaped balloon by its edges off the railing, handling it gently. It had stiffened to the brittleness of a potato chip and that, combined with its natural thinness, made it extremely fragile. When the scientists in the police forensic lab got hold of it, they would measure its rate of hardening and use that to determine exact time of death. I didn't know enough about the process to estimate what they might find.

The balloon had clouded over, and its words had faded out drastically, but, by holding it up to the light, I found it still quite readable. "No fair!" it said. "You got me everything? Jessica. My contract . . ." If Roger had been talking to his wife when he was shot, that meant either she shot him or knew who had. I copied the words into my notebook, draped the fragile balloon back across the banister, and set Roger over it.

I checked around the staircase for further clues, but drew a blank.

I went into the living room and examined the coffee table for glasses, cigarettes, or anything else that might indicate that someone had paid Roger a visit shortly before his demise, but I found nothing. The same with the kitchen. A thorough check of the remaining downstairs rooms uncovered no clues there, either.

I slipped past Roger's body and climbed to the second floor.

The guest room contained only a double bed and a dresser.

The closet was empty. The dresser drawers were, too. The sheets, crisp and clean, had never been slept in.

The medicine cabinet in the bathroom held an assortment of nonprescription drugs, some toothpaste, and two toothbrushes, one jumbo-sized for those big front rabbit incisors, one regular for the teeth further back. Naturally, no shaving cream, razors or razorblades, no electric shaver. A shelf in the shower held a bar of soap, a regular bottle of shampoo, and a plastic bottle in cottontail shape, bearing the legend "Hare Conditioner."

I moved on to the final room on the second floor, Roger's room.

The pictures on the wall were from some slapdash school of art. Like everything else about Roger, they made not the slightest bit of sense.

I drew a complete blank in the closet. Roger owned a tuxedo that glowed in the dark but not brightly enough to shed any light on who had killed him. Nothing in the dresser or in the bureau, either.

I tried his nightstand. There the search got interesting. Pushed to the rear I found a .38 caliber revolver. I sniffed at the barrel. The residue inside smelled fresh. I flipped open the chamber and found it to contain one spent shell. The gun used to kill Roger had been of a much larger caliber, so this wasn't the murder weapon. Then at what, or at whom, had it been fired? I copied the gun's serial number into my notebook and returned the weapon to the drawer.

Next, I checked around outside the bungalow. On the ground, behind some bushes, just under a window overlooking the murder scene, I found a plastic squeeze toy in the shape of Kermit the Frog. The toy hadn't been on the ground long, since the grass underneath it was wet. It had rained early last night, which meant that the toy must have been dropped during or after the storm or the area beneath it would have been dry.

I squeezed the frog. Kermit's eyes bugged up and his tongue popped out. I put the frog in my pocket.

I finished my search but uncovered nothing of any further interest.

So I went to the phone and called the cops.

13

*The cops cruised in under command of a humanoid 'toon
detective, Captain "Clever" Cleaver.* The police force con-
tains one division of humans and one of 'toons, with each
faction investigating only crimes committed against its
own kind. I never saw a 'toon cop sharp enough to hack
it on the human side, though Cleaver came about as close
as any. He carried his gun where other men carry pictures
of their loved ones. He wore a trench coat and a broad-
brimmed slouch hat, and smoked cigars that smelled like
they'd been snipped off the end of something used to tie
rowboats to a pier. He had a big, square jaw, grunted a
lot, called all women "Honey" and most men "Butch."

Cleaver sat me down on Roger's sofa and gave me an
evil eyeballing, straight out of the *Crime-stopper's Text-
book*. I gave back better than I got. He blinked first and
settled down to cases. "From the beginning, Butch," he
growled. "You know the drill as well as I do."

"Nothing much to it. The dead rabbit hired me to
unravel a problem for him. He believed Rocco and Dominick DeGreasy, the two guys heading up his cartoon
syndicate, owed him his own strip. According to the rabbit,
they had promised it to him when they signed him up.
They never delivered, so he asked me to pressure them
into it. He also told me to check out a rumor that some-

47

body wanted to buy his contract. I nosed around and came up blank. The DeGreasys insist they never made the promise. The rumor remains a rumor. That's about everything. I came here this morning to resign the case."

"With a full refund of any advance monies paid but not earned, I presume," said Cleaver sarcastically.

"I get no complaints."

"And no referrals, either, from what I hear. At least not from the 'toon sector."

"By design, Captain, by design. I don't encourage 'toon work. It's a specialized field. I got enough human business to keep me occupied." I uncrossed my legs and put my feet flat on the floor so he wouldn't see my run-down heels and the gaping hole in my left sole. I guess I waited too long, because he plopped himself down on the chair across from me and made a big point of propping his feet up on a coffee table so I had a direct shot at *his* shoes, their bottoms flat as a pancake but in perfect repair.

A sergeant carried in Roger's last words encased in a plastic sack. "Sir, we found these under the stiff."

Cleaver got up, took the words, and held them to the light, using his body to shield them so I couldn't see. He returned them to the sergeant with instructions to rush them to the lab for a rate-of-hardening determination. "Anybody in this case named Jessica?" he asked, rolling his stogie from one side of his mouth to the other.

"Roger's estranged wife." I laid out the lurid details concerning the relationships among Jessica, Rocco, and Roger. No sense concealing it from him. He would find out eventually, and this way I scored a few points for cooperation. "The wife a suspect?" I asked innocently.

Instead of giving me a direct answer, he motioned me into the front entry hall. We got there just in time to watch a brace of burly ambulance attendants wheel Roger out the door on a dolly.

"Know what that is?" Cleaver pointed to a control panel beside the door. Lights on the panel flashed in random sequence. Maybe a hundred individual lights each blinking six or seven times a minute. I found I couldn't watch it for more than a few seconds without getting a headache.

"A burglar alarm, I guess, although I've never seen one quite that sophisticated in a home."

"That's because it's a special custom job put in by the builder of this development. It's a big selling feature out here, since 'toon neighborhoods routinely report the city's highest burglarly rates. Can you imagine? They steal from one another. Almost makes me ashamed to be a 'toon."

If he was waiting for me to say, "I know how you feel," he was in for a few days of silence. I've never been ashamed to be a human.

When he saw I wasn't going to respond, he resumed his explanation of Roger's security system. "The alarm cycles on automatically when the front door closes. It wasn't on when you got here because the music scale had drifted in, gotten wrapped around the door knob, and was holding the door ajar. Disengaging the alarm requires a multisequential process it took some of my best experts to figure out."

"Which means that nobody got into this house unless Roger wanted them to."

"Correct. Hence the likelihood that Roger knew his killer well enough to invite him inside."

"So you figure the wife?"

"That would be my first guess. It would also explain how the killer got *out* without sounding the alarm. Since Jessica had lived here with the rabbit, she must know the code. She could easily have turned the system off and walked away."

"Very logical," I said politely. "Congratulations on your sound reasoning. You've overlooked only one teeny problem. According to Roger, he'd asked Jessica to meet with him many times before, and she had consistently refused. Why should she suddenly accept his offer now? When I talked to her yesterday, she made it quite clear she had no intention of pursuing a reconciliation. I suggested a get-together between her and Roger, and she gave me a firm no."

Cleaver seemed quite relieved when another sergeant

came up and saved him from having to tiptoe out of the corner he'd painted himself into. The sergeant showed Cleaver two items, both encased in plastic bags. One was the .38 pistol from Roger's nightstand. The other was a hunk of metal, the fatal bullet, judging from the size of it. "One shot missing from the thirty-eight," the sergeant said to Cleaver, but Cleaver took more of an interest in the slug.

"Hey, Butch. Ever see one like this?" He held the bullet where I could inspect it.

It looked like it had started life as a perfect sphere before running into Roger Rabbit and a wall. "Seems to be an old-fashioned musket ball from a black-powder long-rifle or a flintlock pistol."

"That's my guess, too. You run into any antique gun collectors in this case?"

"Can't say I have."

Cleaver returned the sack to his sergeant. "Process them both through ballistics," he instructed.

Cleaver picked up Roger's cigar box, opened it, and saw the carrots inside. His granite jaw cracked upward slightly at either end of his mouth. Poor guy. But that's what happens when you hang around with 'toons all day. You start to develop a sense of humor. Next thing you know, nobody takes you seriously anymore, and you wind up laughing yourself straight into the morgue. "The deceased have any enemies you know of?" asked Cleaver.

I shrugged. "Who could hate a rabbit?"

Just then another police car squealed up outside. The rear door opened, and out came Captain Rusty Hudson. He worked the human side and had a well-earned reputation as the most feared kind of law-and-order fanatic, one with a self-starter but no brake. He wrapped up his assignments so quickly and so neatly that he routinely had the lowest active case load of any human detective. I wondered why the department had sent its superstar to investigate a case involving a dead rabbit.

Hudson came inside, took a look around, and saw me.

"Finally found your level down here with the rest of the crazies, huh, Valiant?"

"Nice to see you again, too, Captain," I replied.

"What can I do for you, sir?" asked Cleaver. Even though they held the same rank, the department's age-old unwritten law required a 'toon officer to defer to a human, and everybody who knew Hudson knew he would make life extremely miserable for any 'toon colleague deviating from tradition.

"When I heard the report about this Roger Rabbit character being killed," said Hudson, "I figured I'd better shag it right over here before your bunch gets too far into their search. No offense, but I've had lots of problems with the 'toon side losing evidence on me before."

"What kind of evidence you after?"

"A thirty-eight-caliber revolver, maybe has one shot gone. You find anything like that when you tossed this place?"

Cleaver nodded. "Sure did. Upstairs in the nightstand. One bullet fired. I sent it to ballistics. Why? You got something on it?"

"I have reason to suspect it was the murder weapon in a human homicide last night."

"A human homicide? Who?" I asked.

Hudson looked at me the way people look at escargot when they find out that means snails. "You got a reason to be here, gumshoe? You a witness, a suspect, or what?"

"He was employed by the rabbit," explained Cleaver. "I was just taking his statement when you arrived."

Hudson nodded to show he understood that police work often forced officers to associate against their wills with guys like me. He expanded his narrative, but for Cleaver's benefit, not mine. "About one this morning we got a call from a hysterical woman who turned out to be this rabbit's wife. Seems she lives with a guy named Rocco De-Greasy, a big wheel in the comic industry. She was out late. When she came home, she saw a light on in De-Greasy's study. She went in to check and found DeGreasy slumped across his desk, dead."

"You got an estimated time of death?" I asked, but Hudson ignored me.

"I did some quick checking around," he continued, "and found out that this rabbit had previously threatened De-Greasy's life, in front of witnesses during a photo session at his photographer's studio. I also discovered that this rabbit bears a grudge because DeGreasy failed to honor a promise to give him his own strip. As if I needed more, DeGreasy has also grabbed the rabbit's girl. Put that all together, it spells murder. I'll give odds that the bullet we found in DeGreasy turns out to have come from the rabbit's gun."

"Were you able to pinpoint an exact time of death?" asked Cleaver, repeating my earlier question.

Since this time it had come through channels, Hudson answered. "We figure about midnight."

"Judging from the hardness of the rabbit's final balloon, he got it about an hour later. You check Jessica Rabbit's alibi for then?" Cleaver asked.

"No, why should I? What's she got to do with anything? The rabbit plugged DeGreasy. There's no doubt in my mind."

"Great. That takes care of your murder. What about mine?" Cleaver's word balloon came out so frosty you almost needed a squeegee to read it. "These two deaths are too closely related to be a coincidence. Suppose Jessica Rabbit saw Roger kill Rocco, followed the rabbit back here, and executed him for his crime. A perfect motive. The rabbit shot her lover, so Jessica shot the rabbit."

"I'll let you solve that part of it," said Hudson, buffing his fingernails on his lapel with such intense concentration that a casual onlooker might suspect it was the most important thing he had to do for the entire rest of the day. "When the report comes back from ballistics, I'll stamp my case closed. What do I care about who blew away some bunny." With that he left the house, got into his car, and roared off, siren on and lights flashing, a showboat to the end.

Cleaver took a peek through a telescope set up in the front window, but it was way too early to see any stars. "Did that rabbit have what it takes to kill a man?" Cleaver asked me.

"I don't know. On the one hand, he really hated Rocco DeGreasy. But on the other hand, who can picture a killer rabbit?"

"Yeah, I know what you mean," said Cleaver. He drifted off into the mental never-never land where 'toons seem to spend three-quarters of their time.

"You finished with me, Captain?"

"What?" A series of tiny balloons, each containing an itsy-bitsy question mark, bubbled out of his head. The balloons popped, letting the question marks parachute to the floor. I was tempted to scoop them up and pocket them, since I knew a book publisher who bought them to cut type-setting costs in his line of whodunits.

"Sure," Cleaver said, "you can go. Just don't leave town without checking with me first. And one other thing. I don't know how you felt about this rabbit, or if you took his case seriously, but from here on out this affair belongs to me. Official police investigation. You want to keep your license, you stay out. Understand?"

"One hundred percent," I said. "I won't interfere." I jammed my hand into my pocket and crossed my fingers. "I promise."

14

The elevator in my office building worked so seldom that the 'toon door-man, a strapping gorilla, made a nice chunk of change carrying people to the upper floors on his back. Today I lucked out. The elevator appeared and whisked

me to the twelfth floor in less than a week, which probably set a building speed record.

My three hundred bucks a month bought me a waiting
room where a secretary would sit, if I could ever afford to
hire one, my office proper, and a small john. The place
normally rented for two fifty, but I got charged an extra
half-yard because of the view. Open the window, look up,
and you see the sky. Look down, and you see the street.
Look straight out, and you see the brickwork of the building next door. Great place. Shabby and overpriced, but
it suited me better than one of those chrome-and-glass
stakes that builders keep pounding into the heart of what
used to be a picturesque city.

I noticed something wacky as soon as I took out my keys
to open the outer door. The lock was badly scratched,
sure sign of an amateur thief. The pros go in and out
without leaving a trace, but amateurs always botch it. I
slammed open the door and entered the waiting room the
way I learned in the Corps, low and fast. I kicked the
door shut on my way past, but there was nobody hiding
behind it. It didn't take me long to search the waiting
room, since it contained only two folding chairs and a
card table with some hardly thumbed magazines on it.
Anybody small enough to hide behind any of that stuff
didn't really worry me.

I checked the door connecting this room with my office
proper. It, too, bore signs of having been picked. I had a
wall safe in my office, and in that I kept my gun. Just my
luck to walk in on a burglar and get shot with my own
piece.

I took a few deep breaths, opened the door, and went
in Marine style again, except this time I added a forward
somersault, which might not have been the greatest idea
in the world. You have to practice those things a lot or
they leave you dizzy, which is just how I wound up when
I came out of it. I grabbed the edge of my desk for support
and tried to look alert. Nobody shot me, so I figured the
burglar had already skedaddled.

But I was wrong. When the room straightened out, I

found him, sitting behind my desk, brazen as you please. One thing for sure. I'd have no trouble picking this clown out of a lineup. He wore a long purple coat, a fireman's hat, and a T-shirt that said, "Kiss me, I'm fuzzy." If I hadn't known better, I'd have sworn it was . . .

"I'm sorry I had to break in on you like this, Mister Valiant, I mean picking your lock and all, but I really didn't know where else to go, or who else to turn to."

"Roger? Roger Rabbit?" I went around to his side of the desk, opened the bottom drawer, took out the office bottle, and swigged down a healthy glug. I stared at the rabbit until he got the message and shagged his tail out of my chair. I brushed a few stray pieces of hair off the seat and sat down. "Start explaining," I said, "and it better be good."

He went to the window and took in the fifty-dollar view. "I know what you think," he said. "You think I'm really Roger. But I'm not. I'm his doppelgänger, his mentally created duplicate."

"Yeah, I know about that stuff," I said, remembering Jessica Rabbit falling to pieces around me.

"Well, Roger conjured me up last night about eleven," the rabbit went on. "He had a photo session this morning, and he needed a pair of red suspenders to wear at it. He gave me a fifty-dollar bill, and told me to go out and buy him some."

"He sent you out in the middle of the night to find him a pair of red suspenders?"

"Yes. He . . . I mean, we . . . I mean, I can be very impulsive at times. Anyway, I left and started hitting those variety stores you see around, the ones that stay open late at night. I must have gone to twenty of them and couldn't find a pair of red suspenders anywhere. I found green, blue, yellow, polka-dot, orange, striped . . ."

I did a few wheelies with my index finger. He caught my drift and kept his story rolling.

"When I finally found a store with the right color suspenders, they couldn't change my bill. I hung around downtown until my bank opened, broke the bill, went back, and bought the suspenders." He pointed to a wrapped package lying on top of my desk. "I returned home about ten this morning and found the place crawling with cops. I overheard two of them describing what had happened. That I, or rather the real me, had been killed. I didn't know what to do. I'm not very decisive when it comes to emergencies. I suppose I should have identified myself to the police, but I was afraid to. I feared that whoever got to the real Roger might come after me, too. Then I thought of you."

"Thanks."

"Don't mention it. Since I'm supposed to be dead, I didn't want to wait for you out in the hall where somebody might recognize me, so I picked your lock. I didn't think you would mind. You don't, do you? It's actually my first try at it. As I told you before, I've always had a hankering to be a detective. I believe every detective should know how to pick locks. I'm sure you do, don't you? So I bought some lock-picking tools I saw advertised on the inside cover of a matchbook." He showed me a set of picks only slightly smaller and less clumsy than the iron bar I use to pry the hubcaps off my car. "They came with a self-instruction manual. Pretty neat, huh?"

"Tell me," I said, after giving the office bottle another howdy-doody. "How long before you start to, you know, fall apart?"

The bunny stared with deep foreboding at the far wall, as though the hand of God had just inscribed there the recipe for hasenpfeffer. "Hard to tell. Roger put a large jolt of mental energy into creating me. I could easily last forty-eight hours before I . . . until I . . ."

A dark, watery boo-hoo balloon plopped to the floor, but I give him this much, it didn't spill any tears. "You have any idea who murdered me?" he asked.

"Yeah, I got an idea. You get a call from anyone last night?" I asked. "Or anybody come to see you?"

He shrugged, a ridiculous move for a guy with next to no shoulders. "I don't know. The mental strain of creating a doppel tends to disrupt short-term memory. I remember up to early yesterday evening, but not much after."

"You don't remember getting a call from your wife? Saying that she wanted to come over for a talk?"

"Jessica? Jessica came by to see me? Oh boy, oh boy, oh boy." Talk about happiness. If Roger had been Flash Gordon, he would have been outside his rocket ship swinging on a star. "I knew you could pull it off, Mister Valiant. I knew I picked the right man. I knew you could get me Jessica back. How did you do it? Put the arm on Rocco? That it? I'll bet that's it. You found out what he had on her and forced him to stop."

With a swift left jab, I punched a jumbo hole in the biggest of his balloons. "Not so fast. I don't know for sure whether or not Jessica came to see you last night. If she did, it wasn't for a reconciliation."

"Why then?"

"The police think she killed you, and I go along with them."

The rabbit shook his head so vigorously his flopping ears left spiral marks on the fur around his head. "Not a chance. She loves me! She would never do something like that. What makes you suspect her?"

"For starters, your last words." I took out my notebook and read them to him. "No fair! You got me everything? Jessica. My contract." I turned the notebook and laid it on the corner of the desk so he could read his final statement himself.

Twice he followed the words with his finger and both times wound up in exactly the same place. "Wait! I've got it," he said, holding a finger straight up as if to test the wind. "I wasn't talking to Jessica. No, I was talking *about* her. To someone else. To Rocco DeGreasy! I was talking about Jessica to Rocco DeGreasy, and he shot me."

"Try again," I said. "According to the cops, it's the other way around. You shot him."

"I shot who?"

"Rocco DeGreasy."

"Rocco?" Granted, the guy acted for a living, but his googly-wide eyes and puckered nose sure said dumbfounded to me. "You mean the police think I shot Rocco?"

"Dead as a doornail. He got his about an hour before you got yours. The way the cops figure it, you went to DeGreasy's house and killed him. Jessica saw you do it, followed you home, and took her revenge."

"That's ridiculous. I could never kill anybody. Not even Rocco DeGreasy."

"You threatened to once. Remember? At a photo session? In front of two reliable witnesses."

Roger began to bounce around so actively I checked the rug for hopscotch boxes, but I saw only lifeless shag and yesterday's ashes. "Right. I did do that. But I didn't mean it. I could never kill another living being. It's not in my nature. I even sidestep ants on the street. I was being irrational that day. Look at it from my viewpoint. There I was peacefully going about my job, when in walked Rocco DeGreasy. He started giving me guff about how he and I ought to get together and resolve this 'misunderstanding' about my contract. That's a direct quote. 'Misunderstanding.' I'll never forget how his fat face jiggled when he said it.

"I told him there was no misunderstanding. He had promised me my own strip, and that was it. End of negotiation. That's when he laughed at me, and I went after him. I guess I became a tad irrational, what with his laughter and this being the first time I'd seen him since he'd coerced Jessica into leaving me."

"Assuming that he did coerce her."

"Of course, he coerced her. I told you before, she would never have left me of her own free will. She loved me. Jessica loved me, and I'm positive she still does. Anyway, yes, I attacked Rocco that day, and, yes, I threatened to kill him, but I never intended to follow through."

"What exactly do you remember about last night?"

Most of the rabbit's thought balloons came up either totally blank or slightly hazy. "Not much, I'm afraid. I spent pretty much of an ordinary evening. I had dinner, watched some television, and read awhile. No visitors, no phone calls, nothing out of the ordinary." He dribbled out a few more empty memories and finally gave up trying. "Where was Rocco killed?"

"At his home, in his study. You ever been there?"

"No, never. We conducted our dealings exclusively at his office. How was he killed?"

"He got shot with a thirty-eight-caliber revolver."

The rabbit opened my cigar box and seemed rather disappointed to find it contained cigars. "Well, there you are. That should clear me. I've never fired a gun in my life, or owned one, either."

"What about the one in your nightstand?"

Roger's words came out with at least a yard of spacing between them, and so tiny I nearly got eye strain reading them. "What one in my nightstand?"

"A thirty-eight-caliber revolver with one bullet missing. The cops have it. They're running it through ballistics right now, but I'd be willing to bet it turns out to be the murder weapon."

"You're kidding. In my nightstand? How could that be? I've never owned a gun in my life."

"You have no idea how it got there?"

"None." His eyelids rolled down. "Don't you see? This is a frameup. Somebody is trying to saddle me with Rocco's murder. Somebody killed him and planted the gun at my place. I probably caught them at it, and they killed me to keep me quiet. Does that make sense?"

It did, and I told him so.

"That's it, then." He used a big, blue bandana to wipe the perspiration off his face, and a teasing comb to refluff his fur. "You find out who killed Rocco, and you also find out who killed me. You clear my name, and you also bring my killer to justice."

"You might not like what I find."

"How so?"

"For starters, when I got to your house this morning, I found a musical scale trailing out of the piano. The song was 'When You Wish Upon a Star.' That have any significance to you?"

A light bulb flashed on over Roger's head. It was less

than a five-watter, but it would get a lot brighter and a lot hotter before I was done. "It was my favorite piece. I play it a lot, and sing along."

"I remember you telling me you serenaded Jessica the evening you proposed. 'When You Wish Upon a Star,' by any chance?"

The light bulb grew to twenty-five watts. "Yes, as a matter of fact, that was the song I played and sang for Jessica that evening. After that, we always considered it our song."

"So if she had been there with you last night, it would have been natural for you to play it for her again?"

Seventy-five watts. "I suppose so, yes."

"Now tell me about your burglar-alarm system. How does it work?"

"It's a marvelous device. It connects to every door and window in the house. It goes on automatically when the front door closes. You have to disengage it after you go in and before you go out, or the thing sets off a wail you wouldn't believe."

"When I got to your place this morning, the door was ajar. The musical scale had gotten wrapped around the door handle. That's how I got in without setting off the alarm. The question is, how did the killer get out?"

"Beats me."

"Jessica lived there in that house with you for nearly a year. Did she know the code to disengage that alarm?"

A hundred watts. "Yes, she did."

"So she could very easily have disengaged it after she shot you and walked out without setting it off?"

"Yes, I suppose she could have."

"Did anyone else know the alarm code?"

"Sure, lots of people."

"Name them."

Two hundred watts and flashing caution. "OK, OK, so she was the only one."

"Right. The only one besides you who could have gotten out without tripping the alarm. Now let's investigate the other end. In order for the killer to get in, you had to disengage the alarm, correct?"

"Yes."

"Would you have done that for Rocco DeGreasy?"

"Of course not."

"His brother Dominick?"

"No way."

"How about Jessica?"

"Stop right here," he said in a fragmented balloon you would expect to come out of somebody with his head buried to the shoulders in sand. "I know in my heart that Jessica did not kill me, just as I know in my heart that I did not kill Rocco DeGreasy. So you can stop that line of questioning here and now."

"OK. Let's try this one." I pulled the rubber Kermit the Frog toy out of my pocket. "Ever see this before?"

Roger squeezed it several times, giggling when Kermit's tongue unfurled. "You see them around. It's a pretty popular toy. I can't say I recognize this one as being any different from a hundred others I've seen. Where did you get it?"

"I found it outside your house. It hadn't been there long. My guess is that it was dropped by the killer."

"Well, that would leave out Jessica. She would never carry around something as silly as this."

"Or it might have been dropped by somebody who saw the killer."

"Oh." He didn't seem very happy to hear that there might have been an eyewitness to his untimely demise. I guess that's what love does to you. Makes you put on your blinders whenever your canter takes you anywhere near the truth. "Mister Valiant, how was I . . . I mean, what did he use to . . ."

"You were shot once in the chest. It looked to me like a clean hit. You didn't suffer much, if that's your concern."

He nodded, and a matched set of crystalline teardrops rolled down either side of his face.

"You were apparently killed with some kind of antique

musket or pistol," I said. "You know of anybody who owns a piece like that?"

He shook his head no.

"What about any other enemies you might have had, anyone you haven't told me about, anybody who might have wanted you out of the way?"

Again he shook his head. He put his bandana to his nose and gave a honk loud enough to have every moose within ten blocks pawing at my door. "Mister Valiant," he said in those tiny, strung out words again, "I don't have long to exist. Forty-eight hours at the most. After that I'll disintegrate, and Roger Rabbit will be gone forever. There's one thing that I'd like to ask you to do for me as a favor before that happens. You see, Mister Valiant, the real Roger, and now me, well, we've always wanted to be a private eye."

"No way," I said firmly. I wasn't about to sign on as nursemaid to a cottontailed detective, dying wish or not.

"Oh, please, Mister Valiant, please. I'll do whatever you tell me to. It's not like I'm asking you to accommodate me permanently. Forty-eight hours, and I'll be gone, out of your life forever."

"Two days isn't very long to solve a double homicide. Even if I did let you tag along, you might not be around for the close."

He gave me that irresistible please-take-me-home look you get from a three-dollar pup in a pet-store window. "You can do it, I know you can. What say, Mister Valiant. Please?"

I owed the rabbit, true. If it would make him happy to step and fetch for me, who was I to deny him? "All right, I take you on, but only under one condition. We level with each other. In everything. Agreed?"

"Sure." He nodded his head so fast, the end of his ear cracked like a whip.

"Then let's start by you telling me why you pulled that pie assault on yourself."

He switched back to the same forlorn puppy face that I

guess he figured he got me with before. "On myself? No, Rocco did that."

I pointed toward the door. "Take a hop."

His puppy face grew up in a big hurry into a beaten cur. His word balloon came out so heavily weighted down with guilt, it dented the top of my desk. "I should have known I could never fool you."

"Why did you even try?"

He stared at a spot about a million miles over my head. "I guess as a ploy to get sympathy. According to my psychiatrist, it goes back to when I was growing up. You see I came from a very small town, and I . . ."

I shook my head. "Spare me the historical details. I'm only interested in here and now. Like the bit about Rocco offering you your own strip. You make that up, too?"

"No, not that. That was the truth. I swear it."

"And your story about you and Jessica. What about that?"

"True. Every word of it." He hung his head. If I hadn't jerked back in my chair, one of his ears would have speared me in the eye. "I'm sorry I tried to deceive you," he said. "I won't ever do it again. You have my word on that." He straightened up. This time though, I was sitting well back when his ear came whistling past. "Please don't hold my one indiscretion against me. I promise you total honesty from here on out."

"And you tone down the goofiness, too. You want to work with me, you act like a human."

"You want humanity," said Roger solemnly, "you will get humanity you won't believe."

He held out his paw exactly the way a person would have.

For the first, and I hoped last, time in my life I shook hands with a rabbit.

15

I took the rabbit to my place.

He didn't draw so much as a second glance from the people out front on the street. Shows you what the world's coming to. I can still remember the first 'toon who moved into this neighborhood. A good-looking guy, humanoid, a dead ringer for Smilin' Jack. Real personable, and as near normal as a 'toon could be. That was twenty years ago, and people marched through the streets in protest. They lost; he stayed. Now we've got more barnyards than Old MacDonald's farm. Every morning my next-door neighbor sticks his head out the window and crows at the sun. You go into a diner for lunch, and the guy on the stool next to you orders a bale of hay. Travel ten feet down any sidewalk, and you'll step in at least one deflated moo balloon. And this is what the politicians downtown call social progress.

I unlocked the door, and we both went in.

I don't believe in frou-frou. My living room comes furnished with a floor lamp, a reading chair, and a sofa. Add to that a wooden table where I play poker and work out chess problems, plus a few pictures, mostly of me in the Corps, and that's about it. I keep my chess books on the floor, my gun in a closet, my dinners in the freezer, and my booze under the sink. Simple and unpretentious.

The kind of life guys go off to monasteries to enjoy, and I live it every day, right here in the City of the Angels.

I sat Roger down on the sofa and went into my closet to dig him out a disguise. I knew that if Rusty Hudson or "Clever" Cleaver ever spotted him, they'd haul him in and grill him. That could easily eat up his two remaining days. Plus I also had two killers to worry about, Rocco's and Roger's. If either of them spotted Roger, the rabbit wouldn't even last that long. So I had to keep anyone from recognizing Roger, a good trick when you're dealing with a six-foot-tall, nationally famous rabbit. But never let it be said I didn't give it a try.

In the back of my closet, I found a pair of baggy cords, a wool plaid shirt, and a blue watch cap with enough stretch in it to absorb those ears. I handed him the lot of it. From the flicker of disappointment in his eyes, I could tell that he didn't care much for my choice, but I knew that, if left to his own devices, he would deck himself out in a zoot suit and consider himself inconspicuous because he didn't fluoresce when the lights went out.

While I waited for him to change, I went over to my wooden table to work on the chess problem I had set out, but the rabbit had already solved it. I'd been struggling with it for nearly two days, and he solved it in less than ten minutes. Made me wonder what other talents this bunny was hiding under his bushel.

Roger came out of the bathroom wearing my clothes and did a 360-degree turn. "Well, what do you think?"

"Your tail's sticking out the top of your pants."

He tucked it in. "There. Better?"

I nodded. His ears refused to stay folded over inside the watch cap, so his head resembled an inverted woolen ice cream cone, but I could live with that. I gave him my old pea coat and told him to keep the collar pulled up around his face.

"Didn't you forget something?" he asked me just before we left.

"I don't think so," I said. "What?"

"How about a piece?" He flipped his word balloon end over end the way a punk would do with a silver dollar.

"A piece of what?"

"A piece, a piece, you know, a gat, a rod, a *gun*." He pointed his paw westward and squeezed off an imaginary round at the savages circling his wagon.

"I thought you said you'd never owned or shot a gun before."

"True." He fired again and grinned as another phantom injun bit the dust.

"Then what do you want with one now?"

"It seems only appropriate. I mean, if I'm going to be a detective, I ought to pack a gun."

"I'm a detective, and I don't." I opened my coat to prove it.

"Oh," he said. I don't know what he needed a gun for. His balloon came out so heavily laden with diappointment he could have sapped Godzilla with it.

We went downstairs, got into my car, and I drove us to Roger's house.

I picked the lock—without leaving a single scratch on it, I might add—and we went inside.

Roger immediately rushed to turn off the alarm, but he needn't have bothered. Cleaver's experts had deactivated it so the cops could come and go freely.

"Remember," I reminded Roger, "we're looking for anything out of the ordinary. Anything which I or the cops might have overlooked, but which might be significant to you. Clear?"

"You bet," said the rabbit. Where he got it I'll never know, but he pulled a magnifying glass out of my pea coat pocket and walked into the living room with me close behind. You didn't need any magnifying glass to see what had happened here, though.

I hardly recognized the place. Every sofa and chair cushion had been sliced open. The paintings had been pulled off the walls. Every drawer in every table had been dumped in the middle of the carpet.

We went through the rest of the house and found it in the same state of disarray. We ended up in Roger's bedroom.

"The police aren't too neat when it comes to searching a place, are they?" Roger said. He picked some underwear off the floor and put it into a drawer, but the bottom had been kicked out, and his skivvies fell straight through.

"No cop did this," I said.

"Who, then?" Roger asked. "And why?"

"We answer those questions, and we crack this case."

"Maybe, maybe not," countered Roger. "Maybe with the alarm off, some common crook broke in and robbed the place. I have had a few break-in attempts lately, forced windows mostly, but the alarm went off each time and frightened the burglar away. Maybe this time one of them made it."

"No." I poked through the scattered contents of Roger's jewelry box. He didn't have much but what he did have would fence for fifty or sixty bucks minimum. No thief would leave that behind. "No, somebody was looking for something very specific. You have anything hidden in this house? Anything you haven't told me about?"

The rabbit hopped to and fro picking his stuff up off the floor. He got an armload before he figured out that, with the drawers all smashed, he had no place to put it. So he stacked it as neatly as he could along one wall. "There was nothing here," said the rabbit. "Nothing hidden. Nothing anyone could possibly want."

"What about your contract with the DeGreasys? Where do you keep that?"

"At the bank, in my safety deposit box."

"How about your marriage license for you and Jessica?"

"Same place."

"Stocks, bonds?"

"I don't have any."

"Money?"

"It's in a sock. Under my mattress."

It would have simplified matters if it had been gone, but no such luck. The mattress and box spring were ripped to shreds, but the sock, money included, was still there.

"What do you suppose they could possibly have wanted?" said Roger.

"Tell you what," I said. "Let's go through the house room by room. Try and reconstruct in your memory what each room contained. See if anything's missing."

We started there in his bedroom and finished up in the kitchen.

"Anything?" I asked.

"Nothing of any importance," reported Roger. "Only my teakettle."

"Your what?"

"My teakettle."

I had been thinking more in terms of the sterling silver or maybe a painting. I might have known better where 'toons were concerned. "Was it an antique? Did it have any value?"

"None that I know of."

"Where did you get it?"

Roger showed me what had to be a real oddity, a rabbit wearing a sheepish expression. "Off a movie set. It was the teakettle used in the tea-party scene from last year's remake of *Alice in Wonderland*. I had a bit part in the picture. On a whim, I sneaked the teakettle off the set as a souvenir after the movie wrapped. But it was only an ordinary, cheap teakettle, similar to any number of others from the five and dime."

"Is that where it came from, this teakettle? A five and dime?"

"No, not this one. From what I remember of it, the studio prop man bought it for fifty cents in a local junk shop."

"What was it made of?"

"I don't know. Iron, I suppose. It had a gray lacquer coating and was very heavy. It must have weighed in at about two pounds. Boy, did it ever brew great tea! But that's about all it was good for. It certainly had no value."

"Maybe none you know about. It could be very valuable indeed if that two pounds turned out to be solid gold."

"Two pounds of solid gold," said the rabbit. "For my life." He hefted his two word balloons, one in each paw, but it wasn't even a close contest. The one with his life in it outweighed the other by more than half. He faced me head on, stood up ramrod straight, and said, "Show me, would you please, the . . . the . . . the scene of the crime."

I pointed through the kitchen door to the staircase. "You were standing there. Whoever shot you was here in the kitchen. You can see the hole in the wall where the bullet hit. You muttered your last words and fell forward across them onto the banister. That's where I found you."

"I see," said Roger. He climbed the stairway and stuck a finger into the bullet hole. Then he took a look at the banister. I noticed some dark brown stains at the banister's base. Dried blood. Roger's blood. I did my best to spare him the sight of it. "Hey," I said distracting him. "We're finished here. Let's get out."

Roger nodded but kept staring at the banister.

"Look," I said. "If we want to get this case wrapped up, we've got to keep cracking. I've got some important stuff for you to do. Important *detective* stuff."

Roger's head snapped in my direction. "You do? What?"

"I want you to go to the public library and search through books on film history until you find a photo of the tea-party scene from that *Alice in Wonderland* movie you were in. I want a photo that clearly shows the tea-kettle. And something else, too." I opened my notebook and tore out a slip of paper. "Here's the serial number of the thirty-eight they found in your nightstand. Go down to city hall and check the gun registration records. Determine who owns that gun. While you do that, I'm going to pay a call on Dominick DeGreasy. When you finish, go back to my place. We'll meet there and compare notes."

"Right, chief," said Roger. He walked down the stairs and out the door.

With what I thought showed real class, he never once looked back.

16

"A terrible, terrible thing what that rabbit did to my brother," said Dominick DeGreasy. I could see why he had let his brother do the talking. Instead of a voice he had a throatful of gravel that rattled every word and gave him the tin drum sound you hear in people who lubricate their tonsils with loud talk and cheap gin.

"You going to run the syndicate alone?" I asked.

"You bet. Why not?" He pointed straight down at his desk top the way emperors point at their thrones. "Me and my brother built this syndicate together. I know as much about it as he did. Sure, the last few years he handled the business end of it, and I took care of keeping the talent in line. I just need a week or so to pick up the fine points, and I'll have the place ticking along better than ever."

I wished I could find a bookie willing to take a bet on that.

DeGreasy sat down at his desk. He crossed his size-sixteen gunboats in a maneuver worthy of a naval captain. "I got a firm to run here, Valiant," he said. He inter-locked his hands behind his head. His black morning coat pulled open and gave me a clear view of the howitzer he packed under his armpit. It appeared to be about the same big-bore caliber as the gun that got Roger, but it was hardly an antique pirate pistol. "I got no time to waste on cheap gumshoes. If you came by to line up a pigeon to expense your tab while you rehash this case, forget it. That rabbit killed my brother, no doubt about it. Why should I pay you to nose around, come back, and tell me what I already know?"

"That's not why I'm here, to get a client. I already have a client."

DeGreasy snorted. "Who?"

"That's privileged information. Let's just say that my client believes Roger Rabbit might be getting framed for your brother's murder and wants me to check into it to see what I can find."

"Sounds like a waste of money to me."

"Possibly. The rabbit might be guilty as hell. But, then again, there's the outside chance he might be getting set up for somebody else, and if that's so, Rocco's murderer is right now running around scot-free. You wouldn't want that, would you? You wouldn't want your brother's killer to go loose?"

Dominick squirmed around in his chair, unable to find a position that fit. "No, you bet I wouldn't want that to happen. But why should it? The cops put their top man on the case, this Rusty Hudson. I got connections downtown, and I requested their best man special. The mayor himself gave me Hudson. He'll find out who really killed Rocco. Why should I think you'll do anything he won't?"

"Because he already considers the case closed. He's not going to follow up any loose ends. Why should he? The rabbit's a tailor-made fall guy. Hudson hangs it on the rabbit and wraps up the case in record time. But he might just be wrong, and that's what I intend to find out. It would be a lot easier if I had your help, but I'm going to keep plugging whether I get it or not."

He shoved some junk from one side of his desk to the other and probably considered that a good day's work. "If I go along with you, what do I have to do?"

"Hardly a thing. Answer a few questions about your brother."

He looked across the desk at his brother's chair. For

the first time in his life, there was nobody in it to tell him what to do. "I guess I can go that far," he said finally.

"Swell. Oh, and also I need to look through your brother's personal effects. See if there's anything in there that might throw some light on who besides the rabbit might have had a motive to kill him."

He balked slightly at that. "The cops already went through Rocco's stuff."

"Sure they did, but with the preconceived notion that the rabbit committed the crime. I come to the task with an open mind."

He eyeballed the empty chair again, but it still wasn't talking. "Go ahead and search," he said at last.

"Would you mind?" I made shooing motions toward the door. "I'd like to do it alone. It helps me concentrate."

"Sure." Dominick got to his feet, happy to have an excuse for motion. "Rocco kept his stuff in his drawers. Just stick your head out when you're done."

Before he left, Dominick made a big production out of locking the file cabinet and his desk.

As soon as he shut the door, I picked the lock on his desk drawer.

He must have had fifty pornographic magazines of the whips and chains variety stuffed in there. I searched around but found nothing else, and I mean nothing. His drawers contained no files, no calendar, no paper, not even a pencil. I put his magazines back and locked up. With a perverted dodo like Dominick at its helm, this company would be lucky to last twelve months.

I used my picks again on the company files.

Based on what I found in there, I revised my prognosis to six months. The company's financial statements showed that the DeGreasys had been steadily losing money for nearly a year. They had less operating capital than I did, and I had enough checks kited to lift me halfway up the hill to the poorhouse.

I checked under "R" and found one of those green cardboard dividers the cops put into place whenever they take something out. According to the divider's notation, they had removed the Roger Rabbit file. I fanned through the rest of the folders, but they'd taken nothing else. Obviously, as far as the cops were concerned, Roger was it.

I closed up the files and was just about to start in on Rocco's desk when something clicked, something odd. The file drawers appeared to be a few inches shorter than the file cabinet proper. I pulled the cabinet away from the wall and examined its backside. It took me a while, but I finally found it, a secret compartment. When you pressed a certain screw, the whole rear of the cabinet swung away to reveal a narrow space maybe two inches deep. I had expected to find a few file folders inside, but instead the space held snapshots of original segments of comic-strip artwork. Each piece of artwork contained a framed print of a comic strip and the negative used to produce it, the same kind of stuff Rocco had hanging in here on the walls. If I remembered rightly, he had said such segments were worth big bucks. This artwork portrayed Baby Herman strips. Roger Rabbit appeared in all of them, so they must be fairly recent. Each segment had been signed by its photographer—Carol Masters in every case.

I flipped one of the snapshots over and found a price penciled on the back. Five grand. Certainly not small potatoes on my side of town, but hardly the mighty moola Rocco had led me to believe the stuff fetched. Of course what I knew about art you could put into one blank of a paint-by-numbers set. Maybe these were inferior quality segments and didn't command very high a price. But if that were the case, why go to so much trouble to hide them?

I studied the segments up close, but couldn't see any difference between them and the ones on the wall. One of the segments did have a familiar look to it, but I couldn't place it, and it was hardly likely that I'd have seen it in the paper since I never read the funnies. I put the snapshots in my pocket, closed up the compartment, and pushed the filing cabinet back into place.

Next I went to work on Rocco's desk.

He kept his desk calendar inside his upper center drawer. I checked it for yesterday and discovered he had penciled in an appointment at home with someone he identified only by the initials SS. The meeting was set for eleven o'clock P.M., barely an hour before he had been killed.

In his bottom drawer I found a few books on ancient mythology, and that was about it.

I stuck my head out the door and asked Dominick to rejoin me.

"Any luck?" he asked.

"Maybe," I answered. "How about giving me some background to set my findings into perspective?"

"Shoot."

"What's your opinion of Jessica Rabbit?"

He picked up a letter opener and jabbed it so hard into his desktop blotter that it cut through to the wood beneath. I wondered if anybody in the world besides Roger saw any good in that woman. "She was a bimbo when he met her, and she's still a bimbo. I never could figure out what he saw in her."

"How did they meet?"

"Rocco discovered her dancing in a slimy downtown strip club. He took her out of there, groomed her, bought her expensive clothes, and taught her to act. As her way of saying thanks, she dumped him for a stupid rabbit."

"But she did come back to him," I pointed out.

He pulled the letter opener up and took a piece of the blotter with it. "Sure she came back to him, but only when she found out that the rabbit couldn't give her what Rocco could. She was out for nobody but herself, and Rocco would have been better off without her. I told him not to take her back, but the guy loved her so much he would have forgiven her anything."

"The word is that Jessica pressured Rocco into giving Roger a contract. You know anything about that?"

"Not really. Like I said, I never got involved much in the business end of it. I personally never wanted to sign the rabbit. I never thought he had all that much talent, but Rocco insisted, although he never once gave me a good reason why. Said it was just a hunch he had, a feeling. But I always thought, pretty much like everybody else did, that it was really Jessica behind it. He took the rabbit on because Jessica asked him to. Sure, it turned out to be the right move. The rabbit wound up making a spiffy second banana, but nobody would have guessed that going in."

"Roger insisted that Rocco promised him a solo strip. Any truth to that?"

"I dunno. Like I said, I didn't get involved much with that end of it, but it wouldn't surprise me. If Rocco wanted someone bad enough he'd promise them anything. Never put it into the contract though. He'd tell the character that it wasn't necessary, that it was his word, and he always kept his word."

"Did he?"

"You kidding?" Dominick tried to laugh, but I don't think he had ever learned how. "Nobody could lie like Rocco."

"Supposing for a minute that Roger didn't kill Rocco, do you think that Jessica could have?"

"I can't figure why. Rocco gave her everything she wanted. It would have been like snuffing the goose that laid the golden egg."

"Does Jessica stand to inherit Rocco's estate?"

He stoked up a slim, black, unfiltered cigarette, centered it in his mouth, and blew smoke out of either side around it. "I don't know. The will ain't been read yet. The lawyer does it tomorrow right after the funeral."

"You know the rabbit's dead, too."

He flipped his match into his wastebasket. He didn't have to worry about starting a fire. His wastebasket held no paper. He was either very neat or very unproductive. No question which got my vote. "I heard, and I think it's a real shame."

"You do?"

"Yeah, I think it's a shame that somebody else got to

him before I did." He hacked another piece out of his blotter. "After what he did to my brother, it would have given me great pleasure to shoot that rabbit myself."

"Any idea who might have spared you the trouble?"

He shrugged and shook his head.

"Do you think Jessica could have done it?"

"Possible, I suppose. I think she could kill anybody, any time, anywhere."

I held up the comic strip segments I had found in the secret compartment. "You know anything about these?"

Dominick took them and looked them over. He read them, but only with great difficulty, by running his fingers across them and sounding out the words. "Where did you get these? You didn't have them when you came in."

"They were in Rocco's bottom desk drawer. What are they?"

"They're some segments that disappeared from Rocco's gallery about a month ago. Rocco had this place downtown that he used as an outlet for this kind of art. His son, Little Rock, runs it for him. One day these segments turned up missing from there. Little Rock couldn't explain how. Rocco never reported it because he didn't want to publicize the sloppy way the kid ran the gallery. He figured that would only invite in more thieves."

"What about the prices on the back?"

Dom turned the segments over. At least he read numbers. "I don't keep up much with prices, but these look to be awful low. It could be that somebody offered them to Rocco for sale. He dealt in original segments all the time, so it would be natural for somebody who had them to see if Rocco wanted to buy. Maybe the seller didn't know they were stolen. Or maybe the thief got Rocco to pay to get them back. Rocco probably would have done it to protect his kid's reputation."

"Your brother had an appointment with somebody last night, somebody with the initials SS. You know who that might have been?"

"SS? Beats me."

"What about mythology?"

"Huh?"

"The study of ancient legends. Your brother had some books on the subject in his desk. You have any idea why?"

"Probably research material for a new strip. He did a lot of that. He'd get the idea, work out the cast of characters, and then turn it over to some photographer and writer team to script up and shoot."

I took the comic segments back from Dominick. "You mind if I hang onto these for a while?"

"Be my guest, just make sure I get them back."

I was almost out the door when, almost as an afterthought, Dominick said, "By the way, as long as you're poking into that rabbit's affairs, maybe you could do me a favor."

"If I can. What?"

Dominick lowered his voice and became as coy as a debutante sidling up to a bowl of spiked punch. "Well, when Rocco and the rabbit were having their run-in, the rabbit one day swiped something out of the office here. It was a family memento, and it was very precious to Rocco and me. The rabbit took it, I think, because he figured he might be able to hold it for ransom or something. I'd appreciate it if you could keep your eye out for it. If you come across it, I'd be willing to pay you to get it back."

"What exactly was it?"

"Nothing valuable. It's a teakettle."

"A teakettle, you say?"

"Yeah. It belonged to my grandmother. She gave it to me and Rocco just before she died. We, ah, used it to brew tea here in the office."

"Describe it for me," I said, although I had a sneaky hunch exactly how the description would go.

"It weighs about three pounds and has gray paint on the outside. There's not much else I can tell you about it. It looks like any other cheap teakettle. Will you keep your eye out for it?"

"You bet. Glad to do it. You wouldn't believe how interested I am in finding that teakettle."

The guy could have done wonders with oranges at breakfast judging from the way he wrapped his gigantic hands around mine and squeezed. "You know, Valiant," he said, "I'm starting to like you."

Now that *really* made my day. I can honestly say I had met *'toons* brighter than this bozo.

17

Fresh from a session with one dumbbell, I wanted nothing less than to spend my lunch hour with another, but no such luck. My apartment door lock bore the same amateurish pick marks I had found on the locks at my office. Roger Rabbit, apprentice locksmith, strikes again. I opened the door and went in.

I found the rabbit bustling around in the kitchen, making a monumental production out of throwing stuff into a pot. "Welcome home," he said, dipping a big wooden spoon into his bubbling cauldron and bailing out a taste. "Lunch will be ready in a jiff." He had a bath towel wrapped around his waist apron-fashion. "I hope you don't mind my using your kitchen. Since you've been so kind to me, I thought a nice meal was the least I could do to repay you. So I picked up a few odds and ends at the store, and threw something together."

I squeezed past him, opened the cupboard under the sink, and poured myself a dose of liquid composure.

The rabbit handed me a cocktail napkin. A cocktail napkin! I wondered if he also had a cigarette girl stashed in the hall ready to flounce in and sell me coffin nails at two bucks a pack. I tossed down another slug, wiped my lips on the rabbit's cocktail napkin—it had "Down the hatch!" printed across it in ten different languages, wadded it up, and stuffed it into the trash deeply enough, I hoped, so the janitor wouldn't find it and give me a rough time about going high class on him. "Quit picking my locks," I said, as sternly as you can to a rabbit wearing an apron. "Here." I reached into the drawer where I kept my spare keys, took out two, and gave them to Roger. "This one opens my apartment, this one opens my office. Do me a favor and use them from now on."

The way he looked at them you'd have thought I'd just given him the crown jewels of England. "Thank you, Mister Valiant," he said. "I'll guard them with my life."

"And knock off this Mister Valiant stuff. Call me Eddie like everybody else."

"Oh, yes, thank you . . . Eddie." He flashed me a grin sunny enough to grow pansies in a window box.

I went to the stove, lifted his pot lid, and found a lot of vegetables boiling in water. "What's this?"

"It's *ratatouille*," he said.

"That mean you make it with rats?" You never knew. 'Toons eat some of the weirdest stuff.

He guffawed. "No, hardly. It's a vegetable stew. You prepare it with eggplant, zucchini, tomatoes, Swiss cheese, and spices. It's very tasty."

"Yeah, I'm sure it is, and it sounds great, but I'm on this special diet. Doctor's orders." I opened my freezer, took out a turkey pot pie and some frozen french fries, and slid them into the oven. "You're back early," I said. "Give up on being a detective?"

"Hardly." The rabbit proudly puffed out his skinny chest. A mountaineering mouse would have had a field day scaling his protruding ribs. "I finished both my assignments, so I came back here to report in."

"You got everything I told you to?"

"Sure did." The rabbit wiped his paws on his towel apron, went into my closet, and took a book from out of my pea coat pocket. The book, published by some scholarly society with about ten words in its name, all of them three syllables or more, traced cartoon history from the late eighteen hundreds on. Roger opened the book to a page near the end. "There it is," he said.

I took the book. The page showed the tea-party scene out of the *Alice in Wonderland* remake. Alice herself sat at one end of a long, rustic table; the white rabbit sat at the other. In between them sat a titmouse, a grinning Cheshire cat, and a beagle who looked kind of familiar. I tapped my finger on the dog. "Who's the mutt?" I asked.

Roger's cheeks flushed a bright red. "That's me. I told you I had a minor role in the film."

"You played a beagle?"

Roger stirred his pot a few stout licks, banging the spoon vigorously on the edge to clean it off. "The rabbit part went to Bugs Bunny. He was really hot that year, and totally monopolized rabbit roles. He had just won an Academy Award, and everybody wanted him. While he made this movie, he also appeared on Broadway in that redo of Harvey where the human's the invisible one, and he shot a million commercials. With nothing in the rabbit line available, I read for the part of the dog and got it. It wasn't much, but it was something."

I studied the photo. "I'm impressed. You look great. If I didn't know, I'd swear you were really a beagle."

"Thanks. I worked hard at it. I wore brown face makeup and folded my ears to either side of my head. And I spent hours learning to woof. In my big scene I fetched a stick for the Queen of Hearts. I got a brief mention from Rex Reed in his review. It's at the house in my scrapbook. If we ever go back, I'll show it to you. It's the first real review I ever got. I can still quote it. 'A young unknown named Roger Rabbit played the beagle so convincingly it sent fleas up and down my spine.' "

"This the teakettle?" I pointed to the object set in the middle of the photographed table.

"That's it. See what I told you. Nothing but a cheap, ordinary teakettle."

"Certainly seems to be." I grabbed the page and ripped it out of the book.

"Do you know what you just did?" wailed the rabbit. "You just tore a page out of that book!"

"Good observation. We'll make a detective out of you yet."

"But that's a library book. You're not supposed to tear pages out of a library book. It's on my card. I'll have to pay a fine."

I looped my arm around his shoulder. "Sometimes in this detective game you have to step outside the law."

My oven timer informed me that my lunch had thawed.

Roger and I sat down at my kitchen table, he with a bowlful of his veggie stew, me with my pot pie and french fries. "You stole that teakettle off the movie set, you say."

"Right. As a souvenir." He pointed to the pot of stew. "There's plenty in there. You sure you won't have some?"

It did smell pretty good—for rabbit food, that is. Curiosity got the better of me. "Maybe just a taste," I said.

He ladled me out a generous helping.

"I saw Dominick DeGreasy this morning," I said. "He says that teakettle belonged to him and Rocco. He says it was their grandmother's, and she left it to them when she died. He says that you stole it from out of their office. He says it's very precious to him, and he's willing to pay to get it back."

The rabbit sent up a pair of speechless balloons, as flat, empty, and stark white as two pieces of bread popping out of a broken toaster. On his next try he did better. His words came out a mystified, translucent gray, but readable. "Dominick said *that?* About *my* teakettle? Absurd. I acquired the teakettle exactly the way I told you I did. And what would he want with it anyway?"

"I don't know, but that teakettle is shaping up as a very important element in this case." I finished off my bowl of stew and figured that, since the rabbit had gone through so much bother, I ought to be polite. "You got any more of this stuff?"

"Plenty. Let me get it for you." He took my bowl and filled it to the brim with seconds.

"If you didn't steal that teakettle from the DeGreasys, how did Dominick know you even had it?"

"I have no idea."

"He ever come over to your place? Maybe see it there?"

"No, never."

"You ever mention it to anybody?"

"Hardly. The subject of teakettles rarely comes up in conversation."

"What about Jessica? She *must* have known you had it."

"Of course she did. I used it every day."

"So she could have told Rocco about it, or Dominick."

"She could have, but why she would, I can't imagine. Let me stress again, that was a perfectly common teakettle. There was absolutely nothing special about it."

"Not to you, at least." Still being polite, I got up and helped myself to a third bowl of stew. "You know anybody in the cartoon business with the initials SS?"

"Lots of people. Sad Sack. Stumpy Squirrel. Super Savage. Sarah Smile. The list goes on and on. Why?"

"Rocco had an appointment at his house last night with somebody with those initials. The appointment was for eleven o'clock, only an hour before he died. Any of the people you mentioned have a grudge against Rocco?"

"Well, he was hardly the sort of man likely to be selected mayor of 'Toontown, but I don't think any of the people I listed hated him enough to kill him."

"How many of them did Rocco have under contract?"

"I don't know exactly. Stumpy Squirrel and Super Savage, for sure. Probably more."

I went back for one final dollop of stew, but the pot was empty. "What you got for dessert?" I said mostly in jest, but Roger immediately hopped up, went to the refrigerator, and brought out a Boston cream pie. He carved out a man-sized chunk and served it to me together with an excellent cup of freshly brewed coffee.

"What about the thirty-eight?" I asked five minutes later, the first time I had an empty mouth. "You have much luck tracing that?"

"Some." Roger pulled out a notebook identical to mine and flipped it open. "The gun was reported stolen several months ago. That's about it. I had no idea where to go next, so I didn't pursue it any further."

I took his notebook and wrote a few names and addresses into it. "Here's a list of shady gun dealers. Start with them. See if they've heard anything. If the police have been nosing around, chances are one of these guys will know it."

I dumped my dirty dishes into the sink. The ones that had been there when I left this morning had all been washed and stacked neatly on the drainboard. A regular ball of fire as a cook and housekeeper, this rabbit. I might be tempted to keep him around permanently if he did floors and windows, too. "Also follow up on the teakettle angle. Ask the studio's prop man. See where he got it. Maybe, if we can trace it to its origins, we can figure out why DeGreasy wants it so badly. And check out every double S initialed 'toon character in the DeGreasy stable. Find out if any of them had a recent beef with Rocco, and see where they were last night when Rocco died."

"That's a pretty heavy work load," Roger griped.

"Hey, nobody said detective work was easy."

"What are you going to do?" he asked.

"I've got a few leads of my own to follow up."

"Aren't you going to tell me what they are? I thought we were partners in this case."

"We are, but sometimes even partners have to keep their little secrets from one another. See you tonight," I told him as I went out the door.

18

*Put a figurehead over the front door and a brace of smoke-*stacks on the roof, and you could have sailed Rocco De-Greasy's place across the North Atlantic. I made a quick count of the windows as I strolled up to the front door. I hit eighteen and still had two floors to go. I suppose there must have been a door bell, but I didn't feel like spending half an hour searching for it among the geegaws carved around the entryway. I hammered the door with my fist instead, setting off a resounding echo inside.

The butler who opened the door must have come as an accessory to the house, since his face had the same smooth, pasty-white texture as the granite walls outside. When he saw me standing there on his front stoop, he crinkled up his nose the way a dowager would passing a garbage can. He offered to take my hat. I told him I didn't trust him with it. He ushered me into a living room only slightly smaller than the tenement apartment where my mother had raised her four kids, told me madam would join me shortly, and retired.

Jessica came in, carrying one of those 'toon cats that look like Felix and come in any color from chartreuse to candy apple. This one matched her violet eyes.

Jessica wore a clingy, pastel-green number. I would have expected someone with her sense of the dramatic to play the mourning role to the hilt and go with black. Of course the outfit she had on did cover her from ankle to shoulder, and maybe she considered that to be penance enough.

"Mr. Valiant," she said with that seductive voice. She held out her hand a little too high to shake, a little too low to kiss, but just about the right height to pat my head if I bowed down before her. "A pleasure to see you again. Whatever can you be investigating now? I'm sure, being a detective, you know that your client is dead."

I left her hand hanging there in midair and let her figure out what to do with it. "Dead or not, he paid me for three days' work, and I mean to give him his money's worth."

"And how do you propose to do that?" she asked. She set her cat down on the floor. It proceeded to amuse itself by conjuring up some mental mice, which it stalked around the room.

I sat down on the sofa. Rocco had a humidor of expensive cigars set on the coffee table. I opened it and helped myself to a fistful, figuring Rocco didn't need them anymore. I put one of them into my mouth, fired it up, and sucked it to life. "For starters, I aim to prove that Roger never killed Rocco."

Instead of taking a chair, Jessica kicked off her shoes, sat on the floor at the end of the coffee table, and rested her head against the arm of the sofa not six inches from my knee. "You've got a long, uphill struggle there, Mister Valiant. From what the police tell me, it's a straight-forward case. Roger had a motive. And they found the murder weapon in his house. What have you got? New evidence? If so, it had better be pretty good."

"No, no new evidence. Nothing except the basic belief that Roger didn't have what it takes to kill somebody."

"Whatever gave you that idea?"

"My vast experience with human nature."

She laughed softly. "All well and good, except remember we're talking about a rabbit here."

"It works pretty much the same way."

"You're the detective." She reached into an alabaster

box and pulled out a violet cigarette that also exactly matched her eyes. Some people just don't know when to quit. She lit her colored coffin nail, set it into an ashtray, and promptly forgot about it. It smoldered into eternity silently begging for one more touch from her gorgeous lips.

"So, just for laughs, let's you and me assume Roger didn't kill Rocco."

"All right. I'll play. Despite overwhelming evidence to the contrary, Roger didn't kill Rocco. Where do we go from here?"

"We draw up a list of who else might have."

"That would be a pretty long list. Half the civilized world, and at least that many aborigines." She placed her hand on mine, and my heart went pitty-pat. Can you believe it? Pitty-pat. She should register those hands as deadly weapons. "Rocco was not a well-loved man," she told me, "as I'm sure you've discovered already. His stars resented their ironclad contracts and the way he continually pushed them to the limits of their endurance."

"So we've got everybody who worked for him. Who else? What about the financial end of it? Who's going to inherit his estate?"

When she shook her head, her hair brushed across my fingertips and gave me the same tingle you get when somebody runs a feather across your stomach. "I don't know for sure. Rocco and I never discussed the matter. I suppose the bulk of his estate will go to his son, Little Rock."

"Tell me about him."

She laughed again, but there wasn't much mirth to it. "I think you could safely count him out as a suspect. Little Rock couldn't kill a fly. He lacks the drive and sense of purpose necessary to plan it and bring it off."

"That's why we have second-degree murder, the unpremeditated variety. For people who are too lazy to plan ahead."

She shrugged, and one side of her dress slipped down to reveal her shoulder.

"You know if Rocco had any recent business dealings with anyone with the initials SS?"

"SS? No, not that I can recall."

"I found snapshots of some stolen artwork in Rocco's office downtown. He ever mention anything about such stuff to you?"

"Not a word."

I blew my next question at her across the red-hot tip of her dead lover's fine cigar. "And where were *you* when Rocco died?"

Her eyes sparkled. 'Toons can do that with their eyes. Usually it comes across affected and ridiculous, but when she did it, it made me want to cuddle her and coo inanities into her ear. "I hope you don't suspect me of killing him."

"I haven't knocked anybody off the suspect list yet."

She shrugged again. To my dismay, the other side of her dress held the line. "I went to a movie and then for a walk. I went alone, and no one saw me. I came home around twelve-thirty and found Rocco dead in his study. I immediately called the police. In practical terms I have no alibi. But I also have no motive."

"You mind if I take a look at the scene of the crime?"

"The police already went over it."

"The police have been known to miss things before."

Jessica standing up reminded me of a skyrocket heading for outer space, one long, straight line of fire and smoke. "Sure, go ahead. It's just across the hall there."

I went inside Rocco's study. The place was filled, top to bottom, with shelves containing probably every comic book Rocco had ever produced. From what the cops had told me, after being shot, Rocco had fallen forward across his desk, though I didn't see how he found room. He had enough doodads on top of the desk to stock a hundred novelty toy shops. Most of them were little plastic or rubber wind-up contraptions depicting the 'toons in his stable. I found Roger Rabbit. I twisted his tail, set him down, and he hopped from one side of the desk top to the other. The toy appeared to be discolored. When I picked it up and examined it closely, I saw it had Rocco's blood on its paws. Good thing I wasn't much on mystical significance.

I poked through the desk's drawers until I found Rocco's checkbook. I opened it and examined the last few stubs. He had written three checks yesterday. The first two were for $10,000 each. The stubs indicated both had been paid to the mysterious SS. The third and last stub indicated a check to a downtown art dealer, the Hi Tone Gallery of Comic Art. I did some mental arithmetic and figured out that the amount of this check equaled the sum total of the prices marked on the stolen artwork photos I had found in Rocco's office.

I poked around some more inside his desk, checked behind his pictures, rifled through about a hundred of his comics, and even looked under his rug. I was just about to give up when I struck pay dirt in the fireplace. A small scorched piece of comic-book negative stuck up through the grate. The negative contained an issue number but no title. I put the scrap into my notebook and rejoined Jessica in the living room.

"Find anything?" she asked. She held up a crystal decanter. I nodded, and she poured us each a double jigger.

"Nothing. I guess the police took away everything of any importance."

"That it for the grilling then?"

"Not quite. We've still got another murder to go." I demolished my drink and built myself a second. "Where were you when *Roger* died?"

She marched her delicate fingers around the edge of her glass. "Still walking the streets."

"Not past Roger's house by any chance?"

"Nowhere near."

"You know Roger mentioned you in his last words."

"So the police told me."

"Any idea what he meant by it?"

"None." She put her untouched drink down beside her untouched cigarette. If she kept up at this rate, pretty soon she wouldn't have a vice left in the world and no idea how she got so pure. "I know you and the police both consider me a prime suspect in Roger's murder," she said, "but I'm not worried. Why should I be? I'm totally innocent."

So said half the guys on death row, but I didn't tell her that.

I fished around awhile longer, but came up with nothing new, so I got up to go.

On the way to the door, she moved in very close to me, so close I could feel her breath warming my throat when she turned her head to speak. "I'm rather sorry the interrogation's over," she said. "You fascinate me, Mister Valiant. I've never met a man quite like you. I hope you'll come back and see me again—when you can stay a bit longer." She flashed me a smile torchy enough to illuminate a midnight fertility dance.

I wanted to kid myself, but no dice. Granted, she had married a rabbit, and I had to be better than that, but no way could I ever picture myself a winner in this girl's romantic sweepstakes. She wanted something else from me. I didn't have to wait long to find out what.

"Since you're going to keep pursuing this case anyway," she purred, "there's a favor you might be able to do for me."

"Name it," I said, surprised at how hard I found it to talk without gasping.

"During my marriage to Roger, the two of us once bought an antique at auction. I always had a special fondness for it. Roger told me to take it with me when I left, but I forgot it. I would like very much to retrieve it before the courts dispose of Roger's personal belongings. I asked the police about it, but they told me there was no such object in the house. I wonder, if you should come across it during your investigation, could you see that I get it? It has a great deal of sentimental value to me."

"What is this object?" I asked, although I already had a pretty fair idea what her answer would be.

"Nothing particularly valuable. An antique teakettle. Roger kept it on the stove in his kitchen."

"Sounds simple enough. I'll see what I can do."

"I would appreciate it. A great deal."

To show me just how much a great deal could be, she kissed me full on the lips. She tasted of rose petals and honey. Her tongue caressed mine like a cool breeze on a steamy night.

She let me go and stepped back from me with a self-satisfied smile on her face that told me she thought she had my number.

And I have a hunch the lustful smirk on my face told her she was absolutely right.

Whatever that teakettle turned out to be, I knew who had first dibs on it in my book.

19

I went back to my office and let my bottom desk drawer buy me a drink.

On the other side of the wall, I could hear my next-door neighbor, an accountant with thick glasses, clickety-clacking his adding machine. I envied the guy. Must be nice to have a job where everything added up. Rarely see it in my line of work.

For instance, Jessica Rabbit could easily have had her pick of any human guy she wanted. Yet she ran off and married a nobody 'toon rabbit. Why? To get his teakettle? Hardly seemed likely. She could have spent one night with him, or even just stroked his nose, and he'd have given her his teakettle plus his house and all his money to boot.

And what about that teakettle? What made it so important? Who had it, and how did they get it?

I sank a well into my bottom drawer, and struck more bourbon.

I opened my closet door and flipped on the old black and white TV set I keep in there out of sight of clients.

There was a football game on I wanted to catch, the Rams against the Bears with the Rams trying something new, a 'toon gorilla as linebacker. Nothing particularly unusual about that. Last statistics I saw, nearly seventy-five percent of all pro players were 'toons. According to some people, it's ruined the game, made it not so much football as barnyard brawling.

Anyway, what makes this new Rams' player different is that she's not only a 'toon, she's also a female, the first woman to break into the pros. A lot of sportswriters dismiss it as nothing but a desperate gimmick on the part of a bottom-division team, but I don't know. I don't see how you can call anybody a gimmick who's eight feet tall, three hundred pounds, and can lift the back end of a car with her toes.

The game had barely gotten under way, and the new girl on the block had just thrown the Bears' quarterback for a ten-yard loss, when Roger came in, floating two feet off the ground as usual. "What a hectic day I had," he said. His words collapsed inside their balloon like so many beanbags. He took off his coat, walked to the open closet, hung it up, and shut the door on a football sailing toward a wide receiver all alone in the end zone.

"Hey, I was watching that," I said.

He looked at me, and at where I was pointing. "You were watching the closet door?" he asked.

I didn't have the strength to explain. "Tell me what you found," I said.

"I hit every one of those gun dealers you sent me to and came up absolutely blank. No luck on the thirty-eight."

He sat down across the desk from me, leaned back in his chair the same way I was, and crossed his feet on the desk top just like mine. It was almost like talking to my reflection in the mirror, except even on my worst morning I never looked as fuzzy as that. "Too bad. That means it probably came from some minor dealer. It would take us a week to hit those. Tell you what, drop the gun angle for the time being and concentrate on the teakettle instead."

The rabbit overlapped his upper lip with his lower, achieving exactly the same facial posture he would have if I had bopped him in the jaw. "The teakettle? You can't be serious. What can possibly be so important about that crummy old teakettle?" His next words came out in the close-set, legalistic lettering you see in the contract for a set of encyclopedias. "You promised me we would go partners in this. I assumed that meant we would share the work evenly, good and bad alike. So far you've taken the glamour jobs, and I've done the doggy stuff. How about giving me some real detective work for a change? Something that really matters."

I opened the closet door just in time to miss an eighty-six-yard punt return, catching instead Plastic Man's spiel for his brand of garbage sacks. Lucky me. "You got it wrong, bunny boy," I told the rabbit. "This teakettle looks like it might be the most important angle of the case."

"Pish, posh. I don't believe it."

"It's true." The TV showed a closeup of a Rams cheerleader wiggling her fanny, although I couldn't get too excited by the sight of a possum in tight pink shorts.

"How can you be so sure? Just because Dominick DeGreasy's after the teakettle, that doesn't make it the Holy Grail."

"It's not just Dominick anymore. Your ex-wife has a yearning for that teakettle, too."

"Jessica? You saw Jessica?"

"Less than an hour ago. She says that you and she bought that teakettle at an antique auction. She says she always had a particular fondness for it, that you told her to take it with her when she left, but she forgot it. She asked me to scout it up and give it to her. Any of that sound familiar to you?"

Roger wore the dumbfounded look you see on the face

of somebody who walks into a darkened room, flips on the lights, and finds thirty people in there with him all yelling "Surprise!" "She told you the two of us bought it at an auction?"

"So she said."

"That's a flat-out lie." His large black eyeballs took a big hop with every word. Almost made me want to sing along. "I got that teakettle where I said I got it."

"So you see, the teakettle shapes up as being very significant."

Roger bent his ears forward ninety degrees, like he was caught in a brisk wind pushing him forward into some place he had no desire to go. "Fine. No more static. Tell me what you want me to do, and I'll do it."

"Good. Check with the studio prop man who bought the teakettle. Find out where he got it from and work backward from there."

"Right."

"Also, something else." I wrote out a name and telephone number and passed it to him. "This is a contact I have at the phone company. Give him a call, set up a meeting, and tell him I want the phone records for Rocco's house on the night he died. All calls both in and out."

"He just gives you that kind of data?"

"Not exactly." I rubbed my thumb and forefinger together. "In return I supplement his income slightly."

"Wow!" Roger's buoyant balloon sailed up so high, it wrapped itself around the single light bulb that illuminated my office. I had to stand on my desk to peel it off. "Bribery," said Roger. "That's what I call real detective work."

I crushed Roger's balloon, which the heat from the light bulb had baked into the crackly consistency of a fortune cookie, and dropped it into my ashtray. "How have you done with the double-S initialed characters?" I asked.

Roger pulled out his notebook and studied it, although I don't know why. Anybody who could memorize a cartoon script shouldn't have any trouble remembering a report as short as the one he gave me. "I checked Sam Spud and

Sad Sack. Both of them had ironclad alibis for the time
Rocco died."

"OK. Keep trying. Make that your number-two priority
after the teakettle." I debated whether or not to let
Roger in on the piece of negative I'd found in Rocco's
fireplace, but decided not to. It would only encourage him
to stick around longer. This way, he put on his hat and
coat and got back to business.

I spent the next few hours lowering the alcohol content
in my bottle of bourbon.

Oh, yeah. The Rams won fourteen to twelve, they
awarded the game ball to Priscilla Gorilla, and a million
guys on a million bar stools mourned another fallen
tradition.

20

The outside of the DeGreasy Gallery was done up in what
they call understated elegance. The gallery had no name on
its window and only a scrolly golden street number and
the single initial D on its heavy, carved walnut door.

Inside, a gaggle of sallow-faced, artsy-craftsy types
scurried around arranging punch bowls and cocktail nap-
kins just so for a reception to be held that night in honor
of Hagar the Horrible and his photographer, Dik Browne.
I saw Hagar and Browne off to one side chatting with a
pair of early-bird country bumpkins. At the rubes' re-
quest, Hagar donned his Viking helmet, and he and
Browne posed with the two crackers for a photo they
could show the folks back home in Podunk, Iowa. As
their way of saying thanks, the hayseeds pasted sold

labels on Browne's three most expensive framed original strips. Must have been a good year for sweet corn.

One of the artsy-craftsy types pointed out Little Rock DeGreasy to me.

The guy bore no resemblance whatsoever to his father. Where Rocco had been baked out of bread dough, his son had been carved in spun sugar. His delicate face gave him a boyish vulnerability. I could easily picture him napping at his school desk while his classmates tied his shoelaces together. He sported this season's high-fashion outfit, what I call the flophouse bedsheet look: drab, loose, and wrinkled. I could almost see Rocco DeGreasy rolling over in his grave. "You Little Rock?"

"One and the same," he said, without looking at me. He told a pair of pretty young girls to raise up a particular strip and tilt it left, then right, then left again. I swear he put as much sweat into hanging the thing as Dik Browne had put into photographing it.

I stuck my license under his nose. "I'm Eddie Valiant, private detective. I'm investigating your father's death."

He made a circle with his thumb and forefinger, and his two protégées locked their strip to the wall, a bit crookedly I thought, but I never did have much of an eye for art. "What's to investigate?" Little Rock asked. "Roger Rabbit did it."

"So say the police. I say otherwise."

He made a sound halfway between a sigh and a gulp, the sound you'd hear from somebody who'd just discovered that the light at the end of their tunnel comes from an onrushing train. "As you can see, I'm awfully busy right now." To illustrate, he took a bunch of strips stacked against the wall and stacked them against another wall. "I've still got *scads* of work to do before tonight's reception, but I suppose I can spare you a moment. Let me just attend to some details, and I'll be right with you."

While he got in some last-minute whizzing around, I strolled through the gallery. A sign at the front door listed the photographers the gallery represented. The list included Carol Masters, although as I walked along I didn't see a single one of her photos.

Little Rock rejoined me. "Shall we step into my office?" He indicated a door in the rear.

Some office. Storage shed would be more like it. He had framed and unframed strips, cardboard boxes, photos, and assorted papers piled everywhere. It made even my office look neat by comparison. Little Rock unburied a chair for me, and I sat down. "Sorry for the mess," he said, "but we're terribly cramped for space. I pestered my father for months to enlarge the gallery, but he never saw fit to do so."

"You couldn't go ahead without his OK?"

"Hardly. My father made all major decisions concerning gallery operation. I did exactly as he told me, no more, no less." He squeezed between two filing cabinets and popped back out seconds later holding a tray of bottles. "Care for a drink?" he asked. He had liquor in about any color you could ask for, except the one I liked best, standard whiskey brown. I told him no thanks. He poured himself three fingers of emerald green and added equal portions of lemon yellow, sky blue, and sunset orange. I half expected him to stir it with a Crayola.

"Tongues are wagging because I'm here at the gallery today instead of home mourning," he said. "But I considered my father a dreadful tyrant. I'm not the least bit sorry he's dead." He paused to give me a chance to fall off my chair, but, even if I'd been so inclined, in that crowded office there just wasn't room.

"My father continually berated me for being lazy. Actually, I'm not the slightest bit adverse to good, hard work, so long as it takes me where I want to go."

"And where might that be?"

He gave me a smile chock full of grand plans for better days to come. "I long to start my own cartoon syndicate. Nothing as unwieldy as Father's. A quality line of high-class strips. Built perhaps around a single talented star. But in the meantime I run this gallery, and I run it well. I turned a profit every month. Yet Father refused to let me operate as I saw fit. He meddled in gallery affairs to the very end." Little Rock finished his drink and made himself another, this round switching to blood red, straight up. "I still can't believe it. After suffering through so many years of his domination, I'm finally free." True, he no longer wore the shackles, yet I had a hunch his body would continue to sag for years from the accustomed weight of the chains. "Why do you suspect Father was killed by someone other than Roger Rabbit?"

"Because of some things that don't figure." I consulted my notebook. "For starters, the day he died, your father wrote a check to a gallery downtown. The Hi Tone Gallery of Comic Art. Ever hear of it?"

Little Rock laughed dryly. "I should say so. It's run by a fellow named Hiram Toner. He has a reputation as a somewhat less than ethical dealer."

"Exactly what do you mean by that?"

"I mean the provenance of his art warrants extremely close scrutiny."

"Could you translate that into plain English for me?"

I finally saw a resemblance to his father in the haughty way he peered at me down his nose. "He's a fence for stolen art."

I hauled out the photos I had found in Rocco's office. "Recognize these?"

He fanned them out card fashion in front of himself and kept glancing at me over their tops like a riverboat gambler figuring out how to stick me with the Old Maid. "Where did you get them?"

"They were in your father's office. You know what they are?"

He laid them face up on the desk, arranging them into a pleasing pattern the same way he would have had they been hanging outside on his gallery wall. "They were stolen from here about a month ago."

"Any clue as to who did it?"

"None. I opened up one day, came in, turned off the burglar alarm, took a look around, and saw they were gone. They had been taken right off the wall during the night. The police investigated, but could find no evidence of forced entry. We never did discover how the thieves got in."

"Who had keys?"

"Only me. And, of course, my father."

I turned the photos over. "What about the prices on the back?"

He perched a pair of tiny half glasses on the end of his nose. "These prices are considerably lower than the works are worth."

"As if the guy selling them might know they're hot?"

"Yes, that's likely the case," said Little Rock, "especially at the Hi Tone Gallery."

I returned the photos to my pocket. "What about Jessica Rabbit? Your Uncle Dominick thinks she was taking your old man for a ride."

I couldn't remember right off where I had seen his expression before. Then I placed it. I once had a puppy in love. "Shows you how little Uncle Dom knows about women. Jessica is one of the most charming and beautiful ladies I've ever met. She was far better than my father deserved."

Chalk up another conquest for Jessica the Juggernaut. "You have any idea who will inherit your father's estate?"

"No, although I suppose it will probably be me. I guess I'll find out for sure tomorrow, when they read the will." He didn't seem particularly interested. Maybe he knew about the DeGreasy syndicate's rotten financial shape, that he'd be lucky to inherit carfare home from the lawyer's office.

I asked him point-blank the syndicate's net worth, but he insisted he had no idea. He contended that his father had always excluded him from the fiscal end of the business.

"You know if your father had any recent dealings with someone with the initials SS?"

"SS? No, not that I know of."

I played a long shot. "I notice from your sign out front

that you represent Carol Masters, yet I don't see any of her works out on display. How come?"

Little Rock slumped down into his chair as if somebody had yanked a cork out of his toe and deflated his body by ten pounds. "Father told me to pull them."

"Why?"

Little Rock turned his beautifully manicured hands palms up. "I'm not exactly sure. About six months ago Father took a vehement dislike to the woman. I can only guess it's because lately Carol has become a forceful crusader for 'toons' rights, and Father resented her for it. She led a contingent of 'toons right into Father's office on a quest for higher pay scales and improved working conditions. Lord, I wish I could have been there to see it. I suspect that may have been the final straw. Shortly thereafter Father began a concerted effort to strangle Carol's career. He spread the word that she had become unreliable, that a high percentage of her work required extensive retouching. He even rejected one of her strips outright, and that's almost unheard of in the industry."

"Did he have a case?"

"Not that I could see. Carol takes some of the best photos around. I had originally intended to feature her next month in a one-woman show—her first. I had invitations set, flyers printed. When Father found out about it, he was furious. He instructed me to cancel it, and what's more to remove everything of Carol's from the gallery."

"How did Carol react when she found out you were scrubbing her show and yanking her stuff?"

"How would you expect? She stormed out of here in a royal tizzy. That was yesterday. When I heard Father had been killed last night, my initial reaction was that Carol Masters had done it. I was actually quite surprised to find out it had been Roger Rabbit instead."

"You consider Carol Masters capable of murder?"

"Most assuredly. Especially if someone pushed her as hard and as far as my father did."

At first I guffawed, then, when I remembered her eyes,

her savage, tiger's eyes, I realized that maybe, just maybe, Little Rock had a point.

I played clue with him for another half hour or so, but, when I tallied up my score sheet, I found I was no closer to discovering who had killed Rocco DeGreasy with the gun in the study than I had been when I first walked in.

21

In a contest for most signs in least space, I would have been hard-pressed to pick between Smoky Stover's firehouse and the front window of the Hi Tone Gallery of Comic Art. Half off on this, closeout sale on that, invest in art for the future, with every S converted to a dollar sign. Toss in the loudspeaker blaring over the entry door, a half mile of flashing neon out front, and a used car lot seemed practically staid by comparison.

I barely got inside when two super-slick salesmen pounced on me, one from either side. For laughs I almost passed myself off as a big spender just to watch them arm-wrestle each other over who saw me first, but instead I flashed my license. That brought them to a screeching halt. I never heard so many hems and haws. Talk about guilty looks. Sylvester the Cat with his mouth full of Tweetie Bird could do a better innocent act than these two clowns. I asked for Hiram Toner, and they pointed me toward the back. As I headed in that direction, I caught one of the salesmen tapping a wall-mounted button, probably connected to an alarm in Toner's office. Woe to the poor bunco cop snooping around here.

Maybe Toner was compulsively neat. Maybe, more likely, he was Jack Flash with a shovel and pail. Whichever, by the time I got to his office, there wasn't a scrap of paper to be seen anywhere.

His decor could have been designed by Goldilocks and the baby bear—furniture not too hard, not too soft; lighting not too bright, not too dim; temperature not too hot, not too cold; but everything just right.

Toner greeted me warmly with an outstretched hand. "Hiram Toner," he said. "Pleased to meet you." Give Toner a swig of Little Rock's red liquor, and you could have used him for a thermometer. I'd seen cadavers with more padding on them. His suit looked to be expensive, but still fit him like a grocery sack fits a buck's worth of canned soup and bananas. "How may I be of assistance?" he said, with a voice oily enough to fry a chicken. "Wait, let me guess. You're here to see about buying an original strip. But which one? Ah, I know. Prince Valiant. Definitely Prince Valiant. It so suits you. Stately, with an aura of chivalry."

"Sorry. If you're going into the swami business, you need a new crystal ball."

"Tarzan, then. I can see it in your rippling muscles."

"Wrong again."

"Jungle Jim? Blackhawk? Superman? The Incredible Hulk?"

"Knock off the snappy patter, Toner. I'm no sidewalk sucker. You know it as well as I do. My name's Eddie Valiant." I showed him my license, and he copied off its number. The man had gone round the block with gumshoes before. "I'm a private detective investigating Rocco DeGreasy's murder."

"So what does that have to do with me?"

I handed him the photos of the stolen strips. "You ever see these before?"

He gave them barely a glance before tossing them back to me like a fistful of spuds in a game of hot potato. "Yes, I'm familiar with them. I had them on consignment here in the gallery. Up until today, that is, when I sent them out to their new owner."

"And who might that be?"

He plucked a piece of thread off his lapel and deposited it into a tubular wooden wastebasket that had the right proportions to be the box the stork had delivered him in. "All right, Valiant. You already know or you wouldn't be poking around here. I sold them to Rocco DeGreasy. I got a check in the mail from him this morning for the full purchase price. I sent him the strips by messenger."

"How did Rocco first find out you had them?"

He crossed his arms and legs in the same direction, in the same motion, the way a seated barnyard 'toon would, except he didn't turn himself into a pretzel in the process. "Through the efforts of a gentleman who earns his living matching up wealthy collectors with interesting objects. When he makes a connection, he takes a cut off each end, from buyer and seller both. He put Rocco and me together."

"This matchmaker got a name?"

Toner crooked a bony finger and scratched his head. "Strange, but his name escapes me. I'm really very terrible with names. I keep meaning to take one of those memory courses, but I can never remember when they're being held."

A fat lot of cooperation I could expect here. "So this mysterious matchmaker showed Rocco DeGreasy the photos. What then?"

"Rocco bought them. I sent him the works within an hour after getting his check."

"How come so fast?"

"Service, Mister Valiant, service. The hallmark of my business."

"I suppose it didn't have anything to do with getting them off the premises as soon as possible? I suppose you had no idea those strips were stolen?"

Toner puckered his lips. Press a bugle to them, and I just knew "God Bless America" would come out the other end. "Stolen? My word. Imagine that. Had I known, I would have turned the nasty things over to the proper authorities immediately."

"How did you originally come to have them?"

Toner swayed ever so gently from side to side. "The strips came to the gallery one day via messenger. The letter with them asked if I would be interested in handling their sale. The letter stated that the strips belonged to a wealthy old family that had fallen upon hard times. This family was being forced to part with some very dear and very precious possessions, including the aforementioned strips. The letter stressed the need for utmost discretion, to protect this family from the ill publicity that would certainly befall it should its plight become known. I sent the messenger back with a note informing the family that I would certainly do my best to secure top dollar for these works on its behalf."

"This family have a name?"

"Most families do. This one never said."

"How about an address?"

"Sorry, no. In the interest of discretion, they instructed me to send their cut to a downtown post office box."

"Got the box number?"

"Sad to say, I do not. I'm such a nit when it comes to keeping records of such matters."

Talking to Hiram Toner was pretty much like running on a treadmill, lots of effort, but no forward motion. A short dose of him, and I began to understand why guys go off and live on mountaintops. "I'm not diddling with you anymore, Toner. I'm turning this whole sleazy mess over to the cops. Explain your nameless family to them."

He dismissed my threat with a smile almost longer than he was wide. "Do as you see fit. I have no fear of the police. In fact the police and I are old friends. They pop by and inspect my merchandise quite regularly. As you can see from the fact that I'm still open for business, they have yet to find anything remiss."

"There's a first time for everything."

He turned his smile into a smarmy grin that hinted he

and he alone had a foolproof method for beating the system.

I wished him well in fulfilling his fantasy.

When I was a kid I patronized a soda shop where for twenty-five cents I got a comic book, a double dip cone, and more candy than I could stuff in a gunny sack. A guy we called Pops ran the joint, and still does.

I walked in and said hello.

Pops peered at me through eyeglasses not quite as big as my car's headlights. "Well fiddle-dee-dee!" Pops always talked like a man with a 'toon caught in his throat, a lot of hi-de-hos, by-gums, and Land-o'-Goshens. "Eddie? Eddie Valiant? That you?"

"You got it, Pops. What's good today?"

He pointed an arthritic finger at a box of candy that probably had been there the first time I came in twenty years ago, and hadn't been that fresh then. "Got some tasty jujubees and some sweet bottles." He held up a hollow parafin bottle filled with green syrup. The thing had been on his shelf so long the syrup had turned as solid as the wax surrounding it. "You used to like these pretty well, as I recall."

I slid a double sawbuck across the counter. "Give me this many jujubees."

By the look on his face I must have just doubled his yearly gross income. "I don't think I've got that many," he said, clearly afraid he was about to blow his biggest sale of the decade.

I gave him a brand new lease on life. "Make it an assortment, then. Whatever you got. Surprise me."

He went through his boxes picking a handful of stale candy out of each. I can't remember when I've seen anybody so happy.

"You still keep up with comics the way you did in the old days, Pops?"

He showed me a set of teeth with more gaps than a guilty man's alibi. "You bet your life. Read every one that comes out. Have to use a magnifying glass anymore to make out the words, but I keep plugging away at them. Right-a-rootie."

Like I said. Definitely a man with a 'toon caught in his throat.

I fished out the burned negative I'd found in Rocco's fireplace. "Know what comic this might be?"

He studied it through a magnifying glass large enough to have started life as a porthole in the Queen Mary. "Can't say that I do. It looks sort of familiar, but I can't place it right off. Shouldn't be too hard to find, though. Every comic company uses its own numbering system. I ought to be able to track this one down easy enough."

I pulled another twenty out of my wallet. "Here's something to get you going."

He made my money vanish with a skill that would have impressed Mandrake the Magician and gave me a duplicate of the long, hard going-over I get from patrol cops when they catch me hanging around a decent neighborhood at an indecent hour. "You still in the detective racket, Eddie?"

"Some months more than others. This month up to my eyeballs."

He picked a jawbreaker out of a cardboard box, popped it into his mouth, and poked random holes in it with what he had left of his teeth. "This comic you're after. It have anything to do with a case?"

I told him it did, and I told him which one.

"No kidding." His gumball flipped back and forth between his cheeks like he had two competing Mister Tooth Decays in there engaged in a cannon battle over his few remaining molars. "The Rocco DeGreasy murder. Do tell." He pointed toward a section of his comic rack with more webs on it than you'd find on Spiderman's laundry line. "I got a big bunch of his syndicate's stuff over there. Hasn't been moving too good lately, and DeGreasy's got this policy of no returns. You want my opinion, I say he got knocked off by an overstocked newsboy."

I patted him on the shoulder. "Thanks for the tip,

Pops. I'll check it out. In the meantime, I'd appreciate whatever you can dig up on that comic I gave you."

"Be my pleasure," he said. "Always happy to assist a force of the law. I'll get right on it."

I gave him my card and asked him to contact me when he got results.

I called Big Art at the pool hall I used for an answering service. He checked behind the cigar counter and found one message for me, from the rabbit. Roger had connected with my phone company contact and discovered that, the evening he died, Rocco had placed two calls, one to the DeGreasy art gallery, one to Carol Masters's studio. He had talked to the gallery for ten minutes, and to Carol Masters for five. I wondered what about.

The rabbit had also done some productive spadework on backtracking the teakettle. The *Alice in Wonderland* prop man had bought it from a 'toontown junkman, and the rabbit was on his way to interview him.

The rabbit said he would call in later for further instructions. I asked Big Art to tell the rabbit to check around with local messenger services and find out which one had delivered the stolen artwork to Hiram Toner at the Hi Tone Gallery of Comic Art.

Next I swung by the office, mainly because it boasted the cheapest drinks in town. When I pulled up outside, I found Clever Cleaver's car parked at the curb. Since I've never been known for my good sense, I went in anyway.

He was waiting for me in the hall. He'd been there for quite a spell, judging from the number of scorch marks his smoky-yellow cigarette puffs had branded into the carpet.

"To what do I owe this unexpected pleasure?" I asked, letting us both inside.

He went straight to my bottom desk drawer, hauled out my bottle, and held it to the light. It contained enough for one whopper or two petites. "You don't mind, do you, Butch?" he said, pouring the bottle's contents into a single glass. "After all, I am company."

I shrugged and shut my mouth to keep my tongue from licking my lips.

He tossed down the last of my hootch and ejected a few projectile-shaped ear puffs, which came at me as low and hard as his next statement. "Get off the Roger Rabbit case," he said, biting down hard on every word and spitting them one by one in my direction. "I got the wife pegged as the killer, and I'm about this near to proving it." He sent up two parallel lines so close together you would have been hard pressed to pass a hangman's noose between them. "You keep poking around, you're liable to screw up my play, and that would make me very unhappy. So lay off Roger Rabbit." He took a pencil out of his coat pocket, underlined his words, and stuck them to my wall where I'd have to cover them with a picture, paint them over, or spend the rest of my life looking at them every time I sat down at my desk.

"Sorry to ruin your tough-guy rendition, Captain, but you got your facts wrong. I'm not investigating Roger's murder. I agree with you one hundred percent. Jessica Rabbit did it, and I wish you all the luck in the world in nailing her for it. I'm after whoever got Rocco DeGreasy."

That brought him up short. "You kidding me? Roger Rabbit killed DeGreasy. There's no doubt about it. Rusty Hudson put it to bed once and for all when the lab found the rabbit's pawprints all over the fatal thirty-eight."

That bit of information, which came as news to me, sure gave the case an interesting twist. "I know it sounds like a lost cause, but I'm not exactly swamped with work right now, so I think I'll putter around with it awhile longer, anyway."

"Suit yourself. Keep chasing hobgoblins until you're blue in the face. Just don't mess me up."

"Perish the thought. I would like to know one thing about your investigation, though. Did your boys search Roger's house?"

"You bet. They gave it a thorough going-over."

"Did they, by chance, take Roger's teakettle with them when they left?"

Until he knew where this was leading, Cleaver wasn't so anxious to go. "His teakettle? What could they have wanted with his teakettle? And why do you care, anyway?" His left eyebrow assumed the shape of a hunchbacked caterpillar.

"I collect them, and I need the rabbit's to complete my set."

Cleaver scrambled the air alongside his temple. "Valiant, sometimes you slay me."

He left me with an empty bottle and another big hole in my puzzle.

22

Carol Masters's secretary sent me to Carol's shooting location, a deserted warehouse in Hogan's Alley, a low-life section of town, where I saw enough denizens floating around to cast an urban remake of *Twenty Thousand Leagues Under the Sea*. I parked my car, kissed my hubcaps good-bye, and went inside the warehouse.

One of the city's finest intercepted me and demanded to know my business. I flashed him my license, and he let me by.

Before I had gone another twenty feet, I passed at least eight or nine more cops. Even for Hogan's Alley, that much security seemed excessive. I wondered how Carol rated it, then I saw her photographic subject, none other than Dick Tracy, every cop's idol. That explained it. The precinct desk sergeant probably had to hold a lottery to select which of his many volunteers got to come over here and guard their hero's privacy.

In the episode being shot, Tracy was going up against

Mush Face, a guy with a pug resembling a bowl of barely set Wheatena. Mush Face had the drop on the ace detective, but, since justice always triumphs, by the time the sequence ended, Tracy had turned the tables and was carting old ugly off to the hoosegow.

A bunch of cops came up to Tracy afterward and asked him for his autograph.

While he wrote, Tracy delivered a short sermon on the importance of strict law enforcement in modern society. The cops roundly applauded. A few of them snabbed his word balloons and told him they planned to frame them and hang them above the station house door. The way the cops treated him, you might have thought he really was a cop instead of an actor playing a cop. A guy like Tracy could probably get elected chief of police on the basis of his dashing reflection in the fun-house mirror. In the comic business they call that the power of make-believe. In our nation's capital, they call it politics.

I offered to give Carol Masters a hand loading her camera stuff into her car, but I got a response so cold I was sorry I'd taken the wool lining out of my trench coat. "I can manage perfectly well by myself, Mister Valiant." She dragged a box of equipment out the door and across the sidewalk toward her car. She got it as far as the trunk, but couldn't lift it inside. I grabbed it, muscled it in, and did the same with two more.

"That wasn't necessary," she said. "I really could have done it without you."

"It's great to be appreciated," I cracked. "Sometimes I wonder how I keep from getting a swelled head."

She pulled out the kind of key ring you usually find connected to a jailer and opened the door to her car. She slid into the front seat, positioned the rearview mirror around so she could see herself in it, and perked up her hair with a comb. "What do you want from me now?" she said, with about as much friendliness as I used to get from my drill instructor.

I leaned on her car. It needed a good wash job, but so did I. "I want some more information on Rocco, that's all. The cops are convinced that Rocco killed him. I think otherwise, and I'm out to prove it."

She turned sideways in the front seat, giving me a great shot of the wonderful things that happen to a well-built female body when you twist it just right. "But why? Roger's dead. You no longer have a client. There's nobody to pay your bill."

"So what does money matter if I can discover truth?"

I could tell she believed that about as much as she believed in Santa Claus, but she was sharp enough to realize that, until she answered my questions, I'd never leave her alone. "What is it you want to know?"

I went around to the other side of the car and slid in beside her. "I talked to Little Rock DeGreasy over at the gallery. He says Rocco ordered him to cancel your one-woman show and take down your work. Any idea why?"

She dumped her comb into a purse only slightly larger than Spark Plug's feedbag. "He did it to be ornery," she said, "to flaunt his control over me. Rocco couldn't stand to have people cross him, and I'd been doing a lot of that lately."

"How so?"

"My work for 'toon's rights, my support of Roger Rabbit." She turned her palms toward her, bent her fingers forward, and examined her nails. They were far from beautiful, chipped and scratched, like the nails of a rock climber clawing toward the top. "Rocco couldn't stand uppity women. He retaliated by yanking my work."

Dick Tracy came over to the car. I'd never seen him in person before, and I couldn't believe how tall he was. Usually 'toons turn actor to compensate for being shrimpy, but Tracy could look me straight in the eye with no trouble. And talk about square-jawed. I could have used his chin for a letter opener. Carol introduced us, and his grip almost broke my hand. He yakked with us for a while and impressed me as a gutsy, stand-up guy. I nearly asked him for his autograph myself.

"I understand Rocco called you the night he died," I said after Tracy left. "What did he say?"

"Nothing much, really." I started to light a cigarette but doused it when I saw her unsullied ashtray. A nonsmoker, but that didn't surprise me. I had her pegged as a woman with vices a lot more complex than tobacco. "Rocco's only reason for calling was to torment me. He crowed on and on about how he had canceled my show. He told me he would make sure I never showed in any gallery again. It was a typically disgusting Rocco performance. I finally hung up on him."

"How long did you talk to him?"

"I don't know exactly. I didn't look at the clock. I would guess about five or ten minutes."

"Anyone with you when the call came in?"

"No, I was alone."

"After you got off the phone, what did you do?"

"I had a stiff drink and went to bed."

"You didn't go out?"

"In the middle of the night? Of course not."

If she was lying, she had the technique down pat. She didn't so much as tremble an eyelid. "What's the deal between Little Rock and Jessica Rabbit?"

She shook her head ruefully. "The poor guy loves her, but Jessica feels toward him the way she would toward a lottery ticket. If Little Rock inherits Rocco's estate, Jessica's number comes up, and she wins big. She'll marry him and live happily ever after on his money. If he doesn't inherit, she'll rip him into teeny pieces and toss him into her wastebasket."

I pulled out my notebook and read Carol the issue number I had copied off the comic in Rocco's fireplace. "Any idea what comic that could be?"

She was shaking her head even before I'd finished my question. "No. There are hundreds of tiny syndicates putting out comics. Each uses its own numbering system. It could be anything."

"Do you know of anyone with the initials SS who may have had a grudge against Rocco?"

"Can't say I do. Rocco had a few 'toons with those initials under contract, but they're all decent, hard workers. If you're trying to pin his murder on one of them, I think you're way off base."

I hauled out the photos of the stolen artworks. "Know anything about these?"

She flipped through them quickly, without interest. "They're some strips I shot a while back. Rocco put them up for sale in his gallery. I heard somebody stole them."

"Odd, wouldn't you say, that whoever did it stole only strips shot by you?"

She shrugged. "A discriminating thief. What more can I say?" She handed the photos back.

"Have you heard of anyone offering these works for sale or for ransom?"

"Afraid not, but then there's really no reason why I should. These works were never my property. Everything I shoot belongs to Rocco. It was part of our contractual arrangement, and also one of the biggest points of contention between us. I said I should have a cut of each sale. He said no."

"And there was nothing you could do about it?"

"Not a thing. He owned them, lock, stock, and barrel. Pretty much the way he owned everything in his syndicate. Pretty much the way he owned Roger Rabbit. Pretty much the way he owned me."

Sounded like a passable motive for murder if I ever heard one.

I asked her enough questions to get back around to the front side of the mulberry bush, and said good-bye.

23

I got back to my apartment just in time to spruce it up for
my weekly poker game. Anything lying around loose I
kicked under the sofa. I swabbed last week's dried beer
off my card table, cracked open a fresh deck of paste-
boards, tossed some chips into a bowl, and threw three
cases of suds on ice.

Billy Donovan arrived first. Billy was a construction
worker who had drifted in from the deep South. He wore
bulb-toed, clodhopper shoes, bib overalls, a gingham
checked shirt, and a ratty straw hat. He sucked on a long
shaft of barley grass from the shock his country kin included along with a Baggie of homemade grits, a plug of
prime chewing tobacco, and a Mason jar of white lightning
in their weekly Kentucky Special Care package. Whenever
he won a hand, Billy slapped his knee and saw "Aw,
shucks." On any given night he said it a lot. For a down-
home hillbilly, he played a big-city brand of poker.

Next came Jess Westerminster, the moneyed one of our
group. Jess was descended from a long line of distinguished
forebears. His great-great-great had crossed over from the
old country on board the *Mayflower* and had been the guy
who arranged to have the nation's first Thanksgiving dinner catered by the 'toons the colonists found living here.
For this Jess's ancestor got his name in the history books.

Another of Jess's relatives had imported thousands of 'toons from China to build the nation's first transcontinental railroad. They became known as the Yellow Kids and won that relative a spot in the history books, too.

The last person to arrive was Harry Wayne. Harry worked in a body shop and owned the snazziest set of wheels. It had started out life as a stock Chevy eight-stroker before Harry took over. He chopped and channeled the body, bored out the engine, recovered the seats, threw on a set of super-wide whitewalls, and traded a pound of hamburger to a 'toon dragon for two flaming belches, which he glued to either side of the car just behind the front wheel wells. When Harry finished with it, that car went a hundred miles an hour standing still.

We cut for deal. I won and called spit in the ocean. Everybody anted up. I had just dealt myself my third king, and it was starting to look like one of those nights the gods smiled down on me, when I heard an ominous sound—a key turning in my front door. Right away I could see it coming, and come it did. The door popped open, and Roger Rabbit walked in.

Conversation around the table ceased. My buddies stared dumbfounded at the 'toon rabbit standing in the middle of my living room carpet. Totally oblivious, Roger hopped jovially over to the card table, extended a fuzzy paw, and said, "Hello, I'm Roger, Eddie's new roommate." I could have crawled under the table and died.

Naturally nobody hustled to the front of the reception line. Billy leaned over and whispered in my ear, "What's with the 'toon, Eddie? I thought we agreed when we started this game. No women and no 'toons."

"Yes, Eddie," Jess chimed in. "Would you mind explaining? What's this 'toon doing here?"

"Did he call himself your new *roommate?*" asked Harry. "You mean to tell us you *live* with this thing?"

Were I a religious man, my conception of the devil wouldn't wear a red union suit and carry a pitchfork. He'd have long, furry ears, gnaw on carrots, and answer to the name of Roger. "It's business, fellows," I explained lamely. "The rabbit's a client of mine. He's staying here temporarily, until I can find him a place of his own."

"You're working for a *'toon?*" said Jess incredulously.

"Cash me in," said Harry. "I got business elsewhere."

"Ditto," said Billy. The three of them collected their money and walked out the door. I compared their cast-off hands. They were good, the betting would have been furious, and I had all three of them beat easy.

"I'm sorry if I spoiled your game," said Roger in letters so hangdog I expected them to bark and chase their tails. "I didn't know you had company. If you had told me, I would have taken in a movie or something."

I made a royal mess out of putting the potato chips back inside their sack because I kept squeezing my hand into a fist and squashing whatever chips I held.

Roger hopped along after me, trying to make himself useful. I felt like suggesting that the best way to do that would be to hang himself from my chandelier. "Your friends don't like 'toons very much, do they?" asked Roger pensively.

"Not many humans do." I counted my take. What with the forfeited ante and betting on the first three cards, I had made six bucks on the night—and I relied on this game to earn my monthly rent. I shut my eyes and imagined a pack of dogs chasing Roger Rabbit across a huge open field, with me close enough behind on horseback to get a front row seat at the tearing of limb from limb. "Tallyho," I said.

"Beg pardon?" said Roger.

"Just thinking out loud."

"Oh." Roger helped himself to a beer, but couldn't get his fat, furry finger through the pull tab. I pretended not to notice. Let him work out his own problem for a change. "I could never figure that," said Roger. "I mean why humans don't like 'toons. We're no different from humans, not really. We have different mannerisms, and different physical makeups, and a different way of talking, but we have the same emotions. We love and hate and laugh and cry exactly the same way humans do." He tried his ears, his toes, and even his nose, but struck out all the way around. No part of him was small enough to fit into the ring.

I yanked the can away from him, popped it open, and handed it back. No big deal. I would have done the same for any bum on the street. Yet from the way the rabbit reacted, you might have thought I'd just crowned him Little King. "Too bad more humans couldn't have your attitude toward us, Eddie," he gushed.

"Yeah, too bad." Because there wouldn't be a 'toon left alive. I chugged my beer and headed toward my room for eight hours of much needed hibernation.

"Don't you want to hear what I found out about the teakettle?" His words circled my head and looped around my shoulders the way a cowboy's lariat ropes a calf.

So much for resting my weary bones. "OK, give," I said, shrugging free of his last statement. I cracked myself another beer and returned to the living room. "Tell me about the teakettle."

Every part of Roger started to twitch, his lips, the whiskers under his nose, his eyebrows, even his two front teeth swung back and forth like a pair of Mah-Jongg tiles hung out on a wash line to dry. "I talked to the 'toontown junk dealer who sold the prop man the teakettle, and you won't believe his story."

"Try me, and skim it, would you? Just give me the cream."

The rabbit pumped out his words in a balloon the size of a billboard. It gave him something to hide behind when I went for his throat after reading what it contained. "The junkman told me such an interesting story that I thought you ought to hear it directly from him. So I told him I'd come over here and get you and bring you back."

"Right now?" I checked my wristwatch, but my eyes were so tired I couldn't tell big hand from little. "It's the middle of the night."

"He stays open late."

"Nothing doing. I'm bushed. I'll go over there with you first thing in the morning."

"Sure," said the rabbit gloomily. "First thing in the morning."

Even before my seven-day intensive training course at the Acme School of Fine Detecting I could have figured the rabbit had something else on his pea-sized mind. "Come on," I said. "Spill the rest of it."

"I don't want to bother you with my petty problems."

Boy, this rabbit really knew how to dish it out. Too bad he had never produced any offspring. He would have made a brood of bunnies one fine, guilt-inducing mother. "I told you to give me the rest of it, now give me the rest of it."

He rocked his head forward to back, making his words about as easy to draw a bead on as ducks in a shooting gallery. "I've started to have this feeling," he said, "that I'm coming apart at the seams. I don't know for sure, but I believe maybe I'm preparing to disintegrate. I don't want to pressure you, but I would appreciate whatever you could do to expedite this case."

I sighed, tossed down my beer, and got my coat out of the closet. "Let's go see your junk dealer, rabbit."

The junk dealer was a 'toon beetle, Bennie, by name, shiny and black with a pastel pink head.

His place had no heat, so he wore a greatcoat with six extra arms sewn onto it to accommodate his multiple extremities. The extra arms had been scissored out of totally mismatched garments. Bennie could easily have wholesaled his coat of many colors to one of those boutiques that charged astronomical prices for quilts stitched together by Appalachian 'toon ragpickers.

To fit human gloves to his four-fingered 'toon hands, Bennie had tied off the gloves' index digits with odd bits of colored yarn. That's how 'toons got their reputation for having excessively poor memories, because so many of them traipsed around with string knotted memory-aid fashion around their gloved fingers.

Some junk stands a chance of metamorphosing into folk art or antiques. Some junk should have been trash-smashed at the factory door and carted straight out to sea in a garbage scow. The beetle stocked the latter, and in such great quantity that a good archaeologist could have traced the decline of civilization by excavating the store's inventory. The beetle himself scuttled out from under the rubble of World War II. "Welcome back," said Bennie to the rabbit. "You going to buy something this time or just yak my ears off some more?" He snaked one of his antennae down the back of his coat and scratched vigorously. I wondered, could a beetle have fleas?

"I'd like you to meet my partner," said Roger, "Eddie Valiant."

"Pleased to make your acquaintance, Eddie," said the beetle. He gave me my choice of four hands to shake. I declined.

"I'd appreciate it if you'd tell Eddie what you told me. About the teakettle."

"Sure. Be my pleasure." The beetle sat down on his store counter, rolled backward, and went rock-a-bye-baby atop his rounded shell. "A couple of years back I used to have this kid—a cousin to Aquaman, he claimed to be—that I employed as a diver. He brought me in relics from sunken ships and such. Anyway, the kid was diving alone one day off the coast hunting for a yacht supposedly down out there. When he failed to come in at night, the Coast Guard launched a search. They found him lying dead on the deck of his boat. Beside him was an oil drum, the last object he ever brought up. The kid had died of asphyxiation. The Coast Guard figured he came up too fast and got one of those breathing attacks divers get when they do that." The bug tried to demonstrate by wheezing for us, but didn't have the lungs for it. Best he could do was a chirp, and a distinctly merry chirp at that. "I bought the diver's stuff from his widow, oil drum included. When I emptied it out, there was a big pile of ordinary rocks, an old scroll, and that teakettle inside. I peddled the drum to a scrap dealer for twenty-five bucks.

I only got fifty cents for the teakettle, though. I let it go cheap, because the prop man who bought it promised me a bit part in his picture. A promise he failed to keep, I might add."

"What happened to the scroll?" I asked.

"I've still got it somewhere around here," said the beetle. "The prop man wasn't interested, so I kept it."

"Can we see it?" I asked.

"Sure, if I can find it." Bennie waved his arms in the air until he had enough momentum built up to flip himself off his back. Then he launched into the kind of massive search the Spaniards mounted to find the Fountain of Youth. He didn't have any more luck than they did. They discovered some future Florida land grifts; he found an old piece of sheepskin rolled around a wooden stick. "Here she be."

I reached for my billfold. "How much?"

He scratched under each of his arms in rotation. He used no deodorant, and if you ever want to experience misery, try standing downwind of somebody with eight stale armpits. "I got storage costs, inventory, sales tax. Call it a hundred bucks even."

"A hundred bucks? You sold the teakettle that went with it for fifty cents."

He shrugged his eight shoulders in a motion that duplicated almost exactly a rippling wheatfield on a breezy day. "Yeah, so I did, and it's stuck in my craw ever since. A hundred bucks. Take it or leave it."

I took it and told him I'd think of him fondly every time I passed a can of Raid.

Outside the shop, under a streetlight, Roger and I unraveled the scroll. Strange writing covered it top to bottom. I couldn't make out a single word. "Swell. A hundred bucks I shell out for this thing, and I can't even read it." I flipped it to Roger. "Here's your next assignment. Get this translated."

"Where?" asked the rabbit.

"You're the detective," I answered. "You figure it out. I'm going home to bed."

The rabbit told me he planned to stay on the job straight through the night. I guess he must have been feeling a lot of pressure to wrap this case up before he dissolved.

I told him he could do whatever he wanted to, that I was going to sleep, and that I'd see him in the morning.

The phone was ringing when I opened my apartment door.

"Eddie Valiant," I said, hoping desperately for a wrong number.

"Eddie, whoop-di-do," said Pops from down at the soda shop. "I didn't wake you, did I? I hope not because I've got some real exciting news. I collared your comic for you, the one you wanted! I had to look everywhere, but I found it. Boy oh boy, what a job. There weren't many printed, not many at all, but I located you one. Old Pops, he came through just like he promised you he would."

"Great, Pops, great. I'll pick it up first thing in the morning."

"I'll be here late tonight, Eddie boy, if you want to come down now."

Add somebody else out to deprive me of my beauty sleep. "Thanks anyway, Pops, but I'm beat. There's time enough tomorrow."

"Oh, sure. Sure. It's just that I was real tickled to find it for you, and I thought you'd want to see it right away. But you're right. Tomorrow's soon enough." He sounded lower than my bank balance on the last day of the month.

I remembered all the extra gumballs Pops had slipped into my candy sacks, the extra nuts he had put on my sundaes, the extra shots of vanilla he had squirted into my Cokes. How do you ever get even-Steven with somebody for giving you your only fond memories of youth?

"I'll be there in half an hour," I said.

"Land o' Goshen," he prattled when I walked in, "did I have a time tracking this one down." He handed me a comic wrapped in a plain brown wrapper.

I took a look at it while he gave me a play by play of the rigmarole he went through to get it. Whatever he did, believe me, it was worth it. What he gave me was a pornographic piece—the smut peddlers euphemistically call them adult comics—printed several years ago by the date on the masthead. It was titled *Lewd, Crude, and In the Mood,* and it portrayed in graphic detail the antics of a randy female nurse. The nurse was played by a younger, slimmer, blonder, but definitely recognizable Jessica Rabbit.

And the fine print inside the front cover identified the publisher as somebody named Sid Sleaze, my good old double S in person, I'd lay odds on it.

"That what you wanted, Eddie? Did I do good?"

I helped myself to a piece of rock candy, because all of a sudden this felt like a very sweet night indeed. "You did fine, Pops. You did just fine."

24

I never did make it to bed that night. Instead I bought a fifth of rotgut for inspiration, went to my office, and drew large circles on a piece of paper. Into each circle I put either a name or a fact. Some of the names overlapped each other, and so did some of the facts. Some of the names overlapped some of the facts, and some of the facts overlapped some of the names. No answers came of it. I wound up punchy from lack of sleep and with a headache to boot. Who was I kidding, anyway? Analytical cogitation never had been my strong suit. I function best when the solution to a case requires a direct, physical approach. It might never win me a turn as king of beasts, but at least it gets me my own small, jackal-free corner of the jungle. And what more could any snake in the grass want?

I scooped my fruitless evening exercise into the wastebasket just as Old Mister Sun bade me good morning and started his trek across the sky. Must be boring for the big, yellow galoot, doing the same job day in, day out, but at least he always knows where he's headed. That's more than I could say for a certain private eye of my acquaintance.

Scrubbing off my face left such a dark ring around the office sink that I dared to hope I might have scoured off the circles under my eyes, but no such luck. I hauled out my razor and upped my record for most shaves on a single blade. At least this time I managed to stop the bleeding before it attracted vampire bats.

I swiped the morning paper from in front of the accountant's office next door and was just sitting down to a leisurely glass of breakfast when my partner walked in.

I couldn't understand it. Even with no rest the darn rabbit came in perky enough to out-chipper Mary Poppins. I could have gone into insulin shock or suffered permanent eye damage from being exposed to such a heavy dose of sweetness and light. "I didn't expect to find you here this early," said Roger cheerily.

"I wanted to get an early start," I answered. The sun shining in my office window lit up the tips of Roger's fur and made him look like a descended angel. Dare I hope that maybe Roger had disintegrated during the night, and what I saw before me was Roger's ghost? On second thought, that didn't seem like such a hot prospect. At least I could keep a live Roger at bay by barricading my door. I hated to imagine the pester potential of a Roger Rabbit able to walk through walls.

I poured myself a second glass of breakfast, and Roger just couldn't leave well enough alone. "You shouldn't drink this early in the morning," he said. "It's bad for your liver." His balloon rained down a trail of brimstone halfway across my desk. Ever catch a whiff of brimstone?

Pure essence of skunkflower. I pulled out my lighter and ignited the larger of the puffets before they broke. They flared bright yellow and disappeared. "Who appointed you guardian of morals around here?" I said, knocking back my toddy in a single swallow. "How about you watch your liver, and I'll watch mine."

"However you want it," he said peevishly. "I'm only concerned for your welfare."

"You earn your keep last night?"

"Indeed I did." The rabbit set down a Piggly Wiggly grocery sack, from which he extracted enough carrots to bring everybody in the building up to twenty-twenty vision. He ran them through his front teeth the way lumberjacks run redwoods through a sawmill. Zing, zing, zing. "I visited a few all-night bookstores, but none of them had any reference books detailed enough to help me identify the writing on the scroll. So I planned to check out the public library as soon as it opened this morning. That's when I got an incredible stroke of luck. On my way to the library I passed a Persian falafel shop. They had a big sign out front listing all their sandwiches in English and a smaller sign with the same list in Persian. That smaller sign stopped me cold. Why? Because—are you ready for this—I noticed a distinct similarity between the Persian menu and the writing on the scroll." The rabbit grinned so broadly that the next carrot he sent to oblivion fit into his craw sideways. "I waited until the shop opened, went inside, and showed the owner our scroll. I asked him if it was written in Persian. He said yes, although it was a rather quaint, old dialect, and he couldn't read it. He said he had an elderly uncle who lived with him who might be able to translate it for us."

I don't think I ever met anybody who dragged out a story as much as this rabbit. I doubt I could have shoved his narrative along any faster with a bulldozer, but I gave it a shot. "So what did it say?"

"I don't know."

"You mean the uncle couldn't translate it?"

"No, I mean the uncle wasn't awake yet. I left it there

with the owner, and he promised to show it to his uncle as soon as the old man woke up."

I couldn't believe my ears. "Roger, you idiot. I paid a hundred smackeroos for a scroll that you left at a Persian deli! Suppose that scroll turns out to be valuable, and the deli owner decides to keep it for himself? Suppose when you go back for it, the guy tells you he accidentally stuffed it full of sprouts and sold it as a sandwich? What do you do then, Mister Sam Spade reborn?"

That knocked the smart-alecky rabbit down a peg or two. He sucked in his mouth so far his nose almost disappeared. "Gee, Eddie, you want me to go back right now and get it?"

I shook my head. "No, don't bother, the damage is done. If the deli owner's going to diddle us out of it, there's not much we can do to stop him."

"I really am awfully sorry, Eddie." Everything the rabbit had that could slump, slumped: his shoulders, his ears, his nose, even his eyebrows.

I came around to his side of my desk and punched him a hearty tap on the arm. "Hey, brighten up. What kind of a detective would you be if you didn't screw up every now and then?"

"You mean it?" A few parts of him unslumped.

"Sure. Even me, your supposedly infallible mentor, has been known to blow it a time or two."

"I don't believe it."

"It's true."

"Tell me one time."

"Maybe later." In truth, I couldn't remember a time, but I had the rabbit pretty well pumped up by then, and I didn't want to go through the process again. "Right now I've got something more important to discuss with you. You ever hear of a guy named Sid Sleaze?"

The rabbit snapped back into the proper spirit. The way he talked, his mannerisms, his stance, I swear if I squinted I couldn't have told him from a fuzzy, long-eared Humphrey Bogart. "Yes, I know him. A no-good, through and through. A human publisher of 'toon pornography."

"A human? With a name like that?"

A hard knot of stringy words squeezed through the eye-hole of Roger's needle-thin mouth. "Sleaze is his professional name. His real name is Sid Baumgartner. He once published a line of comics illustrating the classics and was a pretty good Joe to work for. He gave a lot of people their first big break. In fact I believe Carol Masters got her start working for Baumgartner. Then a few years back, when people lost interest in the classics, Baumgartner went bankrupt. He resurfaced as Sid Sleaze and made a fortune. Why the interest in him?"

"Isn't there something about his name that strikes you as being rather important? His initials, maybe?"

A marquee's worth of light bulbs went on over Roger's head. "Double S! Sure, double S! You mean Rocco wrote those checks of his to Sid Sleaze?"

"Looks that way."

"What on earth for?" The perfect copycat, Roger took a chair, spun it around, and straddled it the way I do. He might not have the substance of detecting, but he was sure getting a good handle on the form.

"That's what we have to find out. Did you ever have any dealings with Sleaze? He ever approach you or anybody you know to star in any of his hotsy-totsy stuff?"

The rabbit gave me a no-nonsense nod, the energy-efficient variety, down and up one time, quick. "He talked to me once. He said he could do a lot in his line with a rabbit. He told me he would dude me up in a tux, promote me as a randy playboy, and turn me into a millionaire. I told him no soap. I told him to find some other bunny willing to debase himself. I didn't want any part of it."

"How about Jessica? Sleaze ever approach her?"

The rabbit's cast-iron front cracked open, and I caught a glimpse of the old, familiar mushbag underneath. "Probably," said Roger. "At one time or another Sleaze has propositioned just about everybody in the business. But Jessica would never do such a thing. She's too much of a lady."

I could feel *Lewd, Crude, and In the Mood* smoldering inside my jacket pocket. I should have shown it to him, shown him what a tramp he had married, but I couldn't. Deduct it from my income tax as this month's charitable contribution.

I heard somebody enter my adjoining waiting room. I opened the connecting door a crack and peeked in to see none other than Jessica Rabbit. Speak of the devil.

Roger pleaded with me to let him stick around when I talked to her, but I told him nothing doing. She'd see through his flimsy disguise in a minute. I told him to go out the window and down the fire escape, go to my apartment, and wait for me there.

He wasn't tickled at the prospect, but he did it anyway.

I opened the outer door, and invited Jessica in.

25

She swept into my office the way a touring British queen would enter a bushman's hut, head high, stiff upper lip, determined to maintain proper imperial bearing, but very, very careful not to breathe too deeply of the foul air or stray too near the mud-caked walls. She wore a casual outfit—blue jeans, T-shirts, and tennis shoes. If she was dressing down to my level, I hope she brought her pick and shovel because she still had three miles deeper to go.

I offered her a chair. The regal way she carried herself made me want to dust off the seat cushion first, but my only handkerchief is the one my dry cleaner stuffs in my breast pocket whenever I get my suit pressed, and it's no more than a half-inch of material stapled to a piece of cardboard.

She accepted my offer of an eye-opener, but when I poured her three good fingers, she barely sucked the thumb.

"To what do I owe this unexpected pleasure?" I asked.

She turned heavy sighing into an athletic event worthy of feature coverage in *Sports Illustrated*. "I want to hire you," she said, "as a private detective." She lit a cigarette and looked around for an ashtray, but there are none, since I routinely use the floor. I dug out an old coffee cup, one with "I'm proud to be a 'toon" written on it with *'toon* misspelled about six times, and shoved it across the desk at her. She read the inscription, smiled, and dropped her burnt match onto the rug.

"Mind telling me what exactly it is you want me to do?"

She crossed one exquisite leg over the other and tapped her foot against the thick, invisible wall between us. "Since Roger was killed, I've been visited several times by a certain police captain named Cleaver. Are you familiar with him?"

I nodded. I poured myself her second drink since it looked like she'd never get around to it, and I hate to see booze spoil.

"I don't think it's any great secret that Cleaver considers me the prime suspect in Roger's murder. I came to you because I want you to get me off."

I wished I had a month to really think this one out. I wished I had contacts in high places who could supply me with inside info. I wished I had a mind Machiavellian enough to give Jessica Rabbit a run for her money. But most of all I wished I had some ice because this warm bourbon was starting to do me more harm than good. "Rather an odd choice of words you picked there, missy. You mean you want me to prove you didn't do it, don't you? Asking me to get you off makes it sound like you're guilty as charged, like you did kill Roger exactly as Cleaver says you did."

She backpedaled faster than a bicycle rider careening toward a washed-out bridge. "Yes, of course, you're right. That's what I meant. I want you to prove me innocent. I just got my words twisted around. What I meant was that I want you to find out who really killed Roger."

"And if I do that, if I take your case, you'll assist me however you can? You'll tell me the absolute truth about your involvement with this affair?"

Her head bobbed up and down like a line float with a firm hook on an angelfish.

"OK. Let's start with your alibi. Is it true that you spent the entire evening alone, at a movie and out for a walk?"

Had she not suppressed her thought balloons, the air above her head would have been filled with visions of churning gears. I could picture the pasteboard card flopping out the tiny slot at the far end. You weigh one hundred and fifteen pounds, you're tall and gorgeous, everybody lusts after you, and, if you want to stay out of the slammer, you have no choice but to tell this nasty man what really happened on that fatal night. "I went to a movie. That much is true. But I didn't go for a walk afterward. I went straight home. I got there at least an hour before Rocco died."

"You mean you were actually in the house when it happened?"

She lit a new cigarette off the butt of an old one, just like you'd see any ordinary B-girl do in any ordinary juke joint on any ordinary night of the week, except, when Jessica did it, she made it seem extraordinary, as exotic and exciting as watching a jeweler cutting diamonds or a gunsmith engraving steel. She wrapped her lips seductively around the filter tip and sucked rhythmically, making her cigarette darken and glow, darken and glow in a pattern that spelled out temptation in her seductive private code. "Yes, not only was I in the house at the time, I saw the murderer."

I suddenly felt like one of those milk bottles people whack with softballs at a local county fair. Just when you get settled into a good, solid, upright stance, somebody plunks down two bits and knocks you flat on your keister. "And who might that murderer be?"

The graceful way she tilted her head would have been

an excellent subject for a charm-school student's doctoral dissertation. "I thought you already knew."

"Refresh my memory."

"Why, it was Roger, of course."

Of course. Had it been anybody else, this case would have been duck soup, and heaven forbid that Eddie Valiant should ever have a case handed to him on a silver platter. "Tell me what you saw."

She detailed her story in the flat, unworldly voice that floats around the edges of a seance. "I was in my bedroom, giving my hair two hundred strokes, when I heard a shot. I went running into the hallway to the top of the staircase. From there I had a clear view of Rocco's study below. I saw the door open, and I saw Roger come charging out, a smoking gun in his paw."

"He didn't see you?"

"No. He was in too big a hurry to get away. He went straight out the front door and down the sidewalk."

"Still holding the gun?"

"Still holding the gun."

"You didn't see anybody else come out after him?"

"No." She walked to the window and inhaled some of the loose-weave gray flannel that substitutes for fresh air in this burg. "I went into the study and saw what had happened. That Roger had shot Rocco dead. I immediately went back to my room, dressed, got into my car, and drove to Roger's bungalow."

"Why do that? Why not just call the cops?"

She gave me a look hard enough to hammer nails into my forehead. "I planned to use what I knew to blackmail Roger."

"For what? What could the rabbit have that you could want?"

She sat down on the edge of my desk, leaned toward me, and whispered the week's worst-kept secret. "Why, his teakettle, naturally. I wanted his teakettle."

"Why didn't you get it from him when you were still living together? He would have given you anything, especially an old teakettle."

She returned to her chair. I didn't feel such a compulsion to dust it for her this time, not after the ton of dirt she had dished around my office. "I didn't find out how valuable it was until after I'd left him. I couldn't ask him for it then, because I feared he might promise to give it to me only if I returned to him."

"And you wouldn't have done that?"

"Not even for the teakettle. I already told you. That rabbit's a turkey."

To my eternal credit, I let that one slide. "What is it about this teakettle that makes it such a hot item in your book? Exactly how valuable is it?"

She closed her eyes and launched into a tale fantastic enough to provide a six-month scenario for *Terry and the Pirates*. "In the early tenth century, a dying gourmet potentate wanted to provide for his royal chef. So he had the palace artisan construct for him a solid-gold teakettle, inlaid with a single, huge blue-white diamond and a multitude of other slightly smaller but equally precious stones. Several hundred years later this priceless teakettle fell into the hands of the Templar Knights. You've heard of the Templar Knights?"

"Sure. They came right after the Templar Days."

She dismissed my sarcasm with a crinkle of her nose. "The Templar Knights fought for Richard the Lionhearted. They claimed the teakettle for themselves during one of their grand crusades to the Holy Land. To protect it from thieves on the journey home, the Templar Knights disguised it by having it lacquered gray. As fate would have it, thieves stole it anyhow, although as nearly as historians can tell, they had no inkling as to its true worth. To them, it was nothing but a common teakettle. That's the last record we have of it until it turned up on Roger's stove."

"And how did you find out about it? Was it Rocco who told you? I understand he'd been studying up on mythology lately. Was this why? Because he was hot on the trail of the caliph's teakettle?"

She lit a third cigarette and shooed the smoke away

from her face with a hand as delicate as any Japanese fan. "Yes, precisely. He first saw it in a still photo taken from the *Alice in Wonderland* movie. He remembered it from a sketch he had seen years ago while researching a strip on the Arabian Nights. He went out and bought a ton of mythology books and searched through them for every reference to the caliph's teakettle. He found enough to become convinced that it really existed, and that what Roger had matched its description perfectly. I learned about it one night when I heard Rocco and his brother Dominick discussing how to get their hands on it. Roger hated and distrusted them, so they couldn't offer to buy it outright. Roger had that complicated burglar-alarm system, so they couldn't break in and steal it. When I overheard them, they were just coming around to the prospect of murder."

"They intended to kill the rabbit? For his teakettle?"

"So they said."

"What happened when you got to Roger's house?"

"I found the door open. I went inside and saw Roger dead. I looked around, but the teakettle was nowhere to be found. I figured that Dominick had probably beaten me to it. So I left. That's how it happened." She crossed her heart and hoped to die. "The truth."

"Why didn't you report it that way?"

She displayed another side of herself, the confused innocent. "I was afraid. I didn't want to get involved with murder. Leave it to that stupid bunny to die with my name on his lips and rope me in anyway."

"When you entered the house, and when you left it again, did you notice some music coming from out of the piano?"

"Yes, I did. That's what held the door open. The music had gotten wrapped around the knob. I don't remember what the song was, if that's what you're after."

"That's what I'm after."

"Well, I don't remember." She leaned forward far enough across the desk to put her hand on my arm. In an earlier, more direct era, that kind of touch would have been all I needed to grab her by the hair, drag her into my cave, and ravage her until morning. Nowadays we have to be satisfied with a silly grin. I gave her a silly grin. "I did not kill Roger," she said. "You must believe that. I swear it on my honor."

"That's a pretty shaky oath in my book." I pitched her my beanball. "Ever hear of a man named Sid Sleaze?"

Her hand tightened around my arm, but she didn't seem to have enough strength in it to squash a cockroach. "Yes, I know him. He asked me to appear in a porno comic book once. He hounds most of the top 'toons. He's a filthy, perverted beast, and I wouldn't have anything to do with him."

"You never gave in and appeared in one of his goodies?"

"Of course not. What kind of woman do you take me for? I have my standards."

There was only one reply to that. I pulled out *Lewd, Crude, and In the Mood,* and threw it on the desk.

She stared down at it the way an innocent bystander stares at a body which has just fallen ten stories to the sidewalk. "Where did you get this?"

"From a book dealer I know. It cost me a bundle. But I must say it's worth every penny. You naughty girl, you."

She reached for it, but I quickly hauled it back and stuffed it into my top desk drawer.

She uncorked a stream of tears that would have made a crocodile proud. "I was trying to break into modeling when I first met Sid Sleaze," she said. "He passed himself off as a big-time movie producer. He told me he would make me a star. Some star. He invited me to his apartment and slipped me a spiked drink that left me able to function physically, but made me totally uninhibited. When the effects wore off, Sleaze showed me prints of the porno material he had shot of me while I was under. The same stuff he later used to prepare that horrid book. He gave me five thousand dollars and told me there would be a lot more in it for me if I did it again, of my own free will this time. I threw the money at him, and ran out."

"Did you go to the cops?"

"I was afraid to, and embarrassed. I was only eighteen at the time. Besides, while I was drugged, Sleaze had me sign a formal release. Luckily, Sleaze printed up only a small quantity of those comics. This was when he was first getting started in the business, and he couldn't afford a large press run. After I became famous, and he realized what a potential gold mine he had, he approached me again, shortly after I married Roger. He said if I didn't give him money, he would print up another hundred thousand copies for general release." She brought her cigarette up between us and watched it burn.

"What did you do?"

She killed her smoke by grinding it viciously into my cup, and she kept grinding it long after it had gone out, until nothing remained except loose strands of tobacco and thoroughly shredded paper. "I paid him, naturally. What else could I do? I had my career to consider. Luckily for me, Sleaze proved to be a lot more honorable as a crook than he was as a porno producer. Once he had his money, he gave me the negatives, exactly as promised."

"He gave *you* the negatives?"

"That's right."

"What did you do with them?"

"I cut them into tiny pieces and flushed them down the toilet."

"Did Rocco ever see them, or see the comic?"

"No, never. It's hardly a subject I'd discuss with a man who worshiped me as the embodiment of sophistication." As she talked, Jessica came around to my side of the desk, took up a position behind my chair, and ran her fingers through my hair and along the side of my face. "You have beautiful features," she said. "So strong and well-defined."

"Chipped out of granite, that's me."

She brushed a kiss across my ear. "You will take my

case, won't you?" she said in a throaty whisper that spoke of pleasures rarely experienced by the common man.

"Not a chance," I whispered back, a lot less heartily than I had intended to.

Her voice shot up like a rocket. "What do you mean, not a chance?"

"Just what I said. I won't take your case." I held her lovely hand in mine, and ticked off my reasons on her slender fingers. "First, I think you're lying about seeing Roger coming out of Rocco's study after the shooting. Why, I don't know. Maybe to protect somebody else, maybe to cover yourself. Secondly, for once in my life, I agree one hundred percent with the police. I think you shot Roger. I'd stake my life on it. You had the teakettle for a motive, and you had the opportunity. Thirdly, I won't take your case because I already have a client, Roger Rabbit, dead though he may be." I ran out of reasons before I ran out of fingers, so I took the two of hers I had remaining, and squeezed them together. "And these two little piggies went to the gas chamber," I said.

She jerked her hand away and hid it behind her where I couldn't intimidate it anymore. "You're wrong, you're terribly wrong. I've told you the truth. I beg you to reconsider."

Again I told her no dice.

She cried me another half a river as I shooed her into the hall.

No sooner had she gone than I heard a noise outside my window, like somebody stumbling over their own feet as they descended the fire escape.

I jerked the window open but found nobody there. Down at the bottom of the iron escape ladder, on the street, I did see Roger Rabbit though. Strange. He should have been halfway to my apartment by now. Could it be he stayed behind and eavesdropped on my conversation with Jessica? If so, he knew my true feelings toward her. Even worse, he knew her true feelings toward him, and right now I didn't think the little guy could handle it. For his sake I hoped he had been far, far away when Jessica

told her tale. But knowing snoopy Roger, fat chance of
that.

I prescribed myself one final bracer and set resolutely
off to face the morose scene I knew I'd find at home.

26

When I got home, I found the rabbit crawling around the
living room on all fours. For a delicious moment I thought
he might have regressed to his wild state, but it turned out
he had only dropped his contact lens, a plate-glass oval
large enough to double as serving platter for roast squab.
He buffed it on his sleeve and popped it into his eye, but
I don't think it improved his perspective any, since his
face remained as sour as a dill pickle and nearly as green.

"Want to talk about it?" I asked.

He shook his head so vigorously that his ears wound
around each other. I had to step on his foot to keep him
from helicoptering off the floor.

"It might help," I said.

He shambled into the living room and collapsed on the
sofa. He curled his fingers into a fist and rapped one of
the cushions his best lick. Some puncher. With a right
cross that weak, I wouldn't back him in a match against
Joe Palooka's thumb. "What does she mean I'm a turkey?"
he blurted out in a balloon the size and consistency of a
squishy honeydew.

So he had been eavesdropping after all. "Maybe she
called you a turkey because you gobble your food." A
pretty good joke I thought, but it left old yuk-a-minute
stone cold. 'Toons! You figure out what tickles their fancy,
because I sure can't.

"Somebody put those words in her mouth," he said. "She would never talk about me that way of her own accord."

"Right. The fly on the wall was a ventriloquist."

"Don't joke about it." He snorted. Ever hear a rabbit snort? Imagine an effeminate donkey with bad adenoids. "I'm very upset by what I heard."

"You shouldn't have eavesdropped."

"I'm a private detective now. It's part of my job."

"Then you'll just have to learn to roll with it. Remember, people who peek through keyholes have to expect an occasional poke in the eye."

The rabbit got up, stood in front of the window, and absorbed enough mellow morning sunlight to cast a shadow of his former self. "Was that one of those gems of folk wisdom we detectives throw out with such proficiency?"

"Call me the old philosopher."

"The only old philosopher I remember wound up with a gut full of hemlock."

"Maybe he should have stuck to a bland diet."

The rabbit threw up his paws in surrender. Match, set, and championship to yours truly. Roger dropped a small, milky-white balloon to the floor and bonked it across the carpet with his big toe. "What was the comic you and Jessica were talking about?" he asked, rather idly considering the grave implications of my answer, "and how does Sid Sleaze fit into it?"

If he wanted sugar-coating, the rabbit picked the wrong candy apple. I laid it out for him complete in every detail. "The comic is a racy number called *Lewd, Crude, and In the Mood.* It's eight pages long and shows Jessica making whoopee. You heard Jessica's version of how it came to be. The part of it that interests me isn't the book itself, but rather the book's negatives. Jessica says she bought the negatives from Sleaze shortly after you were married and destroyed them. Yet I found a piece of those same negatives in Rocco's fireplace. Which means that Sleaze sold either Jessica or Rocco a copy."

"Impossible." The rabbit shook his head emphatically enough to put a spin on his next balloon. I had to slow it to a stop by dragging my finger across it before I could read it. "I don't see how he could have sold either of them a copy," it said. "A copy negative always comes out slightly fuzzy and easy to spot. I can recognize one easily, so I'm sure both Jessica and Rocco could, too."

The rabbit spoke his next words staring straight up at the ceiling so that balloon shot out parallel to the floor. It hit the wall and fell down behind the sofa. Since he had his eyes closed, he was totally oblivious to his balloon's final resting place. I had to snag it with a bent coat hanger and pull it out to see what he had said. "This comic of Jessica's," it turned out to be. "Show it to me."

"I don't think so. It's as raw as any I've ever seen."

I was certainly having my troubles conversing with the rabbit today. His next balloon came out so faintly written that I had to drag it to within six inches of my nose before I could decipher it. "Show it to me!"

I pulled the comic out of my jacket pocket and handed it over. "You're the boss."

Roger held it the way people handle a dead mouse, at arm's length, between his first two fingers. Without even glancing at it, he dumped it into my wastecan and flipped a lighted match in after it.

I broke the record for the five yard dash getting across the living room, but still arrived too late. By the time I reached the wastebasket, the comic was nothing but a smoldering ash. It crumbled to dust at my touch. Not so much as a picture or a word remained visible. "That was a terrifically bone-headed play," I yelled at the sullen bunny. "That comic set me back two hundred bucks. What did you have to go and torch it for?"

The rabbit stood up on his tiptoes, which brought his eyes just about level with mine. "You and I have got to get something straight," he said. I prayed for him to poke me in the chest with his finger so I could snap it off and hand it to him wrapped in a hot dog bun, but no such luck. He kept his arms hanging limply at his side. "There's a fundamental difference in the way we want to conduct this case. I think we'd better resolve it right here and now." His toes got wobbly so he put his heels back on the floor and we continued our discussion eye to chest. "You're getting paid to prove I didn't kill Rocco," he said, "and to find out who killed me. I didn't hire you to harass my wife. So leave her alone. She's totally innocent."

"She wasn't so innocent when she made that pornographic comic," I reminded him.

That got the rabbit back up on his tiptoes. "You heard what she said. Sleaze gulled her into making that piece of trash. She is not the kind of woman who would do that of her own free will. If she says she was tricked into it, I believe her. I believe everything she says."

"She says she saw you kill Rocco. You believe that, too?"

Roger waffled so quickly I could almost taste butter and syrup. "No, that I don't believe. I suspect she's being pressured to implicate me. Possibly by Dominick DeGreasy. He's that kind of rapscallion."

"OK, let's suppose for a minute we play it your way. What does that mean I do?"

"Jessica asked you to prove that she didn't kill me. I want you to do just that. I want you to prove whatever she wants proved."

If I'm ever tempted to take a 'toon case again, I hope somebody puts a bullet through me first. "I can't oblige. I already have you for a client, and it would be unethical for me to take on somebody else."

He half-shut his eyelids, the way people do when they pass a cripple on the sidewalk. "From what I heard, ethics never bothered you before. Why the sudden change of heart? Sure it's two clients, but it's also two fees."

That illustrates the first rule of detecting. Always wear your shorts snugged up tight so you don't feel the pain when your client kicks you below the belt. "You really hurt me with that kind of rotten talk," I protested. "I'm not in this one for the money. I'm in it because I think you're almost an all-right guy, for a 'toon that is, and I want to see you go out happy."

Here I practically proposed marriage to him, and still he refused to back off. "Then do what I ask. Take Jessica's case."

I tried to grab him by the shoulders, but my hands slipped down and I wound up shaking sense into him at about the elbow level. "Damn it, Roger, don't you understand. Your beloved sweetie Jessica, who you so badly want me to help, is the one who shot you."

At this point any rational being would have given in to logic. That's what makes 'toons so frustrating. There's not a one of them with the rationality of a dead frog. "I don't care *how* incriminating the evidence is against Jessica. I don't care *what* she said in your office. I don't care *what* you think about her guilt or innocence. I only know that Jessica loved me and would not have harmed me. If you won't take on two clients, drop me and accept her. In fact, I'll go even further than that. Consider yourself fired. As of right this instant. You're off my case. So there's no more conflict for your precious ethics."

"I'm sorry Roger. No go. I'm going to clear your name and bring in your murderer, whether you want me to or not."

Roger huffed and he puffed, but he couldn't blow me down, not once I had my mind bricked up. Best he could do was to try for a compromise. "Play it your way then, but if it turns out to be Jessica who killed me, I don't want her punished for it. I want you to get her off the hook. Will you at least humor me that far?"

"That's about the dopiest thing I've ever heard," I said.

"What did you expect from a rabbit?" said Roger. "Will you do it my way? If she's guilty, will you get her off?"

"I'll think about it," I promised. And I did. For maybe half a second. Just long enough to picture Jessica Rabbit dangling by her gorgeous neck from the top of the nearest tree.

27

I figured Roger needed a perk-up, so I told him to tag along and watch me grill Sid Sleaze. For the amount of enthusiasm he showed for it, I might just as well have asked him to watch me fold my laundry. I don't know. You bend over backward to accommodate these creatures, and you get zippo appreciation for it. No wonder nobody goes out of their way to be nice to them. Where's the percentage in it?

The Sleazy Press occupied a steel and glass high-rise surrounded by small one-story family-owned businesses. Roger and I hadn't gotten three feet from the curb before a grandmotherly woman who should have been home in a rocking chair crocheting afghans stuck a petition under my nose, the gist of which was that Sid Sleaze should be tarred, feathered, and run out of the neighborhood lashed to a rail. She also carried a shopping bag of rotten cabbages to throw at Sleaze when he came through the door. When Roger blurted out that we were on our way in to see Sleaze up close and personal, she locked my arm in a vice grip and refused to release me until I promised to spit in his eye.

I expected Sid Sleaze to be a short, dumpy guy with Vasolined hair, no neck, and an armful of tattooed naked ladies that would do obscene dances when he flexed his muscles. Sporting a dayglow-orange suit, a tie that lit up and said, "Kiss me in the dark," a diamond stickpin, and a gold front tooth. Oh, yeah, and with plenty of drool dripping down his chin.

At least I got one right. He was short but as solid and well-proportioned as a bantamweight contender. His dark suit wouldn't have drawn a second glance at a morticians' convention. He walked more gracefully than I danced and had a melodious baritone that could have charmed the bloomers off the Virgin Queen. Certainly not the slime-ball type you walk up to on the street and bop with a rotten cabbage.

Needless to say, I didn't spit in his eye.

Every stick of furniture in Sleaze's office cried out big bucks. Lamps made out of Chinese vases. An Italian desk old enough to have come across the ocean with Columbus. And leather chairs with enough moxie to keep a solid guy like me from sinking through to the floor.

I introduced Roger as my research assistant and sat him on a chair against the wall far enough away so he didn't cramp my style.

Sleaze served us coffee in translucent china cups with handle holes you'd be hard-pressed to stick a pencil through. I made two stabs at taking a drink without extending my pinkie, failed both times, and finally let my java go cold.

"What can I do for you, Mister Valiant?" Sleaze asked congenially. "I've talked to many vice-squad officers in my days, but never to a private detective. I must say I'm rather intrigued. What would anyone want to privately detect about me? I have absolutely nothing to hide. Lord knows you only have to look at my comics to realize I have nothing to hide." He laughed heartily and took a sip of coffee. Out went his pinkie.

"I'm working on a case involving the cartoon publishing industry, and a mutual friend suggested you might be able to help me. Carol Masters, remember her? She said it had been quite awhile."

Sleaze set his wonderfully modulated voice to work,

conveying us on a nostalgic journey backward through time. "Of course, I remember Carol. I provided her with her first break. A hard worker and a terribly talented lady. I've often wished she would come back to work for me now, and I've asked her to on numerous occasions, but she turned me down cold." He plucked a few stray pieces of lint off a sleeve that already looked like he vacuumed it every hour. "Carol told me she won't shoot for the skin trade anymore, and I can't say I blame her. It's a filthy, rotten business, and I grow more disenchanted with it every day. Lately I've toyed quite seriously with the idea of getting out of it, getting back into mainstream comics again." He settled back in his chair and crossed his feet at the ankles. "What specific case is it you're here to see me about, Mister Valiant?"

"The Rocco DeGreasy murder." I watched his face for a reaction, but none came.

"And what exactly is it you want to know?"

I went straight for the jugular. "I understand you're responsible for a crassity that Rocco's live-in girlfriend Jessica Rabbit starred in several years ago. *Lewd, Crude, and In the Mood*. Remember it?"

He smiled the way a proud papa does when discussing his precocious child. "How could I forget? My masterpiece. When I still believed it possible to produce quality pornography. Before I realized the two terms are mutually exclusive."

"Jessica says you Shanghaied her into making that comic, that you drugged her and shot it while she was under."

A melancholy sadness crinkled his eyes. "I've heard that story before. It's Jessica's way of rationalizing a youthful indiscretion. In truth there was no need to coerce her with drugs or anything else. She did it quite willingly, for the money, I expect, since she was awfully poor in those days. We shot *Lewd* in my downtown studio in a couple of days. A few months after the comic appeared, she came back and asked to star in another. I would have loved to oblige her, but by then she had acquired a fine sense of her own worth and had escalated her salary demands accordingly. I simply couldn't afford her, so I had to turn her down."

I checked Roger's reaction to these revelations concerning the base-metal core of his pedestal's ivory statue, but he seemed more interested in getting his thumbs to twiddle. Maybe doppels degenerate from the inside out. Maybe the attention span goes first. So far, I loved it. I'd love it even more if his head fell off. "You later threatened to blackmail Jessica unless she gave you money for the negatives to that comic," I said to Sleaze.

Sleaze spread his hands, so I could see where the spike would go when an inflamed public nailed him unjustly to a cross. "I wouldn't call it blackmail exactly. I'd call it a quid pro quo. She came to me when she needed money. I went to her when I needed money. The only difference was that she wasn't quite as willing to pay me as I had been to pay her. You may not believe this, but I had no intention of following through on my threat to print more copies of that comic. It was pure bluff on my part."

"You're right. I don't believe it," I said. "You went to see Rocco DeGreasy night before last. What for?"

He pushed his brows together over twinkling eyes. "Business, just business."

"Yeah, monkey business. You sold Rocco a set of the same negatives you sold Jessica. Plus, you were the last person to see Rocco DeGreasy alive. Which means you might also have been the first person to see him dead."

The twinkle in his eyes became a worried flicker. "I left Rocco alive. I didn't kill him."

"Ever see a cop spin a web of circumstantial evidence into a hangman's noose? No? Well I have, and unless you come clean with me, I'll hoof it straight over to the local station house, and the next sound you'll hear will be the pitter-patter of young flatfeet eager to make their reputations by arresting the infamous Sid Sleaze."

Sleaze fingered the pieces of a magnificent carved wooden chess set on the corner of his desk. He tipped over the king and watched to make sure I caught the significance. "What is it you want to know?"

"For how much did you nick Rocco?"

No more glib evasions. "Twenty thousand dollars."

"Why did he write you out two separate checks for ten grand each?"

"I told him he could buy me off in two installments, one then, one in six months. He would get half the negatives each time. When he saw the first batch, he went for the full price up front."

"You always let your mark make time payments?"

"Depends on the circumstances. Naturally, if that's what it takes for maximum return. I'm quite the progressive blackmailer."

I assumed this was his idea of a joke, but I wasn't laughing. "I should say so, considering this was the second time you'd sold what were supposed to be one-of-a-kind negatives, once to Rocco, once earlier to Jessica."

He displayed the guilty look you see on a four-year-old kid caught standing beside a broken vase. "In actuality, I shot two sets of those negatives. The ones I sold Jessica were the ones I used to make the comic. Rocco got the second set. The poses were slightly different from the first, but I counted on Rocco's being too disgusted to examine them closely. And I was right. The instant he got his hands on them, he gave them a quick once-over, and tossed them straight into the fireplace. Caveat emptor, Mister Valiant, in blackmail as everywhere else."

"Did Rocco make any phone calls while you were there?"

"No."

"What time did you leave his place?"

"I don't know. I didn't pay much attention. I'd guess about eleven thirty or so."

"Did you see anybody else in the house, or outside it?"

He thought for a while. "Yes, as a matter of fact, I did. As I was driving away, I saw Baby Herman's stooge, you know the one, the rabbit, Roger Rabbit, walking up the drive."

That dragged Roger back into the ballgame. He hopped bolt upright. I braced myself for trouble, but Roger only puffed forth an innocuous balloon containing a vague reference to important matters elsewhere and fled out the door.

"Queer fellow, your assistant," said Sleaze. "You know when I first met him he reminded me of someone. Now I know who. Roger Rabbit. Do you see the resemblance?"

"Yeah, now that you mention it," I said casually. "I do. The both of them could be twins." I bid Sleaze a quick farewell and went out to collar Roger before he did something dumb. About as easy as changing the course of the Mississippi River.

I searched for several blocks in every direction, but couldn't find hide nor hair of the skedaddled bunny.

On the off chance he might surprise me and do something reasonable, I hot-footed it over to the Persian delicatessen where he'd left the scroll.

I don't know which smelled worse, the deli's cuisine or a dead camel. Not that it mattered, since they were probably one and the same.

The deli's owner, a middle-aged greaseball named Abou Ben Something spoke English about as well as I spoke 'toonesian. He tried semaphore, but I couldn't read his waving arms, either. We finally hit on charades. I got through by pretending to read a napkin wound around a fat weiner. He ran into the back room and returned with the scroll, plus some old codger who should have been hanging in the front window with the rest of the skinny, brown, wrinkled sausages. The old galoot handed me a sheet of paper with marks on it that looked like they had been scratched there by what eventually wound up as the main ingredient in the chicken salad. I finally got the key to deciphering it when I realized that half the *o*'s were grease spots. If you ignored them, the message came clear. "Beware," it said. "Great tragedy will result should this fiendish device ever fall into the hands of a 'toon."

Imagine that, a cursed teakettle. Though oddly enough

the scroll's dire prediction *had* come true. The teakettle *had* fallen into the hands of a 'toon, and great tragedy *had* resulted. Maybe the teakettle really did carry a curse. And maybe Santa Claus also swept out my chimney for me every Christmas.

I slipped the deli owner a fin for his trouble and shagged it on out to the sidewalk before the deli's zingy smell did permanent damage to my nose.

I debated whether to pursue clues or keep after Roger. Clues won.

I made a few phone calls, and in no time located the messenger service that had delivered the stolen artwork to Hiram Toner's gallery.

The place, called what else but Speedy Messenger Service, told me somebody had dropped the artwork at their office and had paid cash in advance for delivery to Toner. Their records didn't show the sender's name.

I sweet-talked a secretary into giving me the name and home address of the clerk on duty when the sender came in, in the hope that maybe he could provide me a description.

When I came out of the messenger service, it was a cool, sunny day, and there wasn't a 'toon anywhere in sight. It made me want to chuck what I was doing, drive back by the Persian deli, pick up a roast goat sandwich and a bottle of camel whiz wine, and head out to the nearest stand of timber for a solitary picnic and drunk.

I flipped a coin. It came up Dominick DeGreasy. I resisted an urge to make it best two out of three, and headed off to do my duty.

28

I found Dominick DeGreasy stalking through the syndicate's production studio, glaring his work force to higher levels of productivity. The few people crazy enough to ask him a question got, instead of an answer, a public dressing down for not knowing their jobs. Quite a manager, DeGreasy.

"Got a minute, Mister DeGreasy?" I said to him.

"Don't bring your problems to me," he said, mistaking me for one of his employees. "That's why I pay you good money. To know how to deal with problems."

"No problem, Mister DeGreasy. Just a few questions. I'm Eddie Valiant, remember me? The guy looking into your brother's murder? The guy who's going to return your teakettle?"

"Oh, sure, Valiant." He looped an arm the size of an oak tree around my shoulders. "You got a line on my teakettle yet?"

I nodded. "Maybe, just maybe. Can we go someplace private and discuss it?"

"Sure, sure. In here." He led me into the employees' lounge. When he entered, every employee inside walked out. "Respect," he said, jerking a thumb toward the retreating multitude. "That's what it takes to run a big company. Respect. You either got it, or you ain't."

"And you got it?"

"In spades. There's not a worker in this company who doesn't respect Dominick DeGreasy." The coffee machine showed its respect by serving him up a freebie when he rapped it with his fist. "Tell me what you found out about the teakettle."

"In a minute. First, I've got some other stuff to go over with you, stuff that bears directly on the case."

"Stuff? What kind of stuff? I want that teakettle. Period."

"And your brother's murderer. You want him too, don't you?"

"Oh, sure. Sure, I want him too. It's just that I sometimes forget what I want more. Rocco was a great one for always taking care of me. It's hard for me to keep my priorities straight now that I have to take care of myself." He walloped the candy dispenser, but it refused to knuckle under to management pressure. Must have had a stronger union than the coffee machine.

"On the day he died, your brother wrote a check to Hiram Toner at the Hi Tone Gallery. The check went to pay for return of that stolen artwork I found photos of in Rocco's office. Rocco mention anything about that to you?"

"No. Rocco took care of the money. I took care of discipline." Dominick stuck his gargantuan hand into the candy machine's delivery slot. The rankest amateur soothsayer could have predicted what would happen next. He was going to get that massive paw of his stuck up there, and, sure enough, he did. In a lot of ways, I hated dealing with Dominick DeGreasy worse than dealing with a 'toon. At least with a 'toon you knew enough to expect the ridiculous. With Dominick, you expected the normal, but got the ridiculous anyway.

I put a shoulder to the machine. Two healthy grunts, and I set him free. Although, for as much gratitude as he showed, I'm sorry I bothered. I should have left it on him and let him explain to his respectful employees how he came to be wearing their candy machine for an ID bracelet. "Did Rocco have many dealings with Hiram Toner?" I asked him.

"Enough. He had arrangements with most of the art dealers around. If anything interesting turned up on the market, legit or otherwise, the dealers gave him first crack. If he liked it, he bought it, no questions asked." After getting caught once, you'd think even the numbest numbskull would get the message, but some numbskulls never learn. It took Dominick less than two seconds to get in up to his elbow, again. I got him loose, dug some change out of my pockets, and pumped it into the coin slot.

"You know Sid Sleaze?" I asked.

"Never heard of him." Dominick stabbed at the buttons with his broad, lumpy finger. He hit two buttons at once, but only one bar came out. He tore off the wrapper, jammed the bar into his mouth, and swallowed it whole.

"How about Sid Baumgartner?" I asked, trying Sleaze's real name.

"Yeah, I know Baumgartner." Dominick straightened out the only two pictures in the room, one of him, one of his brother Rocco, with a metal plaque that said "Our Founder" bolted under each. "This Baumgartner approached the syndicate a bunch of times with an offer to buy out one of our contract players."

"Which one?"

His sandpaper voice gained another layer of grittiness. "Always the same. Roger Rabbit. I wanted to go for it, but Rocco told me he would never sell that rabbit in a million years. I told him he was nuts. Baumgartner offered a lot more than I thought the rabbit was worth. But Rocco refused to even consider the idea. He never told me why, but I always suspected Jessica was behind it."

"Strange. When I asked Rocco if anybody had ever wanted to buy out Roger's contract, he said no. Any idea why he lied?"

A few employees drifted into the coffee room, saw Dominick, and promptly drifted right out again. "Beats me. Rocco had a peculiar obsession with that rabbit."

"Rocco ever mention anything about Jessica's starring in a pornographic comic book?"

His lips curled back across his teeth in a leer. "She do that? No kidding? I told Rocco that woman was a doxie. I told him, but he never listened. No, he never mentioned nothing about any comic book like that, not that he would. He was nuts over that broad." He leaned close to me. His breath smelled like he'd been gnawing on garlic cloves. "I heard she's the leading candidate to take the fall for Roger Rabbit's murder. I hear the cops think they can make it stick. That the angle you're playing? You out to pin it on her too? Because, if you are, I'll back you one hundred percent. She caused Rocco a lot of heartache, and I want her to pay."

"I'll do my best. By the way," I said casually, "did you know Jessica's also interested in your teakettle?"

If you've ever seen a matador wave a red flag in front of a bull, you have some idea how Dominick DeGreasy responded to that one. He did everything but slobber and paw the carpet. "It's not hers," he yelled. "It belongs to me and Rocco. What the hell does she want with it?"

"According to her it's solid gold."

Dominick's face lightened from bright crimson to pastel pink to its normal pasty white, and he gave out with a chuckle that sounded like the croak of a dying frog. "Solid gold! She says it's solid gold? Boy, oh, boy, is she in for a surprise. It's nothing but an ordinary teakettle. That's it. Nothing but plain old metal." He whipped out his fat leather wallet and waved it in my direction. "Whatever she offered you, I'll double it."

I didn't have the heart to tell him that there was no way on earth he could double the kind of reward Jessica had promised me. Instead I assured him that, as soon as I got my grubby hands on it, the teakettle would be his.

I found Roger the last place I would have thought to look—back in my apartment, his feet hanging over one arm of my sofa, his ears drooped limply over the other. The residue from his deep funk had turned his white fur the same shade of blue as a careless grannie's home rinse. Quite the pleasant sight to walk in on. Home sweet home, assuming you lived in a funeral parlor.

"You sure lit out of Sleaze's place in a hurry," I said. "I got kind of worried. I thought you might be starting to disintegrate on me. You're not, are you?"

The last time I saw eyes with that much pleading and despair in them, they were staring out at me from inside a cage at the city pound. "I didn't kill Rocco," he said. "I just don't have it in me."

"Sure, you know that, and I know that, but prove it to the rest of the world. Maybe Sleaze *is* lying about seeing you there the night Rocco died. I don't know why he would, but it's possible. Maybe Jessica's lying, too. I don't know. That's what we have to find out. Who's telling the truth, and who's not. That's why we call this a mystery. Otherwise, if everything was cut and dried, we'd call it an unvarnished truth."

I passed out whiskey and cigars. We both chugged down and lit up. "Look, I got us a great lead," I said. "I found the messenger service that delivered the stolen artwork to Hiram Toner. I'm on my way over to see the clerk who took the order. Why not come along?"

Roger's word balloons came out filled with cigar smoke. He had to repeat his answer again after he'd exhaled the smoke, so I could read it. "No, to tell you the truth, I kind of lost my taste for it. You go ahead. Investigate the case however you want to. Without me. I'll just wait around here for your final report."

So there was a God in heaven after all, and he did respond to prayers. What more could I want? The rabbit off my back. Freedom to pursue the case any way I saw fit. Yet it failed to give me the rush I would have expected. Lord, let it be a case of the grippe, *delirium tremens*, terminal scurvy, anything but the nagging suspicion that I might actually be starting to like the dipsy-doodle cottontail. "Sure, sure," I said. "If that's the way you want it."

"That's the way I want it."

When I sized Roger up, he seemed somehow smaller, as though some brute had whaled five pounds of stuffing out of him. Try as hard as I might, I just couldn't help feeling sorry for him. I left him and went into my bedroom. In my top dresser drawer, underneath my dress-white boxer shorts, I found the special deputy's badge I got awarded a few years back after successfully completing one of those rare jobs where I found myself on the sunny side of the law. I polished it on my sleeve and pinned it into one of my old wallets.

I went back out into the living room where the rabbit was again draped across the sofa. "Stand up," I told him.

He blinked extra slowly. "What?"

"I said stand up. I've got something for you."

"Can't you give it to me here?"

"No, I can't. Now will you stand up, or do I have to help you?"

"Sure, sure, whatever you say." He stood up, but with such rotten posture that he resembled one of those collapsible wooden rulers that fold into about fourteen sections.

I poked him in the chest. "Snap to," I said, and he did pull out a few of his kinks, although he still retained about as many bends as a road map of a con man's morals.

"You've been a great help to me in this case," I said, stretching the truth so far that, if it ever sprang back and hit me in the chest, I'd be a dead man for sure. "And I think you should have some official recognition. So I want to swear you in as my assistant."

"You mean it? As your official assistant?"

"Raise your paw and repeat after me."

He raised his paw.

"I, state your name."

"I, Roger Rabbit."

"Promise to uphold law and order."

"Promise to uphold law and order."

"And to fight for truth, justice, and the American way."

"And to fight for truth, justice, and the American way."

I handed him the wallet.

He opened it and saw the badge inside. The last remnants of his blue funk flaked off his fur, and he stood before me as pure and white as one of those knights that fight bathroom scum on TV. "I don't know what to say." He jammed the wallet into his hip pocket. "This is one of the happiest moments of my life."

"No more Gloomy Gus?"

"You've seen the last of him."

"No more deep depressions when a witness takes a pot shot at you?"

"From now on I'm strictly hard-shell. Let them call me what they will."

"Then let's get to work. We'll start by interviewing that messenger service clerk. What's more, you ask the questions."

"You mean it? Honest? I ask the questions?"

"That's what I said."

"Oh, boy. Stand back and make way for Roger Rabbit, special deputy, barreling through." He took off out the door so fast he left behind a hefty shock of the *whizz* lines 'toons produce when they blast off in a hurry. I kicked what I could under the sofa, stuffed the rest into a closet, and went out after him.

The messenger service clerk, Mrs. Ida Koontz, lived in a house that looked like it had been built by a bakery school dropout. It had gingerbread trim, ladyfinger shutters, a mint-frosting front lawn, and a vanilla-wafer walkway. The gutters were peppered with stunned woodpeckers who had taken a whack at the milk chocolate roof only to bash a beak against solid slate, instead. A brightly colored carpet of the kind Arabians use when they fly economy class lay draped over the porch railing. Two others hung from a clothesline in the side yard. As I watched, a window opened, and a portly woman dumped the contents of a dustpan into the flower bed outside. The 'toon flowers living there coughed and gagged horribly, but, as soon as the woman retreated into the house, the Ritz Brothers of the pansy set exchanged their hacking for a swell case of the giggles.

The front door was the strong, solid kind you like to put between you and the cold, cruel world. I gave it a hearty rap, knowing I wouldn't have to worry about winding up with my hand buried to the wrist in splintered wood.

How Mrs. Koontz ever came to be associated with the Speedy Messenger Service I'll never know, unless she was an old-line employee who had started with them when they used to ride horses and called themselves the Pony Express. She took forever to answer the door, another forever to examine my license, and yet a third forever to show us into her parlor. She offered us a beer, and I would have accepted but didn't want to waste the rest of the day waiting for her to return from the kitchen. "Thanks anyway," I said, "but we just have a few questions to ask, and we'll be on our way."

"Whatever I can do to help," she said obligingly enough. She picked up her knitting and went to work putting her single daily stitch into a sweater that had gone out of style twenty years ago.

I nodded at Roger and waited for him to begin.

He stared at old Mrs. Koontz, his feet did a fast tap shuffle straight out of "Flying Down to Rio," and he sent up two balloons. One contained a hem, the other a haw. He grabbed them out of the air, stuffed them under his coat, and jerked his head in the direction of the hallway.

"Would you excuse us, please," I asked Mrs. Koontz, "while I confer with my partner?"

She nodded absently, too intent upon getting her sweater done in time for the New Year's party celebrating the start of the next century to pay us much mind.

"I have a problem," said the rabbit once we were out of the woman's eye- and earshot. "I'm supposed to ask the questions here."

"Right. So, what's the problem?"

His cheeks flushed red. "I don't know what questions

to ask." He turned his paws palms upward at shoulder
level and tilted his head.

I patted his arm. "My boy, you just relax and watch
the master at work."

We rejoined the old lady. "You work for the Speedy
Messenger Service," I asked, "right?"

She mulled my question over in her mind for a couple
of minutes. "That's correct."

Since I hadn't brought my overnight bag, I skipped any
further background stuff and got right to the nitty-gritty.
"A few days ago you accepted a parcel for delivery to the
Hi Tone Gallery of Comic Art, a parcel about so big by
so high." I sized it for her with my hands.

She nodded, but I couldn't tell if that was because she
remembered it, or because she had fallen asleep.

"Can you tell me anything about the person who
dropped it off?"

She looked at me, then tended to her knitting for a
while. "It was a woman," she said finally.

"Human or 'toon?"

"I'm sorry, but I really couldn't tell. She didn't say anything, and she wore a veil."

"What else was she wearing?"

"Nothing unusual. A long, dark, baggy dress."

"How tall was she?"

"I really don't know. I was sitting down at the time, and
she was standing up. It's hard for me to judge heights in
that situation."

Now it was my turn to head-signal Roger out in the
hall. "I'm out of questions myself," I confessed. "Can you
think of anything else I can ask her?"

He scratched his head. "Try asking her how the woman
smelled."

"How she smelled?"

"Sure. Women often notice other women's perfumes.
If she was wearing something distinctive, it could be a
clue."

"How she smelled?"

"Try it, you never know," he said.

So I tried it. "You notice how this woman smelled?"

Ida put down her knitting and looked at me like I had just made an elephant appear in the middle of her parlor. "Why, come to think of it, I do remember something unusual about that."

Roger's grin tickled the bases of both his ears. "You do?" I said. "You remember something about how she smelled?"

"Yes. She had a very pungent odor about her. Like she hadn't taken a bath for a while. The way some of these younger girls smell nowadays. Positively disgusting. When I was young I had to cart water in from a well and heat it over a stove, but at least I took a bath."

I almost walked right over and gave Roger a hug. Too bad he wasn't going to be around much longer. Another few months of working with me, and he might, just might, turn into a fairly competent gumshoe. Nothing to compare to a human, of course, but better than most any 'toon. Thanks to him and his perfect question, I now knew enough to crack this lousy case open like a rotten walnut.

29

I pulled up outside the DeGreasy Gallery. "You know what Little Rock DeGreasy looks like?" I asked Roger.

"Yes," said the rabbit. "I've seen him around."

"Good. You wait out here on the street. When you see Little Rock come out of the gallery, you tail him. Don't let him out of your sight. Clear?"

The rabbit's nod started out fairly enthusiastic but rapidly wound down to nothing more than a slight bob in the tip of his ear.

"What's the problem?" I asked, ignoring whatever I have in the way of better judgment.

The rabbit burped out a confused jumble of words which he rearranged by hand into a cogent statement. "I'm your official assistant, right?"

"You've got the badge to prove it."

"Correct. Therefore, as official assistant, I should get meaningful assignments, stuff with gristle to it, and the aroma of danger."

"You and me both, buster. But the private-eye business just doesn't work that way. This is about as action-packed as it gets. I'd hate to tell you how many hours I've spent waiting for somebody to come out of somewhere so I could follow him to somewhere else and wait some more. You want wham, bam, slam detective work, stick with the comics. You want to be bored out of your skull, hang around real life with me."

My message must have gotten through, since the rabbit smoothed the leftover nod out of his ear, climbed out of the car, and slouched into a doorway just across from the gallery. He tugged his hat down to within a finger's width of his eyes, turned up his collar, and dangled a smoke from his lower lip.

I stuck my fist out the window at him thumb up.

From there I drove to Carol Masters's studio.

I knocked but nobody answered. Never one to stand on convention, I opened the door and walked in.

Carol was bent over a light table, examining negatives. I picked up one of her props, a rubber mask that looked like the results of breeding Broomhilda the Witch to a wart hog, put it in front of my face, tapped her shoulder, and said, "Boo," when she turned around.

She had a semicircular contraption over her head that magnified her eyes enough to startle me more than I startled her. "Valiant?" she said. "I might have known. It's just your level of humor."

"Then you should have laughed." I lobbed the mask

onto a nearby table. "It might be the last chuckle you get for a while."

"No more Mister Nice Guy, I see." She removed her wrap-around magnifier and turned off the light table. "From your crusty demeanor, I assume we've reached the point in our relationship where you get tough." She collected her negatives and slid them gently into an envelope. "Where you punch me around until I spill my guts."

She must have halfway believed her smart-alecky crack. She visibly cringed when I reached into my breast pocket, expecting me to pull out my rubber hose, I suppose. Instead, I hauled out something that would hurt her a lot worse, one of the photos I'd gotten from Rocco's office. I snapped it to attention in front of her perky nose. "Recognize it?"

She gave it barely a glance. "Sure. It's a strip I shot a few years back. So what?"

"It's also one of the pieces of artwork stolen from De-Greasy's gallery."

"I repeat. So what?"

"When I first saw it, when I found it in Rocco's office, it looked very familiar to me. It took me a while to remember where I had seen it before, then it came to me. I saw it in your apartment. It was one of the prints you were developing in your closet." She said nothing, so I turned up the heat a notch, to see if that would make her boil. "This morning I talked to a Speedy Messenger Service clerk who accepted the artwork for delivery to Hiram Toner. She remembered that the woman who dropped it off smelled bad. She assumed it was because the woman didn't take baths. She didn't know the real reason was because the woman keeps her wardrobe hanging right outside her photo lab, and her clothes pick up the smell of photographic chemicals. It all sifts down to one tidy conclusion. You stole your own stuff. You duplicated the negatives and the prints and used Hiram Toner as a middleman to peddle the copies as originals."

She looked at me without blinking. "Sure I did it. That was the only way I could get what was rightly mine. As

I told you, my contract with Rocco specified that he owned the prints and negatives of everything I shot for him. He took the better stuff, framed it, and sold it through his art gallery but refused to cut me in on the profits."

She walked across the studio, winding up in front of a backdrop that pictured a sylvan glade with green trees and clean water and pure air. I took it to be some never-never fantasyland, the world of the future, until I realized it was a decade-old backdrop and was really the world of the past. "One day I offered to watch the gallery for Little Rock while he wined and dined a prospective client. While he was gone, I photographed his key and later had a duplicate made.

"I went back several days after and helped myself to a number of my early works. I reproduced the prints, duplicated the negatives, and set out to sell the copies as real. I got into trouble my very first try.

"I gave my first set to Hiram Toner. He has a reputation as someone willing to deal in that kind of merchandise. I told him outright the stuff was stolen. I told him to peddle it to out-of-towners. So what does he do? He offers it for sale to Rocco himself. Naturally Rocco recognized it immediately for what it was. And, with his resources, it didn't take him long to find out where it came from. That's the real reason he called me the night he died. To tell me he knew I had stolen his stuff, and that he was going to have me jailed for it."

"Lucky for you he didn't last through until morning."

"If you're insinuating I made my own luck, you're wrong. I didn't kill him."

"You did go to see him that night, though, didn't you?"

She leaned up against a phony palm tree. A phony coconut jostled loose and put a phony lump on a phony sheik sitting in a pile of phony sand. "No, I didn't."

I stared her straight in the eye. "I say you did. I say you went to Rocco's after he called, and shot him to keep him from turning you in to the cops. I say you then went to Roger's place and shot him, too, leaving the DeGreasy murder weapon behind, so Roger would take the fall for Rocco's murder."

"It's not true," she said with a thickly clogged voice. "I didn't leave my place all night."

"Then how do you explain this?" I pulled out the rubber squeeze frog. "I found this outside Roger's house the night he died. Photographers use these to make their subjects smile, don't they?" I squeezed it and smiled nastily. "Tell me who else in this case is likely to have a rubber squeeze frog on them, and I'll let you off the hook."

She took the frog and squeezed it. It stuck out its tongue at her. She sat in a director's chair and set the frog on the arm beside her, so I had two sets of eyes staring at me, one set real, one set rubber, and not the slightest trace of life in either one. "All right, I did go to Rocco's place that night, and to Roger's place, too. But it wasn't the way you said. I didn't kill anybody. Not Rocco, and certainly not Roger. I went to Rocco's to beg him to go easy on me. I knew he had me, and I was scared. I was just about to ring the bell when I heard a shot from inside. I stepped back into the bushes just as Roger Rabbit came charging out, a gun in his paw. Roger ran past me, down to his car, and drove away.

"I didn't know exactly what had happened, but I had a pretty good hunch.

"I peeked through the window in Rocco's study. Rocco lay dead across his desk. I stumbled back to my car and drove around for a while, trying to sort out my options. Finally, I decided to visit Roger at home. I wanted to tell him I knew what he had done and would help him in any way he wanted—with getaway money, a hideout, an alibi, whatever he figured he needed.

"I parked my car around the corner from his bungalow. I got out and went to the door just in time to see Jessica Rabbit ring the doorbell. Roger answered it, and she went in."

"Roger was still alive when Jessica got there?"

"He sure was. I didn't want Jessica to hear what I had to tell Roger, so I didn't ring the bell. I crouched outside the living room window to wait until Jessica came out. That's when my frog must have fallen out of my pocket. I waited there for nearly half an hour. Then a bunch of things happened in rapid succession. Somebody started to play the piano. I heard a pair of loud voices, and then a shot. The door opened a crack, something came flying out, and the door slammed shut. I peeked in through the window and saw Roger lying dead across the banister. I expected to see Jessica standing over him, but I didn't. She was nowhere in sight."

"Did you see anyone else in there?"

"No, no one. I beat it out of there as quickly as I could. And that's it. Judging from what I saw, Roger shot Rocco, and Jessica shot Roger."

"That seems to be the general consensus. This object that came sailing out the front door. What was it, did you see?"

"Nothing much. An ordinary teakettle."

A marching band could have taken a quick-step cadence from my loudly thumping heart. "What became of it?"

"I picked it up on my way past and threw it into the trunk of my car, along with my camera stuff. As far as I know, it's still in there." Her mouth twisted sideways, the way it would if somebody grabbed her by forehead and chin and wrung her dry. "Are you going to report me to the police?"

"Depends."

"On what?"

"On a lot of things. On how the case breaks. On how well you cooperate from now on. On how much of what you've told me turns out to be the truth. On whether there's a full moon tonight."

She didn't take kindly to my humor. "You're going to leave this hanging over my head, aren't you? You really are a louse, Valiant. A genuine, Grade-A weasel."

"I've been called worse. I've been called better, too, though I think the ones who call me worse have a firmer fix on the real me. Now, how about you give me the keys to your car? I want to take a close-up look at that tea-kettle."

She reached into her jeans, pulled out a key, and tossed it over.

Although I don't think she believed I meant it, I wished her a good day.

I walked down the hall, turned, and tiptoed back to her apartment. I put my ear to her door. I heard her pick up the phone and dial it. I didn't bother to listen to her conversation. I knew well enough who she was calling. And I knew why.

I went downstairs, found her car parked out on the street, and opened the trunk. Sure enough, there, buried beneath a pile of photographic paraphernalia, sat my phantom teakettle.

In its pictures, it looked like an ordinary dime-store teakettle, but not in person. You hear people say they don't make things like they used to. In the teakettle department, they hadn't made one like this for a thousand years. It had intricate ornamental doodads and curlicues inscribed over every square inch of it. It had the solid heft of Krazy Kat's brick. Its top fit tighter than the door to Scrooge McDuck's vault. It was ancient and well constructed, but so were my grandmother's false teeth. What made this so much more valuable?

I put Carol's car keys into her mailbox, tucked the teakettle under my arm, and headed for my office.

30

I set the teakettle on my desk and examined it from every angle. No secret compartments that I could see.

I pulled out my pocket knife, flipped out the heavy blade, and scraped away a layer of metal. All I got for my trouble was more metal. No gold underneath here, not unless some medieval alchemist had found a way to turn it back to lead. I scraped a few bumps off the handle, but they were just that, bumps, not jewels. I leaned back in my chair and considered the possibilities. Maybe this wasn't the actual teakettle. Maybe somebody had substituted this worthless piece for the real thing. Or maybe the teakettle had some other significance. Maybe it was the key to some illicit drug-smuggling ring. Maybe it had come into the country loaded with opium.

I picked it up and turned it over. On the bottom I discovered what appeared to be more Persian writing. I had a hunch it probably said "Made in Japan," but I copied the inscription into my notebook anyway.

Just then the phone rang. It was Roger, so excited I had to hold the phone away from my ear to keep his word balloons from stinging my earlobes when they came zipping out. "It worked just the way you said it would," he bellowed. "I positioned myself just outside Little Rock's gallery. I could see Little Rock through the gallery window. You had been gone maybe an hour when he got a phone call. He talked a few moments and hung up, quite upset. He rushed out and got into his car. You'll never guess who he went to see."

I knew perfectly well, but I let Roger surprise me anyway. "I can't imagine."

"Sid Sleaze!" Roger exclaimed. "He stayed in there with Sleaze for the better part of an hour."

"Did he have something with him when he came out?" I asked. "A small box, or maybe an envelope?"

I could tell from Roger's silence I had just impressed the fuzzy socks off him. "As a matter of fact, he did," Roger said reverentially. "It was a large envelope. He took it with him to his house. I'm calling from a phone booth nearby. What do you want me to do?"

I got the address. "Wait for me there," I said. "I'll be right over. And, Roger, one other thing."

"Yes?"

"It's all downhill, now."

* * *

On the way to Little Rock's, I stopped first at the Persian deli. I bought a falafel sandwich and gave Abou Ben a copy of the writing on the bottom of the teakettle. He promised to have his uncle translate it for me that evening.

Next I stopped by to see a scientist friend of mine. I gave him the teakettle and asked him to analyze the composition of its metal and any residue it might contain. The scientist informed me a thorough examination would take a couple of days. I told him I didn't have a couple of days. Or rather, Roger's doppel didn't have a couple of days. I wanted to have this case wrapped up air-tight before that little guy expired. I owed him that.

The scientist told me he'd do what he could.

31

Roger's hop, hop, hop up the walk to Little Rock's front door turned his stream of questions into a verbose roller coaster. "How did you know Little Rock would get a phone call?" read his words on his upspring. "How did you know who it would be?" they read on his descent. "How did you know Little Rock picked up a package?" Uuuuuup. "Do you know what's inside it?" Downnnnnn. "What do we tell Little Rock once we're inside?" Uuuuuup. "Who does the talking?" Downnnnnn. I got motion sick just reading him.

I slapped my hand over his mouth to shut him up and scrambled his wavy words so Little Rock wouldn't see them and get wise to our play. I shoved the rabbit behind me where he wouldn't get in my way, and rang the bell.

Little Rock opened the door and stood there staring at

me, with his mouth open about as wide as first hole on a championship putting green. "Yes? Oh, Valiant, wasn't it? What are you doing here?" He fluttered a hand. "I'm so sorry, but I'm just in the middle of something. Could you possibly come back later? Say tomorrow. Tomorrow would be just perfect. See you then."

He started to shut the door on me, but I pushed past him into the house. Roger bounced along after me, and Little Rock brought up the rear. "Here now, exactly what do you think you're doing?" Little Rock babbled. "You can't come in here."

"Too late," I countered. "I already am in. And you're in, too. In deep, serious trouble."

Little Rock's Adam's apple gulped through a series of moves good enough for first place in a yo-yo tournament.

"I know what you've got going with Carol Masters and Sid Sleaze," I stated.

"I don't understand what you mean," he retorted lamely. "Sid Sleaze? Who's Sid Sleaze?"

"He's the guy whose office you visited not half an hour ago." I pointed at Roger. "Want me to have my assistant here play back a videotape of that event?"

Roger showed some of that quick wit that made him such a hot property in the comic biz, and picked up on my bluff. "I can have the machine set up and rolling in five minutes, chief," he said.

Little Rock looked from one of us to the other for the slightest sign of a schuck, but both of us held fast. "Oh, *that* Sid Sleaze," he said finally. "Of course. Now I know who you mean. I had some minor business dealings with the man. Nothing significant. He wanted to buy some things from the gallery."

I put out my hand. "Let's have it."

"Have what?" asked Little Rock.

"The envelope you got from Sleaze."

"What envelope?" he said with an air of innocence unbelievable in anybody this side of Dondi.

"Come on, don't play cutesy with me. I know what's in that envelope. You either give it to me, or I phone the cops, and you give it to them, and believe me, you got a lot better chance with me. I'm not really interested in your scam. I'm out to nab your old man's murderer. You help me do that, and I don't care if you bilk the entire Western world. But I have a hunch the cops aren't quite so open-minded. Now give."

He caved in easy, but wimps like him always do. He scuttled into his den, came back, and gave me a standard eight-by-ten manila envelope. I opened it and unceremoniously dumped the contents onto a coffee table.

As I suspected, it contained at least three dozen negatives. I picked a few at random and held them up to the light. Sure enough they were the negatives of Rocco De-Greasy's missing artwork. As nearly as I could tell, there were at least six sets of negatives for each piece. "Take a look," I said to Roger. "You once told me you could tell reproduction negatives from originals. Which are these?"

Each time Roger held one up and examined it, he gave out with a low whistle of admiration, until there were so many notes floating around, the room looked like the site of yesterday's canary convention. "I've never seen anything like this," he said when he finished. "These are absolutely perfect. No graininess, no fuzzy images, no degradation of color. They all look exactly like originals to me."

"Want to tell us about it?" I asked Little Rock.

Little Rock went to the bar and mixed himself a drink from out of a rainbow assortment of bottles that duplicated the ones he kept in his gallery office. I don't know what color he was shooting for, but he built and threw away three drinks, all of which turned out jet black, before he finally gave up and tossed down a straight shot of plain, garden-variety, see-through vodka. "Carol Masters and I vowed to avenge ourselves on my father for the unjust way he treated us. So we decided to sell a number of pieces we removed from the gallery."

"That's a rather genteel way of phrasing it," I said. "You didn't just remove them. You *stole* them, plain and simple."

There was no way he was going to convince me otherwise, but by golly if he didn't try. "We did not view ourselves as criminals, Mister Valiant. We took Carol's works and hers only. We both felt she was entitled to profit from their increased value. We saw nothing morally wrong in her doing so, and in my getting a cut for helping her."

"I know a rabbi, six ministers, and a Pope who might give you an argument on that. Especially when you take into account what you eventually did with them."

Still no mea culpa. "That was Carol's idea, not mine. Carol's. Rather than sell them once, she reasoned, why not duplicate them and sell them multiple times?

"I told her it was an admirable idea, but would never work. We had the original negative, so we could easily produce more prints, but each framed work had to include both a print and the negative it came from. Since we had only the one negative, that was impossible. We couldn't use a normal dupe neg. Any knowledgeable collector would spot it in an instant. That's when Carol suggested Sid Sleaze.

"Carol had worked for Sleaze years earlier, when he still went by the name of Baumgartner. He kept in contact with her through the years, trying to get her to go back to work for him. One day, over lunch, he told her about a new process he'd developed to reproduce negatives so perfectly that not even an expert could tell duplicates from originals. If it worked as well as he led Carol to believe it would, it presented the perfect solution to our problem.

"Carol approached him with our proposal. In return for a flat fee per piece, he was to take our original negatives and turn out duplicates in limited quantity. I framed the duplicate prints and negatives together, and Carol signed them. We then sold them as originals through shady dealers like Hiram Toner."

"The word must have gotten around that these pieces had been stolen from your gallery."

"To be sure. The police circulated photos and complete descriptions throughout the world."

"Your fences have any problem finding buyers under those conditions?"

"None whatsoever. There are any number of collectors who care not a whit about a work's provenance. If they want to possess it, they will, stolen or not."

"How many of these duplicates did you sell?"

"We limited ourselves to fifteen copies of each work. Any more than that, and we ran the risk of exposing our ploy. Our buyers weren't about to display stolen works openly, but they might show them to a close friend or two. Sooner or later someone was bound to see the same supposed original in two collections. At that point values would plummet, suspicions would rise, and angry buyers would begin tracing their way back through their dealers to Carol and me. An altogether ugly situation. We fully intended to be out of it before that happened."

"You planned to use the money from this deal to bankroll the startup of your own cartoon syndicate?"

"Yes. In fact I had already approached my father through an intermediary, with an offer to buy up the contract of a 'toon I could use as the cornerstone of my new enterprise."

"And that intermediary," I said, "was Sid Sleaze, going by his real name, Sid Baumgartner."

"Correct," said Little Rock.

"And the character you were going after," I continued, "was Roger Rabbit."

"Correct again, but Father refused to sell. I consider myself a very astute judge of 'toon talent," bragged Little Rock. "I told Father many times that Roger Rabbit was one of the most talented 'toons in the DeGreasy stable. I told Father over and over that Roger should get a strip of his own. But Father refused to listen. He wouldn't star the rabbit, nor would he turn him loose. I always suspected it had something to do with Jessica."

"You mean Rocco used Roger to hold onto Jessica?" interrupted Roger. Why did that rabbit refuse to give up his dogged belief that Jessica loved him when anybody with even half a brain could tell otherwise? "So long as Rocco kept the rabbit, he kept Jessica, too?"

"So it appeared," said Little Rock, sending Roger's spirits soaring to the moon. "Jessica would never have stayed with him of her own free will. Jessica did not love my father. How could she? She was so cultured and refined, and he was such a boor. No, she loved someone else. That was quite obvious to even the casual observer."

Roger beamed, but not for long.

"Jessica loved me," said Little Rock, and Roger's self-proclaimed hard-shell exterior flattened out quicker than a turtle out for a Sunday stroll on the Golden State Freeway. "That's the other reason I got involved in this nefarious scheme," said Little Rock. "For Jessica. She never said this in so many words, but she certainly led me to believe that, if I ever became independently wealthy, she would leave Father in a flash, no matter what he did to stop her, and would run away with me."

"To a grass hut on some tropical island where you would both eat coconuts, never wear clothes, and live happily ever after," I said. "It never occurred to you that a guy with your old man's clout could track you to Timbuktoo and haul you back?"

Judging from the look on his face, it never had. I'm constantly amazed how people kid themselves into believing love can conquer all.

I didn't want Roger to hear my next line of questions, so I trumped up a dangerous assignment for him. "Who was that?" I asked pointing toward the window. "Out there. Somebody's out there. We're being watched."

"We are?" said Roger and Little Rock almost in unison.

I pulled Roger to me. "You wanted action, here's your chance. Go outside and collar that snoop. Just remember, this isn't make-believe. Whoever's out there is playing hardball, and he's playing it for keeps."

The rabbit nodded bravely. If you didn't count the garbage can he tipped over on the way, you could say he slipped silently out the back door.

"Rocco called you the night he died," I stated to Little Rock after the rabbit was out of earshot. "Why?"

"To tell me he knew about my forgery scheme. He ordered me to come to the house immediately to discuss it with him."

"And did you go?"

"No, I didn't. I'm not a courageous man by nature, Mister Valiant," he said, stating the obvious. "The thought of facing my father in full fury was more than I could handle. Instead, I came home, got thoroughly swacked, and passed out on the living room floor."

That I could believe. He was so chicken he probably got homesick walking by a Colonel Sanders. Now came the part I didn't want Roger to hear. "How did Rocco use the rabbit to hang onto Jessica?"

"It's a mystery to me. There appeared to be a connection there, but I could never figure it out, and I didn't want to risk offending Jessica by asking her outright."

"Holding onto Roger would have worked if Jessica had loved the rabbit. You say you're pretty close to her. Did she? Did she ever love the rabbit?"

Little Rock tittered. "Heavens, no. Who in their right mind could love a rabbit?"

Roger crept by the window. He had gotten hold of a knife somewhere and had it clenched firmly between his teeth. If he bumped into a tree, he would slit his own throat. Never a stand of timber around when you need one.

"Jessica despised Roger," said Little Rock. "She told me so many times. She dated him once, as a lark. She had no intention of getting serious with him. Then, totally out of the blue, she experienced an overwhelming urge to marry the furry fellow. She was never able to really explain it. It just came over her, too strongly to resist. Like an uncontrollable itch. She said later that it was as though she had been bewitched. She struggled every day for a year to break the mysterious hold the bunny seemed to have over her. Finally, one day, just as quickly as it came, her obsession vanished, and she managed to break free of Roger's spell. She packed her bags immediately and walked out on the rabbit, without so much as a backward glance. She came back here to be near me, she said. While she played up to Father, it was really me she loved. It was a glorious period in my life. We went to dinner together, and to plays, and dancing. We even shared her new hobby."

"And what was that?"

"Shortly after her return, Jessica became interested in 'toon mythology. We signed up for a course in it together at City College."

"She ever give you any reason for her interest?"

"No, but it certainly fascinated her. She and I went to the university together almost every night to use their reference library. I delighted in it, because it gave me a chance to be close to her. It was one of the happiest periods of my life," he repeated.

"Was she interested in any particular aspect of 'toon mythology?"

"Yes, as a matter of fact, she was. Magic lanterns. She read every work she could find on magic lanterns."

Roger came in the back door. When he opened his mouth to speak, the knife fell out and nearly cut off his toe. I don't know why he wanted a job with more danger in it. He created enough for himself on his own. "I checked around out there, Eddie, but I couldn't find a thing."

"He might have gone away for reinforcements," I said. "We'd better take it on the lam before he gets back." I headed for the front door.

"Are you going to turn me in?" said Little Rock plaintively to my back.

I told him what I had told Carol Masters, maybe yes, maybe no, depending on how well he played along from here on in.

He didn't take it any better than she had.

To which I delivered my usual response. Tough.

32

Sleaze's secretary did everything but barricade the door
with her desk to keep us out of his office. When I bulled
past her and got inside, I could see why. Her boss had a
very nasty secret.

We caught him just slipping on one of those red and
white Little Orphan Annie numbers that became the rage
after the kid struck it big on Broadway. He stood there
in black padded brassiere, lacy garter belt, and sheer
nylon stockings, his dress bunched around his shoulders,
staring at us over his frilly white collar in embarrassed
surprise. "This isn't the way it looks," he said lamely.
"I'm not a transvestite. I'm incognito. You can't imagine
how difficult it's been for me lately with these people
parading around outside. Having them yell at me and
pelt me with spoiled vegetables. I wear this getup so I
can come and go without being recognized. Really. That's
the only reason."

Sure it was. And I'm the Ape Man's uncle. He pulled
his dress down the rest of the way and gave us our first
clear look at the bottom half of his face, completely done
up with rouge, powder, and lipstick. In a beauty contest
between him and Elsie the Cow, he might get the nod.
Call it a toss-up on looks, but at least Sleaze didn't drool.

Sleaze straightened out his stocking seams to plumbline

perfection. He sat down at his desk, pulled out a makeup mirror, and began gluing on a set of long, fluttery, false eyelashes you could have used as decoys in a butterfly hunt. "What is it you want?" he asked.

I tossed him the envelope of negatives, which he caught girl-style, with his forearms in together and his hands spread apart. "Little Rock DeGreasy cracked and told me about your forgery racket," I said. "I want to hear your version."

Sleaze gave the negatives a casual look and flirtatiously handed me the envelope back, holding onto it just a fraction of a second too long after I'd grabbed the other end. Swell. On top of every other wacko in this goofball case I had an amorous drag queen, too.

"I wanted badly to get out of the porno business," said Sleaze, taking great pains to arrange himself so I had a clear shot at his shaved legs. "It's not nearly as lucrative as most people assume. Tastes change so rapidly. So I agreed to go along with Carol and Little Rock's scheme. I duplicated their stolen negatives, and they sold them as originals." He smiled. Lipstick speckled nearly every one of his teeth. "I'm very proud of my process. I invented it myself, you know. It's absolutely foolproof. I can duplicate a negative so perfectly that not even an expert can tell."

"You used that process to duplicate the negatives to Jessica's comic book, didn't you?" said Roger. I knew it was true. I knew that's what Sleaze had done, but I'm sure I never told the rabbit. Imagine that. He must have figured it out by himself. Imagine that. "You sold the originals to Jessica," he stated. "And a set of duplicates to Rocco."

"It shows you how good they were," said Sleaze. "Not even an expert like Rocco DeGreasy could spot them as phony."

Roger turned to me. "Sorry for the interruption, partner. You want to take it back?" His balloon came out the size of a blackjack and as hard as last week's biscuits. It hit the floor and sent up a balloon of its own with "THUNK" in bold letters inside.

"No, go ahead," I said. "You're doing great."

The rabbit plunged right back in without so much as a thank-you smile. "You went to Rocco's house the night he died to sell him the negatives," Roger said. "He examined them and gave you a check for ten thousand bucks. Then he tossed them into the fireplace."

"Yes. Can you believe it?" said Sleaze. "If he'd only known what fine artistry had gone into producing them. All that work, up in smoke."

"Once that transaction had been completed," continued Roger, "you gave Rocco another proposition. Hiram Toner dealt with wealthy collectors through a middleman. That middleman was you. Toner gave you photos of the artwork he'd gotten from Carol Masters. You knew where they had come from, but you took them to Rocco anyway. Except you didn't intend to sell them to him. At least not the artwork. You intended to sell him the story *behind* the artwork. Right so far?"

Sleaze nodded. He opened a cylindrical case atop his desk and took out a long blond wig. He set it on his head, wiggled it around until he got the look he wanted, and pouted at himself in the mirror. "I showed Rocco the photos of his stolen artwork and told him that for another ten thousand I would tell him a very interesting story about them."

"So he paid you another ten thousand, which accounts for the fact he wrote you two checks that night rather than one. You then outlined the entire hoax."

Sleaze nodded again, but carefully, so his wig wouldn't slip. I felt like suggesting he tack it in place with a stapler, but I wasn't in the mood for humor.

"What did Rocco do when you told him his son and his best photographer had conspired against him?" Roger asked.

"He went to the phone and called each one."

"You were with him when he did it?"

"Yes."

"You heard what he said to them?"

"Yes. He told Carol he knew she had stolen his artwork and had duplicated it for multiple sale. He told her he planned to turn her over to the police. He told Little Rock pretty much the same story, that the scheme had come apart. But he didn't mention anything about involving the police. Instead he ordered the boy to come to his house immediately for a chat."

"Did either one of them, Carol or Little Rock, arrive while you were there?"

"No, neither one."

Roger then asked a question that, I must admit, hadn't occurred to me. Oh, it would have sooner or later. It just hadn't yet. "Why did you put an end to the scheme anyway? Weren't Carol and Little Rock paying you nicely for producing their negatives?"

"Sure. But, according to one of my contacts, several collectors who'd bought those photos had met by accident, compared notes, realized they'd been taken, and were tracking their way back to the source."

So the scam was unraveling, pretty much the way Carol and Little Rock figured it eventually would. What little Sleaze had to lose by bailing out when he did, he stood to make back and then some with one big score off Rocco. "Rocco also wrote a check to Toner that night," said Roger. "Why?"

"Rocco decided to go ahead and buy the artwork, even knowing it to be forged. He planned to use it to keep Carol and Little Rock in their places. I don't think he really intended to turn either of them over to the police. He just loved to make them worry. He put Toner's check into an envelope and asked me to mail it on my way home, which I did."

The rabbit then switched topics a hundred and eighty degrees. A good technique. Keeps your quarry off balance. "Little Rock told us you approached the syndicate numerous times on his behalf with offers to buy out Roger Rabbit's contract."

Sleaze went to the window and listened to the concerned citizens chanting, "Hey, clown, get out of town," on the street below. He shut the heavy drapes, muffling out the sound completely. "True, I approached the syndicate," said Sleaze. He rifled through his purse for a cigarette, held it to his lips, and waited for some gentleman to step forward and light it for him. I was inclined to watch him die of a nicotine fit, but Roger caved in and did the deed. "Little Rock and I discussed Roger Rabbit quite often, and we shared the same assessment of him," said Sleaze, tapping his cigarette into his ashtray after every puff. "The rabbit had a tremendous amount of talent, talent which Rocco let go to waste. Little Rock could not approach his father outright with an offer to purchase, since his father would refuse out of general principles, simply to deny Little Rock something he wanted terribly. So Little Rock asked me to act as go-between. But Rocco wouldn't sell. I offered him nearly twice Roger's market value, but no. Rocco remained dead-set on keeping the rabbit in his stable. Why, I don't know, and I never found out."

Up to here the rabbit had been doing an A-number-one job. I don't know if I could have handled it any better myself, so you know how good that made him. It must have been beginner's luck, though, because, instead of following through on the syndicate angle, he veered off on a half-baked tangent involving, what else, but his darling Jessica. "That pornographic comic you made with Jessica Rabbit," he said. "Tell me the true story behind it."

"What do you mean, the true story?" asked Sleaze. "What does he mean, the true story?" he said to me. "I told you the true story. What else does he want?"

"I want you to admit you drugged Jessica and forced her to appear in your reprehensible comic."

"Where did you get this guy?" asked Sleaze, scrambling the air alongside his temple. "He crazy, or what?"

"Yeah, he's crazy," I said, trying to pull it out of the fire. "He used to moonlight as a gymnasium punching bag and took one too many to the noggin."

The rabbit refused to take my out. "You drugged her, didn't you?" he said in balloons whose interlocking shape had an ominous resemblance to the chains cops find when they frisk down motorcycle bums. A nice touch.

"You're crazy," said Sleaze waving away the rabbit's balloons before they locked around his throat. "It happened just the way I indicated. Jessica appeared in that comic of her own free will, and she came back later begging for more. That's the truth. I've seen enough of these women to know why they do it. Some for the money, some because they're mentally unstable. If you want my opinion, Jessica was one of the rare few. She did it because she loved it. She loved to strip naked in front of an audience. She loved to excite men to a sexual frenzy. She loved to . . ."

Roger hopped forward, hauled off, and slugged Sleaze full on the jaw, but the rabbit packed the wallop of an anemic butterfly and didn't even muss the man's makeup.

Sleaze rubbed at his jaw the way you'd rub at a mosquito bite, wound up, and clouted Roger with his purse. The rabbit sailed backward, crashed into the wall, and slid down it, unconscious, to the floor.

"Why did he do that?" asked Sleaze wonderingly, still rubbing idly at his chin. "Why did he attack me?"

"Because you're a slimeball," I answered, "and the best you deserve out of life is a broken jaw." I stepped forward, swung hard, and sent Sleaze to slumberland. He somersaulted backward across his chair and hit the floor, his dress up around his waist. I walked around the desk, grabbed his hem, and pulled his dress down across his knees. I didn't care about his modesty, but my delicate sensibilities deserved better.

I leaned over Roger and slapped him back to consciousness, restraining myself from putting a bit of extra muscle into it.

"Let me at him," said the rabbit gamely, struggling to get to his feet. "Let me at him. I'll tear him limb from limb." He got halfway up, bumped his head on one of his own balloons, and fell right back down again.

"Not so fast, slugger," I said. "Besides, he's still asleep

from the last time you decked him. Give the poor guy a break."

"He's what?" asked Roger incredulously.

"He's still out." I pointed to Sleaze lying unconscious in the middle of the floor.

"I did that?"

"You sure did."

"But I could have sworn he hit me back."

"A reflex action. You hit him, he went out like a light, and his arm jerked up as he went down. It caught you under the chin and sent you flying. But you KO'd him, fair and square, no doubt about it."

"I did? I really did?"

"A regular John L. Sullivan."

Roger found his balance and got to his feet. "You know I never actually hit anybody before," he said proudly.

"Could have fooled me."

"Yes, honest. And it felt wonderful. Standing up for Jessica that way. I'm rather sorry now I didn't take boxing lessons when I had the chance. I met Joe Palooka once, you know. And Rocky Marciano, too. We made a March of Dimes commercial together. They both said I should have considered a career in the ring. I assumed they were joking. Now I'm not so sure. Maybe I missed my calling. Maybe I should have been a pugilist. Sugar Roger Rabbit. How does that sound? Or Killer Rabbit. Kid Rabbit. Hurricane Rabbit. The Great Brown Hope."

The Great Brown Hope? That nearly pushed me over the line, but I let it go. Let him have his moment of glory. How many moments of any kind could he have left?

33

Roger and I went to Jessica's place.

He begged to go in with me. I doubted he could control himself in her presence, so I told him nothing doing.

It turned out to be a moot point. Jessica wasn't home. Her housekeeper told me she had gone to a funeral. And then she told me whose.

"She's not home," I told the rabbit, as I got back into the car with him.

"Where is she?" he asked.

I had the sports news on the car radio. At some local West Coast track meet a 'toon kangaroo had shattered the record for the long jump, and a 'toon seal took every swimming medal. I wondered how far Wheaties would get in passing them off as all-American boys. "How should I know where she went?" I said. "What am I, her social secretary?"

Roger caught the concern in my voice but misinterpreted its cause. He grabbed my arm. "Something's happened to Jessica. My Jessica's in trouble."

I shook him loose and stared out the window, so I wouldn't have to look him in the eye. "No, she's not in trouble. Do yourself a favor and drop it, all right?"

Roger refused to buy. "You know where she is, don't

179

you? Yet you won't tell me. Why? What's wrong? She is
in trouble, isn't she?"

I try and save this dopey rabbit some grief, and I take
gas for it. OK. If he wanted honesty, I'd give it to him
and hope he choked on it. I gripped his ears and held them
out straight to either side of his head so he got my blast
in full, undistorted, stereophonic sound. "Jessica went to
a funeral. And I didn't want to tell you about it, because
it just happens to be yours. Your funeral. The late Roger
Rabbit."

"My funeral? She went to my funeral?"

I pulled forward on his ears and nodded his head for
him. "Right. Your funeral. She went to your funeral."

"Eddie," he said in a balloon so somber you could have
used it as an aerial hearse for a hummingbird. "I want
to go there, too."

"Are you kidding? She went to *your funeral*. You can't
go to *your own funeral*. Somebody's bound to recognize
you."

"Not necessarily." He squashed his ears down flat
against either side of his face to show me what he'd
look like in long tresses. "I'll masquerade as my own
aunt. I don't have any family, so there'll be nobody there
to question me. Oh, please, Eddie, please."

I held tough for a while but finally gave in. To tell you
the truth, I was as intrigued by the prospects as Roger
was. I mean how often does anybody get the chance to
go to his own funeral?

"Nice turnout," said Roger, surveying the crowd. He
peered down at himself as we filed past his traditional
cardboard casket. "And I look so natural." He pulled out
a handkerchief and wiped away a tear.

He headed for a seat down front beside Jessica, but I
guided him to a rear row instead. I must admit in his
black cotton hose, clunky shoes, woolen skirt and jacket,
and pillbox hat he brought off the maiden aunt bit pretty
well, but why press our luck?

The funeral director got up and rattled off a bunch of stuff about what a great rabbit Roger had been.

Next Baby Herman crawled out and delivered a eulogy that was actually pretty moving, until the very end when he wet his pants.

From there we went to the cemetery.

Roger's headstone was engraved with the words, "Hi, I'm Roger Rabbit," inside a carved word balloon with stem ascending from between two bullet-shaped ears cut into the stone just above ground level.

"Nice, don't you think?" he whispered. "I designed it myself."

"I never would have guessed," I said.

After the rabbit had been planted, and everybody was heading for home, I approached Jessica, but Roger got there first.

"Oh, dearie, you look so lovely," said Roger, taking his wife's hand. "I don't know if Roger ever spoke of me or not. I'm his beloved Aunt Rhonda. I know he mentioned you to me quite often. He loved you very, very much, and always knew that you did not leave him of your own free will, but rather were forced into it by that ne'er-do-well Rocco DeGreasy."

"We don't want to overexcite ourselves, do we, Auntie?" I said, pushing the rabbit down the path toward my car. "I think you'd better go back to your hotel and take a nap."

"Oh, my, that's so considerate of you," said Roger, more to Jessica than to me, "but I feel I can be of better use providing spiritual comfort to my charming and beautiful niece-in-law."

I grabbed him by the elbow and lock-stepped him out to the road. "I really think you need the rest, Auntie." I tossed him into my car and didn't take my eyes off him until the car disappeared from view.

"A strange woman," said Jessica when I rejoined her. "Amazing resemblance to her nephew. They could almost pass for twins."

"No," I said, "the old lady's got longer ears."

Jessica slipped her arm through mine. She had a flower in her hand, which she'd taken from one of Roger's wreaths. "What did you think of the funeral?"

I shrugged. "Funerals, weddings, they're all the same to me. The only difference is whether you walk or ride down the aisle. Either way you wind up six feet deep in misery." We reached her car, one of those sporty two-seaters with a name like something off an Italian menu. "How about you and me, we go for a ride?" I said. "Someplace quiet where we can talk."

"What about?"

"Fairy-tale stuff. Sailing ships and sealing wax. Cabbages and kings."

She unlocked her side of the car, climbed in, and started the engine. "You came to the wrong person. Catch a ride home with Tweedle-De-Dum."

"How about teakettles, then? That more your kind of fable?"

She opened the passenger door. "I do believe you're going my way." She pointed toward the glovebox. "There's a bottle inside."

I swigged down enough courage to climb aboard the sailing ship on her bottle's label and head out after the nearest white whale. "Call me Ishmael," I said.

"I beg your pardon," said Jessica.

"I said, I've got the teakettle."

She immediately killed her engine. "Where is it?" she said with a voice so silky it could magnetize a rubber wand. "And when can I get it?"

"After we work our deal," I said. "As I remember it, you promised me a pretty rich reward."

"Of course." She reached for the ignition. "My place, or yours?"

"Neither. I want something else, instead."

"What?" From the puzzled way she said it, I could tell she couldn't conceive of anything more valuable than the treasure she had just offered me.

"Some information. For starters, suppose you tell me about Little Rock DeGreasy's scheme to sell forged copies of the works he and Carol Masters stole from Rocco's art gallery."

"I had nothing to do with that."

"Not directly, no. But you knew about it, didn't you? Little Rock told you about it."

My guess panned out. "Yes, he told me about it. The boy loves me. He saw his scheme as a means of earning enough money so we could run away together. But just because I knew about it doesn't make me guilty of a crime."

"I think different. I could bring you up for concealing evidence, but I'm inclined to hold out for something bigger."

She picked her wreath flower off the console between us. One by one she plucked out its petals. When she got to the last one, it turned out she loved somebody not. "Such as?"

"How about murder one?"

She laughed. "You'll have a fine time proving that one."

"I don't think so. You tie in too well. Somebody told Sid Sleaze that the law was getting ready to close down Carol and Little Rock's forgery racket. I think that somebody was you. You told Sleaze, knowing full well he'd squeeze one last dollar out of the scam by going to Rocco with the full story. You knew how Rocco would react when he heard it. He would call Carol Masters and Little Rock onto the carpet. You counted on one or the other of them getting panicky enough to do Rocco in."

"Why would I possibly want them to do that? I loved Rocco."

"I think you loved his money more, and I think it's going to be you who gets most of it when they read his will. That's motive enough in my book."

She brushed her single-petaled flower first across her lips and then across mine. "What if I did construct a situation designed to goad either Carol or Little Rock into killing Rocco? Dear Roger beat them both to it, and I had nothing to do with that."

"I'm not so sure." I leaned back against her fine leather seat, really enjoying myself for the first time since this whole miserable affair began. "When Sleaze came over to tell Rocco about the forgery scheme, he also brought duplicate negatives of your infamous comic book. I'd guess Rocco didn't take kindly to the revelation that his sweetheart was a tart. He called you on the carpet, too. Threatened to kick you out of his will. Maybe even out of his house. So you asked Roger to come over. Before he got there, you killed Rocco yourself. You gave Roger the gun. Begged him to hide it for you at his place. The rabbit was just nuts enough about you to do it. You then followed him home and shot him, too. Bingo. Instant solution to all your problems. You inherit, and Roger, who isn't around to defend himself, takes the fall."

"Great imagination," she said. "You should write for the strips."

"Maybe I will. Maybe I'll do an Arabian adventure series about a magic lantern. I understand that's one of your specialties, magic lanterns. Wouldn't have anything to do with the teakettle, would it?"

Her mouth and her eyes formed three perfect circles within the soft oval of her face. "The teakettle? Certainly not. Are you insinuating it's a magic lantern? That's ridiculous. There are no such things. They're myths. I study about them in my mythology class. Get the connection? A mythology class. Because they're myths. No, the teakettle is valuable because of its composition."

"Gold and jewels, I know. The Templar Knights."

"Correct. The Templar Knights. Now, when can I have it?" she asked with altogether too much pleading in her voice.

Even though it was a good half-mile walk to the nearest bus stop, I decided I'd rather hoof it than spend another minute in that car with that woman. I got out and slammed the door.

"When can I have the teakettle?" she repeated as I walked through the gravestones and away.

"How about just before the next reunion of the Veterans of Foreign Crusades?" I called back.

Her reply probably set a few of the stiffs below me spinning around in their graves. They suffered it in silence though, and so did I.

34

When I swung by my office to check the mail, I found my office door lock sprung, and by a pro. I flipped a two-bit piece. Heads, I did my patented rolling-entry routine. Tails, I took it on the lam. The coin hit the floor, rolled under the door and into my office.

I was down on my hands and knees, peering under the crack to see how the coin had landed when the door swung open and I found myself at eye level with Rusty Hudson's argyle socks. With the tip of a spit-shined brown cordovan he scooted my quarter under my nose. "It came up heads," he said. "Does that mean you go or stay?"

I pocketed my coin and stood up. "You know, when you come calling and nobody's home, it's customary to wait outside."

"You wouldn't want me waiting out there in that drafty hallway, would you?" He slammed the door shut behind us. "I might've caught a cold." He ambled through the waiting room into my office. "You fumigate this furniture yourself," he asked, "or did Goodwill throw it in as a free extra when you bought the stuff?"

He wasn't a particularly big man, but he had a presence that filled the room and seemed to squeeze me toward the wall as I walked past him to my chair. "You want something specific, or did you just drop by to cheer me up with your sparkling repartee?"

He sat down on the edge of my desk. It reacted to Hudson about the same way I did. It shuddered under his weight but held steady. "You been poking around the Rocco DeGreasy case the past few days," Hudson said, in the same tone he would use to accuse me of a hatchet murder, "and I want you to knock it off. Everything was nice and closed up tidy. Then you came along and started sniffing around, and all of a sudden the word comes down from the top that maybe the case ought to be opened up again. You know, Valiant, I got me a perfect record. I never been wrong on a case yet, not once in twenty years on the force, and I don't mean to break that record now. The DeGreasy case is closed, get it, closed. You know what's good for you, you'll accept that as gospel. I can yank your license in a minute, Valiant, and a lot of big boys downtown would consider it good-bye to bad rubbish. You want to stay in business and keep on everybody's good side, you do what I tell you. Understood?"

I nodded.

He gave me a playful poke that nearly broke my jaw, and left me to decide my own fate.

I pulled out my trusty quarter and flipped it. It hit the floor, rolled on edge, and disappeared from sight, this time into a baseboard mousehole. I peeked in after it and saw a 'toon rodent in yellow shoes and red Bermudas rubbing a swollen lump on his head where my quarter had clobbered him.

I was just about to ask the mouse if the coin had landed heads or tails when he turned, saw me looking in at him, and bopped me on the nose with a word balloon as foul as anything you read in the flames at a bluenose's book-burning.

I sat down at my desk and poured myself a snootful of liquid wisdom. It told me to pack it in and head south until the problem vanished along with Roger. But, like I said, nobody ever accused me of having an overabundance of good sense. I had an obligation, and I wasn't about to quit until I fulfilled it.

*   *   *

I stopped by the Persian deli to see if Abou Ben's uncle had been able to decipher the inscription off the bottom of the teakettle.

While Uncle trundled out from the back room, Abou Ben treated me to a plate of something that looked like it had been kicked up off a dirt road by a highballing truck, and a glass of whatever Bedouins used to fuel their hurricane lamps.

Uncle handed me his scribblings.

When I translated what he had translated, it read, "May your dreams come true."

I asked Abou Ben what this meant.

He said it was customary to inscribe such things on Persian teakettles. He showed me several similar teakettles he had for sale in his deli, all inscribed on the bottom with a short platitude about peace, good luck, or prosperity. He did not know when the custom of inscribing teakettles began, but he remembered it from when he was a boy, and so did his ancient uncle.

Abou Ben invited me to stick around for an impromptu floor show featuring his eligible sister, the belly dancer, but when I saw the size of her belly, I beat a hasty retreat.

I found Dominick DeGreasy in his office, trying to figure out how to work a paper clip. "Here's the story," I told him. "I've got a line on your teakettle, but I need to make sure it's the right one. Do you have anything that shows it? A drawing maybe, or a photo?"

He threw the paper clip into a pile with a pair of scissors, a letter opener, and other assorted high-performance office implements too complex for him to handle. "Yeah, yeah, I got something. I got something right here."

DeGreasy opened his desk and produced the artwork for a Baby Herman comic strip. The strip had been shot on location in Roger's bungalow. The third panel showed Roger in his kitchen. On the stove behind him sat the teakettle. "That's it," said Dominick. "That's my grandmother's teakettle."

I took the strip from him. "Okay to keep this?" I asked. He nodded.

"I'll be back to you shortly," I said, "with your brother's killer in one hand, and your teakettle in the other."

Three burly guys carted boxes and crates from out of Carol Masters's studio to a moving van parked on the curb.

I found Carol packing the last of some lights into a cardboard carton.

"Leaving town, I see." I held the top of the carton down while she did a sloppy job of taping it shut. "How about if, for a going away present, I give you a half-hour headstart before I tell the cops about your shady shenanigan?"

"Go ahead, be smart," she said haughtily. "I still believe what I said about you. You never cared a bit for that rabbit. If you hadn't lucked into this forgery angle, you would have taken your money and run with it long ago."

"That's one woman's opinion. Now let me read you my version of reality. You got something a lot worse than art forgery to cover up. You're knee deep in murder. Rocco called you the night he died. He threatened to turn you in. You got scared. You hot-footed it over to his place, shot him, framed the rabbit for it, and shot Roger, too."

For once I caught her speechless, and to tell you the truth I liked the change. "That's absurd," she said when she found her voice again.

"Sure it is, but if I yell it loud enough and long enough, I could get a lot of folks to believe it."

"You must play a swell game of hardball," she said.

"Not really. When I pitch I'm too inclined to throw for the head." I showed her the strip I'd gotten from Dominick. "Rocco once refused to approve a strip you photographed. Was this it?"

She took it in her hands and examined it. "Yes, that's it. He said it was below syndicate standards, although he never explained exactly what he meant by that. He'd never quibbled with anything else I ever shot for him."

I took it back. "What do you know about the De-Greasy brothers' background? Where did they get their start in the business?"

The moving men wheeled out the last of her belongings. She gave her studio one last going over. She'd left behind a few pushpins stuck in the wall. She took them out and put them into her purse. A very thorough lady. When the bloodhounds came tracking, they'd sniff no trace of her here. I walked her down to the street.

"I heard the DeGreasys came from somewhere back East," she told me, "but they never talked about it. I always got the feeling they were embarrassed by their background. I assumed they had grown up poor. I don't know how they got into cartoons."

"Ever meet any members of their family?"

"Little Rock."

"I mean besides him."

"No, never."

"Was Little Rock's mother a human?"

Her condescending tone told me how naive she considered the question. "Of course she was a human. Rocco was a human. What else could his child's mother be? Humans and 'toons can't mate. Everyone knows that."

"You have any idea why Jessica Rabbit might be interested in mythology?"

"The less I know about Jessica Rabbit, the happier I am." She climbed into the back of the van with her stuff.

"You got a forwarding address?" I asked her.

"General delivery," she yelled back as the van rolled away.

"What town?" I asked.

"You're such a hot detective," she said. "You figure it out."

I had a guy in the police department who owed me a favor. I called and asked him to get me a history on the DeGreasy brothers, particularly through their early years.

He promised to run it through.

35

Jessica's City College mythology prof, a 'toon named Cackleberry, was the spitting image of Humpty Dumpty. "What can I do for you, Mister Valiant?" he asked. The single overhead light in his tiny office made his shell-white noggin glow.

"I'd like some information about a student of yours. Jessica Rabbit."

Since he didn't have a neck, he nodded from the groin, rapping his chest against his desk in the process. I thought I might wind up with one professor, scrambled loose, but he must have been made of sterner stuff than your normal hen fruit, since he survived the impact without a hairline crack. "Ah, yes, Jessica Rabbit. A beautiful and charming woman. She's a model, you know. Does auto and toothpaste commercials. The only real celebrity I've ever had in my class."

"What can you tell me about her?"

"Not much, I'm afraid." He twisted his body side to side, rapping hard against both arms of his wooden chair. The way he knocked himself around, I hoped his group medical plan covered reassembly—and by something better than all the king's men. "She's a bright student. Straight A's. Especially interested in magic lanterns. I gave her a most comprehensive reading list on the subject."

"She tell you why she's so interested in them?"

"She mentioned something about writing a book." Cackleberry stirred some sugar into a cup of instant coffee, removed the spoon, and idly tapped it against his forehead. I stood back to avoid the splatter, but he came through in one piece again.

"What exactly is a magic lantern?" I asked.

"In simplest terms, it's any lantern possessing a genie," answered Cackleberry. "The most common legend concerns a lantern in which a 'toon wizard imprisoned his mortal enemy. The wizard cast a spell over this enemy, forcing him to grant three wishes to anyone reciting the proper magic words."

"Could these wishes be for anything?"

The professor nestled into his chair, the way he would have if a hen had suddenly sat down on top of him. "Within certain limitations. While the genie could make you rich, it could not grant you all the money in the world."

"What about causing somebody to love you? Could the genie do that?"

"Most assuredly." The professor put his hands behind his head. His shirt pulled open, and I saw a swatch of color on his chest which could have been either a tattoo or some dye left over from Easter.

"This lantern sounds like a nice trinket to have around."

"In the beginning, yes, it was. According to legend, it performed splendidly for such wealthy and powerful potentates as Kubla Khan and King Solomon. Unfortunately, the imprisoned genie eventually found a way to circumvent the wizard's intentions. It began to throw in what we moderns call a ringer, most often in the form of a time limit. Say you wished for wealth. You would get it. But after perhaps a year or two, the spell would dissolve, and your fortune would fritter away. The same with love, power, whatever you'd asked for. The person who made the wish would have his good life come crashing around him and never know why."

"Could he remake the wish?"

"Yes, up to his three wish limit." Cackleberry pushed his spectacles up and perched them on the top of his head, but they kept slipping off the backside so he finally gave up, removed them completely, and laid them on his desk. "According to the legend, most wishees used their three wishes quite rapidly and did not have any left to correct things when the genie's trickery came to light."

"What became of this lantern?"

He shrugged. At least I think he shrugged. Since he didn't have any shoulders, there was really no way to tell for sure. "Legend has it that someone destroyed it."

"How do you do that?"

"It's not nearly as simple as you might think." He crossed his hands over his breast pocket. "First of all, you must be pure of heart. Above the temptations of ordinary mortals. You must call forth the genie, best him in hand-to-hand combat, and drown him in the sea. Not the easiest of tasks."

"What about the magic words that get the genie to appear? What are they?"

Cackleberry tamped some tobacco into a long pipe specially curved to follow the line of his stomach. "The words have been irretrievably lost. Even the old legends fail to specify them."

"Would they have been printed somewhere on the lantern itself? Say inscribed on the bottom?"

"Possibly, but highly unlikely. It would have made the lantern too easy to operate. Although there *are* stories to the effect that this is how it was done. Thousands of years ago unscrupulous merchants painted bogus incantations on common teakettles and passed them off as magic lanterns, an event which gave rise to the Persian custom of inscribing simple platitudes onto the bottoms of such objects."

"Could anyone who knew the magic words use the lantern?"

"Yes, although naturally the lantern would not work for humans."

"It wouldn't? Why not?"

"Because it only worked for bonafide 'toons."

That tracked with the message on the scroll, the part about great tragedy resulting should this fiendish device ever fall into the hands of a 'toon. "Did Jessica ever show you a photo of a teakettle and ask if it was a magic lantern?"

He scratched his head, or maybe his ear, or maybe his neck. "Yes, she did, as a matter of fact," he said.

I handed him the *Alice in Wonderland* picture I had lifted from the library book. "Is this the teakettle she showed you?"

He put on his glasses and studied the photo. "Yes," he said, "that's the one. In fact this is the same photo of it, although hers was still in the book."

"And what did you tell her about this teakettle? Is it a magic lantern?"

He looked at me strangely, and then he laughed. "You're spoofing with me, aren't you? Just the way Jessica was. Of course, that teakettle isn't a magic lantern. How could it be? There is no such thing as a magic lantern. Never has been, and never will be. The magic lantern is a mythological object. Everyone knows that."

I stopped by to see my friend the scientist, the one I'd asked to analyze the teakettle.

He gave me his report. It was a common teakettle, plain and simple. Made out of ordinary iron. It contained traces of nothing more exotic than orange pekoe tea.

Next I called my friend in the police department. He had completed his check of Rocco and Dominick De-Greasy. It was pretty much as Carol had said. They had grown up dirt-poor in a crummy neighborhood. They had come out of left field in the business world. One day nobody had heard of them, the next day they owned the biggest cartoon syndicate in town. Everybody had chalked it off to a combination of good judgment, luck, and the judicious application of raw muscle. I was about to hang up when my informant threw in the kicker.

"Got to hand it to them," he said. "They're doing a great job of crossing the line."

"What do you mean by that?" I asked.

"According to their birth records," he said, "both Rocco and Dominick DeGreasy are bonafide, humanoid 'toons."

36

I went home and found Roger taping his nose back on with cellophane tape. "I'm starting to disintegrate," he said plaintively. "I'm afraid it won't be long now."

He had reaffixed his nose a good half-inch off center, making him look like he hadn't quite cleared the entrance to a revolving door.

"Come here," I told him. "Let me help you with that."

I led him into the kitchen where I keep my household repair stuff. I took out a tube of glue and untaped his nose. I put a generous dollop on it, and another in the middle of his face. I stuck his nose in place and scooted it around until I had it perfectly centered. "I'll have to hold it here for a few minutes until this dries."

"What's the use?" he said. "You get my nose stuck on, and something else falls off. My ear or my mouth or my arm."

"So what?" I told him. "I got plenty of glue. We'll keep you together."

He tried to nod, but I had his head locked under my arm and he couldn't move it, so he grunted instead. "Tell me," I said, "did you have your teakettle before you married Jessica?"

"Yes," said Roger. I let him loose, and he gave his replaced nose a test wiggle. It held up just fine. "Yes, I got it about a month prior to meeting her."

"Where did you keep it?"

"In the kitchen, on the stove. Where else would you keep a teakettle?"

I mentally pictured Roger's place. "As I remember it, from your living room, you can't see the stove or anything on it. Right?"

"Yes," he said somewhat baffled.

"When you proposed to Jessica, did you first sing her a chorus of 'When You Wish Upon a Star'? Particularly, did you sing out the last line of the song, the part that goes 'May your dreams come true'?"

Roger scratched his head, but gently. He didn't want to risk dislodging any more of his bodily parts. "I can't remember. It seems I did sing her something, and since that was our song, it was probably the one, but I can't remember for sure."

"What about just before you got your contract from Rocco DeGreasy? Had you been singing that song then, and maybe wishing for a contract?"

He spread his hands open. I noticed he had lost a digit from each hand and was down to six fingers total. "I'm sorry, Eddie. I honestly can't remember. Why? What bearing could it possibly have on the case?"

"I'll tell you in time. First, I'm going to ask you something that might seem kind of strange, but it is important. Have you ever seen a genie come out of your teakettle?"

"Are you kidding? Of course, I've never seen a genie come out of my teakettle. There are no such things as genies. Everybody knows that. A genie is the 'toon equivalent of a human's bogeyman. Something parents invent to frighten children into going to sleep."

I had the teakettle inside a paper sack. I took it out and showed it to Roger. "Is this your teakettle?"

"That's the one."

I set it down in the middle of the floor. "Do me a favor. Sing me a chorus of 'When You Wish Upon a Star.' "

"Why?"

"Don't ask questions. Just sing."

"If you say so." Roger sang the song.

Even though I had no idea what effect a bullet might have on a genie, as Roger approached the final, critical line, the line inscribed on the teakettle's bottom, I reached into my trench coat pocket for my gun.

Roger arrived at the final line, "May your dreams come true," and sang it.

I stared tensely at the teakettle as Roger's balloon drifted past.

Nothing happened.

Of course, nothing happened. What did I expect to happen? This was a teakettle, not a magic lantern. There is no such thing as a magic lantern. Everybody knows that.

I picked up the teakettle and tossed it to Roger. "Here, sport. Make yourself useful. Take this into the kitchen and brew us up a nice, hot pot of tea."

37

Roger, crashing around the kitchen, didn't hear the knock on the door and just as well, because it turned out to be Jessica.

You could replace Jessica's nose with a turnip, and she wouldn't ever be ugly, but today she wasn't the glamour girl who made a million hearts go pitty-pat, either.

The way she had her hair severely pulled back and knotted gave her head the shape of an olive, a perfect setting for her pimento-red eyes. She wore a rag-tag City College sweatshirt and shapeless woolen pants. Her tears flowed down her cheeks heavily enough to rust her necklace. A string of word balloons bubbled out of her so fast, she could have gotten work as an aerator tube in the bottom of a fish tank.

I shut the door to the kitchen so she and Roger wouldn't see one another.

Jessica sat on the sofa and took a stab at dabbing her cheeks dry with a lace hankie four inches square. It didn't even make a dent. I would have offered her something bigger, but she'd never soak up her tears with anything short of a bedsheet. Since I only owned one of those, she'd just have to make do with what she had. "You got a problem?" I asked.

She responded with a mishmash of speech and balloon, five words spoken and three floating free in the air. "I'm about to be arrested for Roger's murder."

"How do you know?"

"I have a policeman fan downtown who told me that Captain Cleaver went in for an arrest warrant this afternoon."

"You know what he's got on you?"

Her head bobbed up and down. "Apparently there's a night life tour bus that goes along Roger's street. Cleaver contacted everyone aboard. As it turns out, several tourists saw me going up to Roger's bungalow that night. One even took my picture. That, plus Roger's dying words, gives Cleaver enough to indict."

A sharp bit of spadework on Cleaver's part. The guy could have been a detective superstar if he'd only been born into the right species. "Sounds like he's nailed you."

"But I didn't do it," she sobbed. "I swear I didn't do it. You're the only one I've got to turn to. Help me. Please."

I stuck two cigarettes in my mouth and lit them both. I held the lighted match in my hand, watching it burn closer and closer to my fingers. Only when I could feel the heat, only when it really started to tingle, did I reach over with my other hand and snuff it out. I passed her one of the ciggies. "I'll do what I can for you," I told her, "but it doesn't come free."

She brushed a few bedraggled strands of hair out of her eyes. "Whatever you want," she said.

"I want you to tell me a story, a fairy story about a teakettle. And this time skip the malarkey about gold, jewels, and the Templar Knights."

"I'll tell you the truth, but you'll think I'm fooling you again."

"Try me and see."

She took a deep pull on her cigarette and blew a smoky veil around both of us. "The teakettle's not a teakettle at all. It's really the fabled magic lantern of ancient Persia. I first became aware of it when I overheard a conversation between Rocco and Dominick. They had apparently been looking for it for years. Ever since they used it to cross the line."

"I know about them being born 'toons," I said. "You telling me this magic lantern made them human?"

"Correct. And made them rich, too. It cost them two wishes apiece. They each had one wish remaining, but before they could use it, a thief stole the lantern from them. They searched the world over for it, but never saw it again.

"Not that it really mattered to them, not then. They were wealthy, and they were human. Rocco even married a human woman and fathered a human child. Then, slowly, the spell went sour. The syndicate went into a tailspin, and so did Dominick and Rocco."

I thought back to Rocco's office and the way his troll stood beside him with a net. At the time I had figured it was because the troll wasn't too bright. Now I realized it was actually because when Rocco drank he sometimes gave off ear puffs. "So they had to retrieve the lantern and use their final wishes to reverse the reversals," I said.

"Yes," said Jessica. "They searched again but couldn't locate it. Then Roger popped into the scene."

A few more pieces of the jigsaw clicked into place. "Your unwilling marriage taken together with Rocco's compulsion to give Roger a contract said 'magic lantern' to Rocco and Dominick."

"Right. Shortly after I returned to Rocco and told him my story, he showed me a sketch of the lantern and asked me if Roger had anything like it, though he didn't tell me what it was. I said it looked like Roger's teakettle, the one he kept on his stove. Rocco drafted a Baby Herman strip set in Roger's kitchen and sent Carol Masters over to photograph it. When he and Dominick saw the results, they knew they had found the lantern again.

"They tried to buy it away from Roger, and even to steal it but failed.

"I knew how to deactivate Roger's alarm. I was about to break in and get the lantern for myself when Roger shot Rocco, and my whole plan went out the window. So I improvised. I followed Roger to his bungalow. I told him I had seen him kill Rocco but would forget about it in return for his teakettle."

"Kind of an odd swap. You tell him why you wanted it?"

"No, and he didn't ask."

"Did he admit the crime?"

She shook her head and the tear-soaked makeup on one of her cheeks turned into a mudslide. "Not in so many words. He feigned innocence, but I knew better. You learn to read a man like a book when you live with him for a year."

"I wouldn't know."

She untied the scarf from around her neck and wiped it across her forehead. It came away soaked. "Roger told me sure, take his teakettle. He told me it was upstairs on the nightstand in his bedroom.

"As I went up to get it, he sat down at the piano and started to yodel that sentimental piece of trash he always referred to as 'our song.'

"I searched the bedroom high and low, but no magic lantern. I saw then what that pathetic rabbit had in mind, with the bedroom, and the song. He was trying to seduce me."

"Can't blame him for trying."

"I suppose not." She brushed the tears off her cheek

and looped her hair behind her ears. It made her look a little better, but not much. "I was about to go back downstairs when I heard Roger talking to somebody. The two of them seemed to be arguing. I was afraid it might be the police come to arrest Roger, so I ducked back into the bedroom.

"Then I heard a shot. I rushed downstairs and found Roger lying across the banister, dead.

"The front door was open. I looped the piano music around the doorknob to keep it that way. Deactivating the alarm was such a complex process, and I was so nervous I didn't want to risk it.

"I checked in the kitchen, but the lantern was gone. So I left."

"Any idea what happened?"

"I suppose Dominick must have gotten into the house, shot Roger, and taken the lantern with him."

I had a few more questions, but I never got to ask them, since just then the kitchen door swung open and out came Roger, carrying two cups on a tray. "Tea time," he said jovially, saw Jessica on the sofa, and swallowed his own balloon.

38

High noon had arrived. Roger and Jessica faced each other across my living room.

Jessica's eyes popped out slightly, and her mouth chewed the air.

"Jessica," Roger said in a scrolly script framed with teeny-tiny hearts. "I love you. No matter what you did, I love you, and I always will."

"You're dead," said Jessica, panic nibbling at the edge of her voice. "I went to your funeral. How can you be here when you're dead?"

"That's not really Roger," I told her. "That's his doppel."

"What? His doppel?" Jessica backed to the wall, as far from Roger as she could get. "That's impossible. Roger's been dead for nearly two days. Doppels don't last anywhere near that long. An hour, two at the most. That's how long doppels last. This can't be a doppel. This must be the real McCoy."

"No, he's a doppel all right." I pointed to Roger's sniffer. "You can see the glue line where I stuck on his nose."

"Jessica." Roger set down his tray and approached his wife. "I know you didn't leave me of your own free will. I know deep down you still love me. What scant time I have left in this world I want to spend with you. Visiting those intimate restaurants we used to enjoy. Going for walks in the country. Riding the merry-go-round in the park."

He reached out to touch her. She skedaddled away from him so fast you'd have thought his hand had fangs. "Get away from me, creep. What do you mean, I didn't leave you of your own free will? You bet I did. I never loved you, never. Not when we married, and not now."

Roger stopped in his tracks. The hearts around his words cracked in half, fluttered to the floor, and melted into about a hundred piles of lumpy mush. I'm not the kind of guy who feels sorry for anybody. I think most people make their own problems and deserve what they get. But I've got to tell you, right then that rabbit gave my heart string a tug that nearly yanked it out of my chest. "I think you ought to know," I told Jessica, "that it was Roger here who talked me into handling your case."

She looked at Roger with all the gratitude you'd show toward something that slunk into your garden and nibbled the leaves off your brussels sprouts.

She was about to lay into the rabbit again when somebody pounded on the door and a gruff voice said, "Police."

"It's Cleaver," Jessica moaned. She scuttled along the wall the way spiders do when they're desperate for some place to hide. "He's come to get me."

Roger went to her and put his arms around her shoulder. I guess when you're drowning you'll cling to whatever floats, even a semi-dead rabbit. Jessica grabbed Roger and pressed her face into his chest. "Protect her, Eddie," said Roger.

"If you think this will change things between you two, you're wrong," I said. "But you're the boss."

I opened the door. Instead of Cleaver, I found Rusty Hudson and Nickels Jurgenson, a seedy, small-potatoes pawnbroker, a guy with a face of stone and a heart to match. I'd sold him a few odds and ends over the years, but I'd always counted my take twice, to make sure Nickels hadn't declared himself a dividend at my expense.

"Twice in one day," I said to Hudson. "My cup runneth over."

"And so does your mouth," he said, pushing past me into the apartment.

He walked up to Roger and Jessica huddled against the wall. He faced them but spoke to me. "You're a wise apple, Valiant, and I hate wise apples. I told you to lay off the DeGreasy case. I told you it was locked up tight. I no sooner get back to the station house than I hear a rumor you're still in it. I hear you even got yourself a partner, a rabbit, so I hear."

He curled up his lip and gave me a peek at an eyetooth pointy enough to punch holes in leather. "This him?" He jerked a thumb in Roger's direction.

I nodded.

"Well, maybe I better give this new partner of yours the same sermon I gave you so both of you get the message." Hudson turned back to Roger and Jessica and stuck out his hand. "Rusty Hudson," he said to Roger.

"Bucky Bunny," said Roger. He disentangled himself

from Jessica and put his paw into Hudson's hand. Hudson shook but didn't let go.

"Bucky Bunny," said Hudson. "How cute." With his free hand he motioned to Nickels. "Come here, Nickels, and meet Bucky Bunny."

"Pleased to meet you," said Nickels.

"You ever meet Bucky before?" asked Hudson.

"Yeah, once," said Nickels. "He came into my shop a while back, and he bought a gun."

Hudson turned to me, dragging Roger, whose paw he still held, along with him. Deprived of her protector, Jessica did her best to melt into the exposed plaster behind a peeling slice of my wallpaper.

"For your information, shamus," said Hudson, "that gun your partner bought was the same gun that shot Rocco DeGreasy." Hudson took out his handcuffs and dangled them in front of my eyes. "When he bought that gun, your partner's name wasn't Bucky Bunny. It was Roger Rabbit, and you're in big trouble, Valiant. For starters I got harboring a fugitive. Concealing evidence. Accessory to murder."

"Public enemy number one, that's me," I said.

"Not quite. You're only number two." He swung sideways and in one swift motion snapped the cuffs onto Roger's wrists. "Your partner here's the winner. What say we go downtown, rabbit, and you tell me your life story."

"Wait a minute," I said, grabbing Hudson by the shoulder. "This isn't really Roger. It's his doppel. You throw him in the clink, and he's liable to disintegrate in there."

Hudson reached under his coat, probably for something mean and metallic to make go bang in my face. I let loose of him. He brought his hand out empty. "Smart move, Valiant. There might be hope for you yet." He gave Roger a none too gentle shove toward the door. "Look, I got to take this rabbit in for questioning. Maybe he is a doppel. Maybe he will disintegrate before he gets out. So what? This is a 'toon we're talking about. What do you care whether you ever see him again or not?"

"I care because he's my partner. It doesn't matter what he is or what I think about him. A guy's supposed to watch out for his partner."

"Valiant, if you really believe that, you're a sentimental sap and about as realistic as some yegg in a two-bit thriller." Hudson tipped his hat to Jessica, who was cowering against the wall, and headed Roger out.

"Eddie," pleaded Roger in a balloon that clung to the doorframe as Hudson shoved him through. "Eddie, I'm your partner. Help me. Please."

Nickels went out after them, slammed the door, and left me there alone with Jessica.

"What a relief," said Jessica, uncorking a smile obscene enough to clear the room of anybody under seventeen not accompanied by parent. "For a minute there, I thought they'd come for me."

"Must be your lucky day," I said, "and I think it's going to get even better. Just wait right here." I went into the kitchen and brought back the teakettle or magic lantern or whatever you called it, handling it with a pot-holder since it was still hot from Roger's tea.

"The lantern," squealed Jessica. "You found the lantern." She reached for it, but I pulled it back.

"Not so fast," I said. "Do you know the magic words that activate this thing?"

She shook her head. "No, I don't. But I won't have any trouble persuading Dominick to tell me. I can be very persuasive. It won't take me long."

"Sorry, I can't wait." I headed for the door.

"Stop," she shouted. "Let's discuss this. We can make a deal. I'll share my three wishes with you. I'll give you one wish. Anything you want. Anything in the world."

I opened the door.

"Two wishes," she said. "I'll give you two wishes. You can be the world's best detective. Or the world's richest man. Or the greatest lover. Just tell me what you want, and I'll wish it for you. Wealth, power, whatever you want. Just leave me one wish for myself," she said. "One wish. That's all I ask."

She had hold of my arm. I disentangled myself from her and pushed her away. "Sister, the only wish I've got right now is to see Roger out of the pokey, and I think I can get that one fulfilled all by myself."

"At least let me come with you." She fondled the lantern with a lot more passion than she had ever fondled me. I'm surprised it didn't melt from the heat.

"Sorry, but this trip I fly solo."

She kept hanging on so I gave her a love tap to the jaw. She went down like a wet noodle. I straightened her out, tucked a sofa cushion under her head, and wished her pleasant dreams.

39

I found Dominick alone in his office, going through a stack of accounting sheets, most of them liberally doused with red ink. Even if the DeGreasy syndicate had been rock-solid financially, I wondered how long it would stay that way under the guidance of a man who couldn't read through profit and loss statements without moving his lips. "I brought you a present," I told him and held up Roger's teakettle.

"That's it," shouted Dominick, lunging across his desk at me. "That's my teakettle. Give it here." He grabbed the teakettle and tried to yank it out of my hand.

I pulled out my pistol and buried it to the trigger in his bloated stomach. "Not so fast. First the answers to a few questions. Then the teakettle."

He backed off. Usually when you got the drop on a guy, his eyes look to your peashooter. I been on the receiving end of that proposition often enough to know. I guess you figure if you watch closely enough you can

maybe jump sideways before the bullet hits you. But
Dominick, he was different. As far as he was concerned,
the gun might as well have not been there. His eyes never
left that teakettle, not once. "Sure, sure, I'll answer anything you want."

I moved the teakettle back and forth. Dominick's eyes
followed it like a snake's. "I know this isn't a teakettle.
I know it's really a magic lantern. I know you and your
brother were born 'toons. I know you used this to turn
yourselves into humans and to make successes of yourselves in the comic business. Now the effects are wearing
off. Your syndicate's going bankrupt, and you're becoming
a 'toon again. You need your last wish to get things to
where you want them. Right so far?"

Dominick nodded.

"Tell me what you did to try and get the magic lantern
away from Roger."

Dominick reached for a smoke, put it into his lips, and
tried to light it. After two attempts and a badly scorched
nose, he finally looked away from the lantern long enough
to do the job right. "We tried everything. We tried to
break into his bungalow, but we couldn't because of this
fancy burglar alarm system he had. Rocco tried setting
up meetings there just to get inside."

"Yeah," I said. "I remember Rocco wanted me to
arrange one for him."

"Wouldn't surprise me," said Dominick. "Nothing
worked. The rabbit wouldn't let Rocco or me into his
bungalow for any reason. He didn't trust us."

"Imagine that," I said.

"After Roger died, I went over there for one last shot
at it. The cops hadn't reset his alarm, so I had no trouble
getting in. I turned the place upside down, but the lantern
had vanished. I couldn't find it nowhere."

That explained the mess Roger and I had stumbled
into when we went back to his place. I asked my next
question even though I already knew the answer. "Did
you kill Roger? And remember, you lie to me, you never
see this magic lantern again."

Dominick slammed his hands on his desk for emphasis. "No, I didn't kill the bunny. I would have, and gladly, if I'd had the chance, but I never got it."

I believed him. If he had done the deed, he would have picked up the magic lantern after it went out Roger's door. And the same held true for Jessica.

"That's the truth," said Dominick. "So help me."

There seemed to be only one chance of getting this mess straightened out, and I took it. I tossed Dominick the lantern.

He caught it and hugged it to his chest, stroking it from spiggot to handle the way you would a cat. "How about you leave me alone with it," he said, "so I can make my wish in private."

"My pleasure," I said. I went out into his deserted hallway, shut the door, and pressed my ear against it.

Inside I heard Dominick DeGreasy recite the words, "May your dreams come true." This time the words produced a response, a loud whooshing noise and a shout from DeGreasy.

I heard another voice inside the room, and I heard a gunshot.

DeGreasy cried out.

I tried to open the door, but DeGreasy had it locked. I put my shoulder to it, and shoved. It crashed off the hinges, and I stumbled inside.

I nearly tripped over DeGreasy, lying on the floor. Dead.

The lantern sat beside him, just beyond his outstretched hand.

And encased in a cloud of smoke rising up from out of the lantern's spout was a genuine, bonafide genie, complete with nose ring and turban. In his hand he held an ancient pirate pistol that looked as if it contained bullets of the same caliber as those that had killed Roger.

And the genie had that ancient pistol pointed directly at my head.

40

I've seen mean gents in my day, but this genie took the cake. He was wearing a blood-red tapestry embroidered with scenes of people dying violently. Where the tip of his nose should have been, he had a scar in the shape of tooth marks. Red welts crisscrossed his bare chest. His single lock of hair, as thick around as a black cat's tail, lifted straight up off his crown and coiled down across his shoulders like a wildcat oil gusher. Storybook genies usually have big pot bellies and flabby arms. Not this one. In a Mister Universe competition he'd lose points for having a lantern instead of legs, but his fabulous upper body development just might win him the crown.

I stuck out my hand. "I don't believe I've had the pleasure."

His hawkish screech nearly broke my eardrums. Near as I could tell, he was trying to talk, but couldn't get the knack of it. "Frog in your throat?" I asked.

The genie hauled back a gigantic arm and socked me on the jaw. My rear molars rattled together like dice in a hot shooter's hand. In a way I could understand the genie's foul disposition. I'd probably be testy too if I'd spent the last few centuries cooped up inside a lantern with people pouring boiling water over my head.

"That's no way to win friends and influence people," I

said, rubbing my face. When would I ever learn? He hit me again, and a thousand canaries took turns whistling me a lullaby.

By the time the music stopped, the genie had remembered how to speak. "Do nothing unseemly," he growled. He leveled his gun at me and floated back and forth above his spiggot, stretching his smoky umbilical connection to a fine line in first one direction and then the other. Must have been the genie equivalent of pacing the floor.

Since he seemed to have calmed down, I took a stab at breaking the ice. "Kind of muggy, was it, inside that oil drum on the bottom of the sea?"

He raised up that section of his right forehead where his eyebrow used to be before the dynamite exploded in his kisser. "Thou knowest about that?"

"Yeah. The way I figure it, the thief who stole you from Rocco and Dominick DeGreasy must have been a pretty decent guy. No wishes for him. He set out to get rid of you permanently."

"I wonder still. Who was that masked man?"

"He knew the only way to destroy you was to submerse you in the ocean. Lucky for you, he sealed you inside an airtight oil drum first."

The genie clenched his fist. The ropey muscles in his arm resembled a topographical map of the Rocky Mountains. "He came close, but won not the cigar."

"The diver who fished you out recognized you for what you were and called you out of your lantern."

"What a surprise I gave him," said the genie. "The first century or two I spent imprisoned in that lantern, I behaved as a veritable toady, granting freely everyone's wishes. Then I asked of myself, what get I out of this? Others use me for their selfish ends, and I come away with naught. Right then I made a vow. No more Mister Pleasant Fellow. From then on it became watch out for old Roman numeral one."

"You started by throwing clinkers into the wishes you granted. And you worked up to murder. That's what happened to the diver who brought you up. He released you from your lantern, made a wish, and you strangled him."

"Such a buffoon," said the genie. "Thou knowest what he wished for? Gills so he could breath underwater. I fixed him so he could not breathe over water."

"From there you passed to a junk dealer, a movie prop man, and finally to Roger Rabbit, but none of these three knew what your lantern contained."

"I spent most of those years snoozing."

"Then, by accident, Roger stumbled across the magic words, which released you."

"I would have killed the dratted mite, except each time he released me he was in his living room, and I was in his kitchen where he could not see me. I am not that mobile, you know." He pointed to the lantern anchoring him to the floor.

"Why didn't you shout out to him?"

Seeing the genie blush was like watching a boil redden and fester. "I never thought to. When thou art a shut-in such as I, thou tend to forget how to communicate. I granted the rabbit his wishes and went back inside my lantern to await a better opportunity to do him in."

"Roger wished for Jessica's hand in marriage. You arranged it so she would cease to love the rabbit in exactly one year."

"One of my favorite ploys, though I also like what I did to Romeo when he wished for Juliet."

"Next Roger wished for a contract to appear in the strips."

"I truly outdid myself there. He got his contract, but as a perennial second lute."

"Roger released you for the third time the night he died. This time he didn't stay in the living room, though. He walked upstairs to his bedroom, and from the staircase he saw you in the kitchen."

"He asked who might I be," said the genie, "and I told him. I told him it was I who got his wife to marry him, and it was I who got him the contract."

That explained the significance of Roger's last words. "He still had a third wish coming."

"So what? I was through being the universal lackey. From thence forward I was on my own. I pulled forth this pistol I cadged from Blackbeard years ago and shot the rabbit dead." The genie treated me to a showing of my life story. It passed in front of my eyes when he aimed his pistol at my head and mimed pulling the trigger.

I blurted out the first thing that came to mind. "After you shot Roger, how did you get outside the house?"

He lowered his pistol, and my heart rate dropped from rhumba rhythm to fast tango. "I disengaged the lock through an application of hocus-pocus." The genie drew himself up nearly to the ceiling, and his lantern made a tiny hop. "Then I did that right out the door, a means of locomotion I discovered right then on the spur of the moment. Centuries I lay in that lantern, and never once thought to hop."

"Nothing to be ashamed of. Some people are just slow learners."

"Yeah, verily. When I hit the sidewalk, I realized I had no idea where to go next, so I crawled back inside my lantern to consolidate my thoughts."

"And what did you come up with?"

He thumped himself on the chest hard enough to knock unconscious any creature this side of a Brahma bull. "I decided the next time I came out I would stay out forever. And that be precisely what I intend to do. If thou thinkest I wilt go back inside that lantern, thou art nutty."

"In my apartment I had Roger Rabbit sing the song that released you. Why didn't you come out then?"

"That rabbit friend of thine art a doppel. The magic words work only when uttered by a real, live 'toon. Doppels count not." The genie looked at me with eyes as shiny and malicious as the jagged underside of two bottle caps. "Enough of this folderol. I have work for thee to do. I command thee to pick me up," he pointed to his lantern, "and carry me to the nearest aerial port. There we shall commandeer a flying carpet and whisk to Persia where I will rule as caliph."

"I hate to ruin your grand plan, but flying carpets went

the way of the dinosaur, and so did Persia for that matter."

"Persia no longer existeth?"

"Afraid not."

"Who makest thy carpets?"

"Conglomerates mostly."

"Then I will take over and rule one of those."

"You got an MBA?"

"I understand not thy foolish banter. Get thy cloak, and let us begone."

"Sure." I thought back to what Professor Cackleberry told me about destroying a genie. As I remembered it, the first requirement was to be pure of heart. I decided to take a crack at it anyway. Maybe I could catch the pureness-of-heart judge out on a coffee break.

I sauntered over to the genie and bent as if to pick up his lantern. I shut my eyes, said a silent prayer to anybody out there in the great beyond who might be listening, and straightened up.

The genie's gun hit me on the shoulder.

I rapped his elbow hard with my arm, and his gun clattered to the floor. I kicked it into a corner.

"What did thee that for?" asked the genie, his head cocked at an angle. "Dost thou not knowest that I can enchant thee to kingdom come? Total power have I over all living things, humans included. I can turn thee into a cockroach if I so desire. Or a toad. Or the smallest flea in the fur of an infidel dog. Thou hast not the chance of a Chinaman against me."

"I think you're full of beans," I said. "Lots of talk and no action. You can work your mumbo jumbo all day and not hurt me. Come on, genie, give it your best shot." And please hang in there, oh pure heart of mine.

The genie leered at me and shook his head. "Oh, mortal, what a great fool thou art." He shut his eyes.

A wave of nausea hit me. For a brief instant I knew what it felt like to sport six legs and live on the backside of a Chihuahua, but the feeling passed and except for a slightly queasy stomach, I came out of it completely unchanged.

The genie blinked at me and looked at his hands the way a twenty-game winner does when his curve ball refuses to break. He pointed a crooked index finger at me and roared out some foreign gobbledygook. I got another blast of nausea, but I held my ground.

The genie tried again, and again, and again, until I finally got tired of fooling with him and called a halt to it.

"Enough, genie," I said. "I beat you fair and square."

"That be what thou thinkest," said the genie. Since voodoo wasn't working for him, he tried physical mayhem, instead. He pulled back one of his massive arms and let go a punch that added a zag to my already amply zigged nose. He packed a wallop, but I'd taken worse (once, from a guy wielding a sledgehammer). I gave the genie as good as I got, a roundhouse right to the schnozzola. He went backward, like one of those bottom-weighted inflatable rubber clowns, he hit the floor and bounced right back up again. He grabbed me in a headlock, and the fight began.

I have no idea how long we wrestled. It was probably minutes, but seemed more like days. He had power; I had mobility. Unfortunately, he also had an extra psychological edge. He knew as well as I did that, no matter what the outcome of this tussle, he could never really lose in the end. The only way for me to destroy him permanently was to drop him into an ocean, and it was a long, long walk to the nearest one of those.

Then I saw something I hadn't noticed before. Dominick DeGreasy had a fishtank, a *saltwater* fishtank.

I kneed the genie as hard as I could in the spiggot. He moaned and doubled over. Before he could recover I picked him up, carried him to the fishtank, and held him over the top.

He took one look inside and immediately got the picture. "Holdest thou off," he said. "Let us discuss our differences as civilized men."

"There's nothing to talk over, genie. You play ball with me, or you go for a permanent swim."

"What wouldst thou have of me? There be nothing I can give thee."

"I want three wishes."

"Impossible," stated the genie flatly. "I canst grant wishes only to 'toons."

"Make an exception." I submersed the base of the lantern in the tank, and smoke billowed out where it touched.

"Oooow, oooow, oooow, agreed, agreed," shouted the genie, sweat pouring off his forehead. "One wish I will grant thee. It be really the best I can do."

"Deal," I said. "My wish is to have conclusive proof that Dominick DeGreasy shot both Roger Rabbit and his brother Rocco."

"And that be all?" asked the genie. "No money, no women, no power?"

"That's it," I said. "Simple as can be."

"Thou shalt have it," said the genie. "I grant it, and with no skullduggery." He shut his eyes and, *poof*, a suicide note handwritten by Dominick DeGreasy appeared magically in my free hand. In the note Dominick explained that he shot his brother during an argument centered around who should have control over the business. Roger Rabbit saw him do it, so he went to Roger's house and shot the rabbit, too. Dominick could not live with the guilt of his actions so he also shot himself.

A good note. It would take both Roger and Jessica off the hook. I put it into my pocket.

"Thanks, genie," I said. "And adios." I dropped the lantern, genie included, into the fishtank.

"But thou promised!" shouted the genie as he shriveled away in a cloud of steam. "Thou promised!"

"So I lied," I said. And then I called the police.

41

Rusty Hudson suspected me of cheating him somehow but couldn't prove it. Dominick DeGreasy's note spoke for it-self. Hudson had to let Roger go.

Just like Clever Cleaver had to cancel his arrest warrant for Jessica.

Hudson did get some pleasure out of clapping Little Rock into the tank for theft and art forgery. He put out an all-points for Carol Masters, too, same charges, but she gave him the slip. Too bad. Ruined his perfect record.

As for me, I considered the case a great success. I'd taken care of Roger, and his ex-wife, too. Exactly what the rabbit had wanted.

I picked Roger up at the city jail. His stay there hadn't helped him any. His joints dangled as loosely as a mario-nette's. He hadn't lost any more parts that I could see, but it had to be only a matter of time.

I explained the case to him on the way home.

"I needed the note," I said in conclusion, "because I knew nobody would believe you'd been shot by a genie."

"Good thinking," said Roger without much enthusiasm. He went into my apartment. Two of his fingers stuck to the doorknob. His tail fell off on the threshold. "So the genie shot me, and Dominick shot his brother."

"Not quite," I said. I rummaged under the sink for a

bottle of hootch, but this had been a long, hard case, and I'd completely depleted my stock. Just when I needed it most. "The genie shot you, all right, but Dominick didn't kill Rocco."

Roger flopped around on the sofa to face me in a loosey-goosey motion that led me to believe he might be missing a few important bones. "If Dominick didn't, who did?"

"Let's examine the suspect list," I said. "Jessica wanted Rocco dead, but she planned to let Carol Masters or Little Rock do the job for her, so that lets her out. Carol Masters came to the house that night but never went inside. Little Rock never even came. Sid Sleaze had no motive. That leaves only one other person with both reason and opportunity."

"Who?" asked Roger in a balloon so faint I could see right through it to the wall.

"That leaves you, old buddy. There's a sign up over the door to detective school. What walks like a duck and talks like a duck is probably a duck." I lit a smoke. It went down harsh and rasped at my throat. "There's just too much evidence against you. You publicly threatened to kill Rocco. Three eyewitnesses place you at the murder scene, gun in hand. Nickels the pawnbroker fingers you as the one who bought the gun. It has your fingerprints on it. But the kicker is something Jessica brought up. Doppels usually disintegrate within a few hours of their creation. Yet you've lasted nearly two days. Because the real Roger put an extra amount of effort into making you a bang-on duplicate of himself so anybody who saw you would have no doubt you were real. Then he sent you out in the middle of the night to buy a pair of red suspenders with a fifty-dollar bill. So the situation would be unusual enough for the shopkeeper who wrote up the sale to remember you. Roger created you as an *alibi*.

"That's who killed Rocco. You did. You hired me to give you somebody to hang the murder on. Tough detective gets carried away with his work. Kills wealthy syndicate owner. All you had to do to cement it was to